TANGLED UP IN YOU

First published in the UK in 2024 by Studio Press Books,
an imprint of Bonnier Books UK,
4th Floor, Victoria House, Bloomsbury Square, London WC1B 4DA
Owned by Bonnier Books,
Sveavägen 56, Stockholm, Sweden

bonnierbooks.co.uk

1 3 5 7 9 10 8 6 4 2

ISBN 978-1-80078-944-9

Written by Christina Lauren
Designed by Marci Senders
Production by Giulia Caparrelli

FSC www.fsc.org MIX Paper | Supporting responsible forestry FSC® C018072

A CIP catalogue record for this book is available from the British Library
Printed and bound in Great Britain by Clays Lltd, Elcograf S.p.A.

TANGLED UP IN YOU

A MEANT TO BE NOVEL

CHRISTINA LAUREN

STUDIO PRESS

This book is dedicated to every other wildly beating fangirl heart out there.

CHAPTER ONE

REN

Fragile morning sun sent its thin, golden fingertips dancing across a fresh blanket of snow. The view was spectacular; even the barest hint of light turned the ice into diamonds, transformed each blade of grass into a menacing shard of emerald. It was the kind of view to be taken in with a long inhale and sweeping gaze.

Maybe another day.

Ren Gylden's boot made a satisfying crunch as it smashed through the hard, lacy surface of last night's snowfall. Her sharp whistle cut through the still air, drawing her animals right up against the fence.

With a full bucket in each hand, she whistled again and pressed her back against the gate, pushing up on her toes to unlatch the lever with her butt. She was met with a chorus of snorts and clucks as she opened the gate and entered the enclosure.

"Today's the big day." Unable to meet their eyes, she kicked the gate closed, crossed the barnyard, and set her buckets down. She dumped one slop bucket into the trough, saying, "I know you're all happy for me, but maybe you're worried, too."

Her favorite pig, Frank, nudged her leg with his muddy nose, and she stepped out of his way, letting him have a go at breakfast.

"Yes, this is a big change," she continued, "but don't worry. I've told Steve everything he needs to do to take over the morning chores during the week."

Dumping the rest of the slop at the low end of the trough where the smaller piglets could reach it, she said to them, "It'll be the first time in your lives that someone else is feeding you. I wonder if any of you will notice."

Sitting down on one overturned bucket and leaning back against the chicken coop, she patted her lap for the tomcat, Pascal. As if his legs were spring-loaded, he hopped up, landing gracefully. "What do *you* think of all this, huh?" she asked, scratching him between his ears. "Are you going to miss me? I wish I could be in two places at once. Here and there. I'd love to hide behind the oak tree and watch how you all react tomorrow morning."

Pascal flexed his right paw, pressing his claws into the thigh of Ren's thick denim overalls.

"You don't think it'll be any different? Yeah, me either." She exhaled, long and slow, her breath condensing into a white puff. "Not for you, at least."

The cat purred.

"For me . . . I don't think it'll ever be the same again." She leaned her head back, closing her eyes and focusing on this exact moment—the sharp dawn air, the snuffling of the pigs rooting in their breakfast, the hypnotic pecking of the chickens at the dried corn and barley—rather than the one she'd be facing this time tomorrow. Tomorrow was a yawning black of unknown. For as many books as she'd read in her lifetime, Ren had never found one that taught a woman like her—raised away from society and off the grid for most of her twenty-two years—how to live in the real world.

Still, she was so ready for the change, she could practically taste it.

Another whistle cut through the air, her father calling her back to the cabin. When she opened her eyes, the sun had fully tipped its yellow cap over the crown of the mountain. It was her cue.

Pascal, sensing the shift in her energy before she even moved, hopped off her lap. "I'll be back every weekend," she promised to his retreating form as he slunk away from the pigpen and disappeared under some brush near the barn. "Go make me some kittens."

With a grin, Ren gathered her buckets and gave Frank one last pat on the head before heading back to the cabin to load up the truck.

But for the very first time in her life, she didn't feel like leaving the homestead.

Hesitation was the last thing she'd expected to feel today. She'd made a countdown calendar last month and pinned it to her wall. She'd even started packing up her hand-carved trunk a week ago—and she barely had anything to put in there to begin with. In the days leading up to the move, she'd driven her parents to exasperation with the singing and the dancing and the *What ifs*. There had been something about this brand of her excitement that couldn't be muted.

Until now, she supposed.

All that was left was to lift her new trunk into the bed of the old truck and climb in, right into the middle, where she'd be sandwiched between Gloria and Steve all the way to Spokane. But Ren couldn't seem to make her legs move.

It didn't make sense. It wasn't like she'd never left the homestead before. On Tuesdays and Saturdays, the family would go to the farmers markets over in Troy and sell their honey, jams, and every kind of seasonal fruit and vegetable imaginable. Every Monday, Ren would take the truck by herself up to the library in Deary, where Linda would hand over the new stack of used books that had come in. And once a quarter, the three Gyldens would drive to Moscow for fuel, feed, and any other business they'd need to get done.

But this time, getting in the truck felt different. It was a permanent rip down the page. Ren had never spent a single night away from the land since they'd moved here when she was three, and now she'd be living five days a week in a college dormitory with a stranger, home only on weekends. Every day she'd be sitting in a room full of people—different rooms, full of different people—who had spent their whole lives in situations that were completely foreign to her. This—going to college—had been Ren's dream ever since she was little, but now that she was standing there facing it, anxiety gnawed at her gut like a termite on a fence post.

Would her parents truly be okay without her? Gloria had never been good at getting the pilot light back up when it went out overnight, and Steve couldn't easily bend to reach it anymore. It was late January, and as cold as it would get all year; the firewood was budgeted for heat, not cooking. What if the stove went out and they didn't have any way to light it until Ren came home? Would they go down to the Hill Valley Five and Dime to use the phone? Would they even know what number to call?

And the pilot light was only one small thing. When there was work to be done—and there was, always—it was all hands on deck. The garden and fields didn't check the calendar; they wouldn't care if it was finals week. The old milk cow, Callie, wouldn't care if Ren had a paper due. And what if Steve poured both slop buckets into the highest part of the trough, where the piglets couldn't reach? What if he forgot that Gloria's old chestnut mare, Poppy, was allergic to alfalfa and accidentally threw a few cubes into her feed?

For as long as she could remember Ren had wanted to attend school, but it had only been recently—when the desire for deeper knowledge had grown into a living, pulsating shadow in her chest—that she'd finally wondered what on earth was stopping her. Her parents' unwillingness to enroll her in school growing up had mostly been rooted in their philosophy about living free of society's influence and a general mistrust of the ways of the modern world, but they'd taught her well, hadn't they? Ren knew what mattered: honesty, humility, hard work, and self-sufficiency. And she was an adult now; in theory, she could make her own choices. But Ren knew she was too tightly woven into the life of the homestead to unthinkingly do whatever she wanted.

It was only as she was standing there beside the truck, ready to pack up, that Ren felt the more practical weight of her parents' longtime hesitation: They *needed* her. On a homestead of this size, six hands were always better than four, especially when two of those hands—Ren's—were younger and could do over half the work. Leaving might be the most selfish thing she'd ever done.

Her parents had known she was applying to university in the same way they'd known when she was building a wind-power system from old scraps from Mr. Mooney: She'd disappeared down the road for a few hours every day, and then the new power source appeared. But at least when she connected the wind-power to the grid, Steve and Gloria had been happy to have electricity all day, every day. When the acceptance letter from Corona College landed in their PO Box, Steve and Gloria stared at it on the dining room table like Ren had dumped the slop bucket there by mistake.

"There's nothing they can teach you out there that you can't learn right here," Steve had said.

Gloria had nodded. "There's influences out there that'll poison your thinking."

"Is this about you wanting more books?" Ren's father had asked. "We'll take you to the big library over in Moscow."

The truth was that none of them had expected her to be accepted—at the age of twenty-two, Ren had never stepped foot in an actual classroom—so she hadn't properly prepared her argument by the time the thick white envelope landed.

It sat unopened on the small dining table for a day and a half, an uninvited guest in their home. Ren finally made the only argument she had, the one she knew would appeal to their biggest fear: "We need to better prepare for this cycle of drought and flood. Our crop yields are smaller every year, and if I'm going to live here the rest of my life, I need to make sure this land can support me once you're gone. I need to see what the world outside has learned so I can bring it home."

Gloria and Steve had exchanged looks.

Steve had asked, "Who's gonna pay for it?"

"They offered me full tuition and board."

Ren's parents sat with it overnight, then, in the morning, laid out the ground rules.

She would live in the dorms Monday through Friday. Every weekend she'd be home, where she'd still be expected to complete her weekly chores. She was not to tell people the location of the homestead or specifics about their way of life, and if she ever felt the modern influences pressing in on her, she'd tell her parents immediately. She was to avoid technology as much as possible and outside of classwork was forbidden from searching the internet. If they sensed any change in her disposition, they'd withdraw their support, and she could either come home or stay away forever.

But when it came down to it, there was no knock-down-drag-out fight, because the truth didn't need to be said aloud: Her parents couldn't legally keep her from leaving even if they wanted to.

And now she was right on the cusp of doing just that.

"Too late to be scared now, Rennie," Gloria said with her trademark blend of exasperation and weariness. It was what Ren had always admired most about her mother; she didn't waste time sugarcoating anything.

"If you're going off to school," Steve said, coming up to unlatch the gate of the pickup, "you're gonna have to carry your own weight." It was what Ren had always admired most about her father; he made sure she'd never had to rely on anyone else.

"I'm going to miss you both," Ren told them earnestly. "I'll write letters every day so you have something to find in the post office when you go to town on Wednesdays."

With a quick, deep inhale, she bent at the knees and hefted the heavy wooden trunk into the bed of the pickup. Ren closed the tailgate and latched it shut with the long metal pin before turning to look back at the only place she'd ever called home. The roof of their little cabin was covered in a soft blanket of snow from the previous night, but in the warmer months a fifty-year-old oak tree gave them shade, as well as the best branches to climb. Behind the cabin, the fields stretched on as far as the eye could see. Ren said a silent and temporary goodbye to the animals huddled together there, braving the wind to soak up weak tendrils of the late-January sun.

Gloria broke through her reverie: "What are the rules?"

Ren blinked back to focus on where her mother stood holding the passenger door open. "I can leave the dorms for meals, class, or the library," she said, and adrenaline pricked beneath her skin just thinking about it.

"No boys, no booze," Gloria said. "No restaurants."

"No internet, no makeup," Steve added from behind the wheel, and Ren coughed out a laugh as she slid to the middle of the bench seat.

"Makeup! Me?"

"You just wait," Gloria said. She hauled the heavy truck door closed behind her. "College coeds will try to get you to do all kinds of frivolous things. You want to learn, so go learn. Leave the nonsense to everyone else."

"I have a solid foundation about what matters," Ren recited confidently. "Boys and booze and makeup don't."

"That's right." Steve turned the key, starting the gruff, rumbling engine.

Ren knew better than to let any hesitation about this adventure leak free, but with the sound of the truck's engine turning over, nervous excitement bubbled up in her chest, dislodging the tiny worry floating right at the top: "Do you think it'll be okay that I'm starting late?" The beat of silence that followed made her lungs immediately constrict with regret. "I only mean—"

"What's this 'starting late'?" Steve asked sharply. *Starting late* was the worry Ren tried to keep in this whole time—well, one of a thousand about what this experience might really be like—that starting college four years later than everyone else and coming in halfway through the school year because of the fall harvest was going to make her stand out when all she wanted was to blend in.

"That's some cyborg programming hogwash right there," he continued, shifting the truck into gear with a clunking thud. "Who says you have to start school at a certain time? Who says you need school at all?"

"You read every damn book in the libraries all across Latah County," Gloria murmured. "You probably know more than those brainwashed teachers anyway."

"I know that's right." Steve eased the truck down the long driveway. "And if I hear one speck outta you about five-year plans or summer enrollment or study abroad, I'm yanking you outta that place so fast your head'll spin. This is gonna be hard on your mother and me, what with you not here pulling your weight. We're already moving everything around this season so you can take care of your chores when you're home on weekends."

Ren nodded, feeling immediately chastened. "Yes, sir. I'm very grateful, I hope you know that."

"Sometimes I wonder."

"Every Friday," Gloria said with finality. "Five o'clock sharp, we'll be there to bring you home."

"Yes, ma'am." Ren looked across her lap to the passenger side-view mirror, to where the last nineteen years of her memories receded behind them with the homestead until they were just tiny specks of brown broken up by naked trees. "I'm sure I'll already be outside waiting."

CHAPTER TWO

REN

If Ren were asked to describe the Corona College campus, she would probably just open her mouth and sing. Holy moly. She thought the homestead was beautiful, but she'd never seen anything like this. There were lawns that stretched for as far as she could see. Fluffy sugar maples that would turn vibrant in the fall. Regal pine trees that reached, tall and spindly, to the clouds. With the small Lake Douglas and a sharp bend in the Spokane River at the heart of the campus, Ren felt like she'd left her homestead to enter a jeweled, glimmering heaven.

Gloria and Steve didn't seem to share her enthusiasm for the view, but that was no surprise. Closer to Spokane, when Ren had become ever more talkative in her excitement, they'd grown fidgety and restless, lips pressed so tight the edges grew pale. As they exited the freeway, their eyes had lingered on graffiti and billboards, storefronts advertising sales on laptops and phones, piercings and tattoos. Their silence had been brittle, but at least it allowed Ren to let loose her wild flurry of dreams. She imagined echoing lecture halls with some of the greatest minds in the sciences and humanities. She imagined attending a Socratic seminar and standing in front of a group of her peers, speaking her opinions aloud. She imagined long nights spent studying at the library, tucked away inside a polished oak carrel, devouring her assigned reading.

Gloria consulted a map, navigating them closer, and the campus Ren had only seen in photos rose before them: the stone arch signaling the boundary between surrounding neighborhood and college, the wide lawn of the Commons, and, at the apex, the regal brick face of Davis Hall. On this day before the new term began, students were everywhere outside even in the dreary weather: standing in groups, walking in pairs, crossing streets without a thought to the cars around them, calling to each other in greeting after the long winter break. Stuck in the middle seat, Ren longed to be near the side window. She wanted to press her face as close to the view as she possibly could.

Gloria exhaled a disgusted huff at the sight of so many of Ren's peers with their necks bent, eyes directed at the bright screens of their phones. Steve scowled at two students kissing openly on the sidewalk. Her parents' judgment had become a heavy, palpable presence, but as the truck rumbled down the manicured Corona Drive, nothing could interrupt Ren's joy. She was finally doing it.

She was going to be a college student.

The old red truck groaned around a final street corner, and her dorm, Bigelow Hall, rose into view. The exterior was two-tone brick, broken up by stretches of long rectangular windows with warm yellow lights glowing inside.

Ren leaned forward to see all the way to the top through the windshield. "It looks so fancy," she whispered.

With a rumbled settling of the engine and a tiny puff of exhaust, they parked at the curb in a space marked LOADING ZONE.

Ren scrambled out after Gloria, stretching her arms to the sky and spinning in a slow circle. "Look how beautiful it is!"

After giving her a handful of seconds to take it all in, her mother waved her to the back of the truck bed. "Come on, Ren. Give us a hand."

"If they tow my truck," Steve began as Gloria took hold of one trunk handle and Ren took the other, "I'm gonna raise hell."

With that, they followed Steve inside to find Ren's new Monday to Friday home: room 214.

Bigelow was an all-female dorm—a requirement of her parents if she was going to be allowed to live on campus—and her dorm room was objectively unremarkable: two twin beds, two wardrobes, two small desks. Even so, Ren was immediately in love. The room was neatly split down the middle, with exactly one half decorated chaotically in a collage of photos, postcards, ticket stubs, and posters of rock bands, and the other half—Ren's half, she realized—left starkly white. The mattress on her bed was bare, the desk empty.

A blank slate. It sent Ren's pulse soaring.

A girl stood from her desk chair when they entered. She was tall and pale, with thick dark hair, and dressed entirely in black. Ren tried to mask her double take at the various piercings through the girl's nose, ears, lip, even what she thought was a real piercing through the girl's septum, like an actual bull.

"Hi," Ren said, holding out her hand. "I'm Ren. I'm your new roommate."

"Yeah." The girl shook it, limply. "Miriam."

"These are my parents, Steve and Gloria." Who, unsurprisingly, were studying Miriam and her room decor with silent disapproval.

Miriam let out a quiet "Cool."

"Are you enjoying Corona so far?" Ren asked.

Miriam's eyes flickered to Steve and Gloria and then back to Ren. "Sure. It's fine."

"Have you chosen a major yet?"

"Communications."

Ren felt her brows slowly rise and fought the urge to make a good-natured joke. Instead, she said only "How wonderful."

Her parents were always sparse with their words, and Ren never had a problem being the chatterbox of the family. But the mood right now didn't seem to call for friendly small talk. Ren found herself facing a social brick wall as awkward silence settled over the room and Miriam fidgeted with the rings on her fingers before slowly returning to her chair, shoulders stiff.

Ren turned back to her parents, whispering, "Do you want to stay for the campus tour I have in a half hour?"

"Nah." Steve shoved his hands in his pockets, looking uncomfortable. "We've got the drive home to make."

It felt so abrupt, after everything, for them to leave so unceremoniously barely five minutes after arriving. But Ren knew her parents too well to see it going any other way. They hardly spoke to people in town back home; they sure weren't going to draw out a sentimental goodbye with Miriam sitting right there. Ren's excitement shaded bittersweet as she rushed to hug each of them in turn. "Okay. Be safe. Thanks for bringing me." She stretched to kiss each of their sun-weathered cheeks. "Don't worry, I remember the rules."

With one more "Be smart, Ren," and a final look to caution her against the dangers of city life, Steve gestured for Gloria to lead them back outside.

Ren knelt on her bed, staring out the window to watch her parents climb into the truck and disappear back the way they came. Apprehension swarmed inside her chest like bees on honeycomb. She was *here*. She turned, ready to dive into college life. A hundred more questions for Miriam popped up, each begging to be answered.

But her roommate spoke first: "Your parents seem pretty chill."

There was a weight to her words that Ren couldn't quite translate. "Chill?"

"Easygoing." Miriam moved to sit on her bed, crisscrossing her legs. She pinned her elbows to her knees, rested her chin on steepled fingers. With her black T-shirt, black leggings, even chipped black polish on her toes and fingernails, Miriam looked to Ren like a beautiful shadow stepping right out of Bram Stoker's world and into the modern day.

Ren smiled. "Oh, they are *very* easygoing. I mean, with everything going on at home, I'm lucky they let me do this."

Miriam's dark brows furrowed, bloodred lips flattening. "I was being sarcastic. They seemed seriously intense."

"Oh." Sarcasm. Right. Ren had never been good at spotting it. "They don't like the city much," she explained.

Ren wasn't unintelligent. She'd read enough contemporary literature to know that her upbringing was unconventional, and she was sure Miriam wouldn't be the last person at Corona to notice or even call her out on any perceived weirdness. Ren didn't dress like other women her age; everything she wore was handmade or purchased secondhand. She didn't watch live television or listen to the radio; she wouldn't catch many of the slang or cultural references at school. She knew most college freshmen weren't twenty-two years old, and she knew even fewer would be obligated to go home to their parents on the weekends. Modern-day freshmen gained fifteen pounds and learned their limits with alcohol. They flirted and "hooked up" and lost their virginities to people who broke their hearts afterward.

But Ren also knew that most freshmen couldn't build a bug zapper using a six-volt battery, some wooden dowels, and a black light, or craft a portable generator out of a solar panel recovered from the county trash heap and a twenty-dollar inverter. There would be more ways than one that Ren wouldn't fit in. Her goal was to show every person she met that she had something unique to offer, and that she wanted to learn from them, too.

Miriam stretched out and rolled to her stomach, swiping her thumb across a small screen. Ren craned her neck to get a better look at the person Miriam was watching do their makeup.

"Do you have your own mobile phone?"

Miriam went still before slowly turning her head. A flat "What?" floated out of her mouth, carried on a disbelieving smile.

"In your hand. Is that yours?"

Her roommate blinked. "Yes . . . ?"

"I've seen some people with them at the farmers market, and

I've read about them. But I've never held one. The technology is amazing."

"They told me you were coming from a farm," Miriam said. "I—" She mimed an explosion coming out of her temple. "Like, I do not even know how to process that you've never held an iPhone before." But even so, she didn't offer to hand hers over, and Ren mentally logged this: People are protective of their devices.

"Have you lived here all year?" Ren asked.

"Yup."

"Who was your roommate before?"

Miriam didn't look up. "Her name was Gabby. She flunked out."

"What does that mean?"

"It means that she failed her classes."

Okay, so basically what Ren thought. "How?"

Miriam laughed. "Uh, by never going?"

"Oh." Ren studied the other woman, trying to puzzle this out. Someone would enroll in school to . . . not go to school? "Why didn't she go?"

"How would I know?"

"I don't understand."

"Well," Miriam said, "that makes two of us."

"Was she nice?"

"I guess."

"What did she study?"

Miriam huffed out a laugh. "Obviously she didn't study anything."

"I just meant . . ." Ren let the thought trail off. *Maybe Gabby hadn't found the right thing,* she wanted to say, but didn't bother. Somehow, suddenly, the idea that there was a passion buried inside everyone felt starkly naive. "Where did you grow up?"

Miriam bit her lip and looked over at Ren. "I'm sorry. I'm not trying to be rude, but I kind of need to do this right now." She pointed to the phone screen, where the person was now drawing a flower on their eyelid, and then put a small white earpiece in each ear before rolling to face the wall.

Ren pulled her trunk from where Steve had tucked it beside her bed and began unpacking. On top were her prized possessions: a set of new paintbrushes, tubes of oil paints and colored pencils, thick paper, and sketch pads. Wrapped carefully just beneath them was the treasured painting that had hung above her bed since she was capable enough to put the memory down on canvas: a handheld sparkler lighting up the night sky. The style seemed amateurish compared to what Ren was able to create now. The sparks of fire looked like blossoms in her childish strokes, and the cornflower twilight didn't nearly capture the vibrance of the sky in her recollection; the stars weren't nearly as sharp. But even so, the crude painting managed to convey the scene permanently tattooed across the inside of her lids. Once she'd painted the brilliant explosions of light, she never stopped: Ren had painted them across the walls of her room, the headboard of her hand-carved bed, the inside of the barn, the outside of the chicken coop, and, of course, pages upon pages in her notebooks.

Assuming she wasn't allowed to put nails in the dorm walls, Ren propped the canvas on her desk and moved to unpack everything else: clothes, a towel, her bedding, her brush, toothbrush and toothpaste, and her going-away-to-college treat: a block of her favorite farmers market honey soap wrapped in wax paper. All of it was neatly stowed away in her armoire in a matter of minutes.

Buried beneath all that was her beloved collection of fiction. Willa Cather, James Joyce, Zora Neale Hurston, Jane Austen,

Agatha Christie, Franz Kafka, and Shakespeare, all found at the local thrift store or flea market. Each one—whether hardy hardcover or well-loved paperback—was carefully lined up on the top shelf of the new-to-her desk, with the second shelf reserved for her favorite reference texts: the *Oxford English Dictionary*, *Roget's Thesaurus*, Strunk's *Elements of Style*, Kovacs's *Botany*, Abramowitz's *Handbook of Mathematical Functions*, the *CRC Handbook of Chemistry and Physics*, *Gray's Anatomy*, Sagan's *Cosmos*, Hawking's *The Theory of Everything*, *Integrated Chinese*, L'Huillier's *Advanced French Grammar*, *The New World Spanish/English English/Spanish Dictionary*, and her set of well-loved German textbooks.

Ren stepped back, assessing. Unlike Miriam's half of the room, this space didn't look lived-in quite yet, but it would. The last item in her trunk—her small wind-up clock—was set right in the middle of the desk, where it ticked comfortingly, telling Ren that she had fifteen minutes until she would need to leave for—

"Is it going to do that forever?"

Turning, Ren found her roommate staring over at her. "Is what going to do what forever?" she asked.

"That clock." Miriam lifted her chin to Ren's desk. "That loud ticking."

Ren's stomach dropped. "Is that going to be a problem?"

"It sounds like a bomb. You know, they make digital clocks in this century."

This time, Ren easily read her roommate's tone, and her confidence wavered. "I'll look into it."

With a sigh, Miriam rolled onto her back. "Just order one from Amazon."

Ren paused, sure she'd misheard. "Order a clock from the Amazon?"

Miriam barked out a disbelieving laugh. "It's a *shopping* site." She quickly tapped her thumbs to her screen and then turned the phone for Ren to see. "For like twelve dollars, it can be here tomorrow."

Ren didn't know how to tell Miriam that twelve dollars was about all she could spend in a month, let alone within her first twenty minutes on campus. "That's a good idea," she said with a grateful smile. "I'll definitely order one."

But for now, she opened the back of her clock and disengaged the mechanism from the hands. Luckily, she still had her watch—hand-wound by force of habit, and always reliable—which showed she only had a handful of minutes to get to where she needed to be.

Ren ducked to peek out the window, and, as if it was preening under the attention, the sky cracked with a roar of thunder and the clouds opened up in a downpour.

A laugh drifted over from the other side of the room. "Welcome to Spokane."

"So I've heard." Smiling, Ren rebraided her long hair, wrapping it into a twist that fit beneath her beanie.

Her roommate's voice again rose out of the quiet. "Your hair is so pretty."

"Thank you." Ren had a strange relationship with beauty; to her mind, strength and capability were beautiful, but photographs in magazines on the racks at the Hill Valley Five and Dime often featured models who were fake tanned, emaciated, and staring idly out into the distance. Strangers had complimented Ren's waist-long golden hair frequently enough that she had to believe it was objectively pretty, but as for the rest of her, she'd never had the faintest idea.

Miriam watched Ren slip into her big coat. "Where are you going?"

Ren looked over her shoulder as she tugged on a boot. "I have an appointment to meet another student at the Registrar's Office in ten minutes."

Miriam sat up, attention suddenly piqued. "Who are you meeting?"

Ren pulled the sheet out from her coat pocket, glancing down. "Doesn't say." To herself, she read the short letter from the dean again—

Ren,

We're delighted to welcome you to Corona College. I am aware that this will be your first experience with school of any kind, but your test scores leave me more than confident that you're up to the task. I've arranged to have a student meet you at the Registrar's Office in the atrium of Carson Hall at 1:30 p.m. on January 31, the day before spring semester classes begin. He will give you a tour of the campus. Please stop by my office at some point in your first week here so that we can chat. I know our campus newspaper is very interested in speaking to you! Your story is quite unique.

Should you have any questions, please don't hesitate to reach out.

Best,

Dr. Yanbin Zhou, PhD

Dean of Corona College

Her stomach tilted uneasily at the prospect of interviews with the school paper, but after everything Dr. Zhou had done for her, she would find a way to make it work within her parents' guidelines . . . somehow.

"Does it say he or she?" Miriam asked.

"He." Ren looked up. Her roommate's expression had gone razor sharp. "What?" she asked. "Should I not go?"

"Definitely go. I think you're meeting Fitz."

"It doesn't say Fitz here."

"It's Fitz. If the dean arranged it, it's absolutely him. Dean Zhou loves Fitz."

"Should I be scared?"

Miriam laughed. "Only if extremely sexy and charismatic men scare you."

Ren immediately dove for this chance to play along: "Like John Travolta sexy? Or Patrick Swayze?"

Miriam burst out laughing. "Oh my God, Ren, you are a trip." She slid from her bed and walked closer, typing something on her phone. "Have you ever seen Austin Butler?"

"Who?"

She turned her phone to face Ren. "He played Elvis."

"Oh," Ren said, frowning. "I only know Kurt Russell to have played the King." Miriam stared at her, and Ren obediently turned her eyes to the screen, saying, "He is indeed very handsome."

"If you took the raw confidence of Florence Pugh, the bone structure of Austin Butler, the charm of Jenna Ortega, and multiplied it by the effortless sensuality of Timothée Chalamet, you'd have Fitz."

Ren had no idea who any of these people were, but agreed, "That does sound very sexy."

"He's a senior, and everyone falls for him. But it's a trap, Ren."

"A trap?"

"He's charming as hell and will flirt with you until your pants are on the floor. And that's all he wants."

Paling, Ren shook her head. "I don't think—"

"Do you hear me?" Miriam cut in, pointing a cautionary finger. "Be smart. Because his ego is bigger than Alaska." The much-taller woman bent at the knee so that the two were eye-to-eye. "Are you from Alaska?"

"Idaho."

"Well, I take it you know how big Alaska is."

Ren nodded, mentally fortifying herself at the prospect of meeting an attractive man with an ego that was nearly seven hundred thousand square miles.

"Good. So don't let him seduce you."

A flush crawled up Ren's neck. "Oh my gosh, would you stop suggesting that?"

"I mean it. He'll only break your heart."

Flustered, Ren turned to open the door to flee. But when she was only a few steps away, Miriam leaned out of the doorway. "Ren!"

She turned. "Yeah?"

Her roommate's voice reverberated up and down the packed hallway: "Do not let that man into your pants!"

Ren felt every pair of eyes land squarely on her back as she walked the straight path to the stairwell. She'd studied in every moment of her free time—studied hardest these last few months in preparation for college. But a new truth was very quickly becoming apparent: Some things in life were impossible to prepare for.

CHAPTER THREE

REN

Ren took one step outside of Bigelow Hall and rain seemingly poured from an immense overturned bucket in the sky. On this final day of January, the wind was nothing compared to what it could be out in the middle of the fields, but here it was rain that flew sideways, the buildings pressing it all together and then shoving it forward like a colossal mouth blowing a million icy darts. She wrapped her scarf up around her face, leaving only her eyes visible beneath her beanie, zipped up her coat, and covered the whole of her head and neck with her giant hood.

One step, and then two. In the hazy light of midday, the world seemed at once too big and too small; wet sidewalk stretched out in every direction, and yet even a block in the distance was obscured from her view. Ren felt like a blind mouse at the center of a maze. Her heartbeat was a deafening gallop in her ears.

"You can do this, Rennie," she whispered, pulling out the folded campus map she'd printed at the Deary library last week when her new student orientation packet arrived, shielding it from the rain with her body. She'd circled all of the important places she had to be: Bigelow Hall, the Registrar's Office, dining services, and each of the buildings where her six courses were held. The Registrar's Office, where she was meeting this Alaskan-egoed Fitz, was located inside Carson Hall, which looked on the map to only be a couple buildings over. Even so, it was hard to get her bearings. There weren't her usual landmarks here—the hills to the east or the tall stretch of aspen to the west. The sun wasn't visible at all, and the river was obscured by buildings. Here, it was only structures and sidewalks and asphalt in a seemingly uniform stretch of wet concrete no matter which way she looked.

But her direction, the map indicated, was to the right. Past Willow Lawn, past the Stills Center, to the building just bordering the main quad. Ren hauled the door to Carson Hall open with all her weight and stepped inside, where she was immediately sealed up in the dark, quiet atrium.

Shaking the raindrops from her coat and stomping the water off her boots, she looked up into the shadows of the interior of the building. For the day before the start of spring term, it was surprisingly quiet, echoing in its emptiness. Just as the outer door sealed shut, another opened somewhere on the floor above her, and the sound was followed by the jogging squeak of sneakers on stone. From the second story of the building and down the wide set of central steps, a figure descended—a man—with soft dark hair and shoulders so broad Ren immediately had the impression he'd be able to carry a newborn calf with ease.

Diffuse light from the tall window behind her caught his face as he approached, and if this person walking toward her was Fitz, she should have listened more closely to Miriam, should have asked questions: what he studied, where he came from, what exactly his tricks might be. The key to surviving, Steve always told her, was to know everything she could about every possible threat she might encounter. And the way her heartbeat reacted to this man, with that face and those shoulders, screamed THREAT PROXIMITY ALERT.

He came to a jogging stop a couple feet away and pulled a white headphone from one ear. "Ryan?"

"Ren," she corrected, trembling inside her bulky coat. It wasn't so much that he was good-looking—though he was, with shaggy hair he'd tucked behind one ear and strong arms extending from his T-shirt that made Ren think she could put him to great use in the fields. It was the way his warm brown eyes regarded her so steadily from beneath thick, dark brows, like he sensed a secret about her that she didn't even know yet.

She lifted her chin. "My name is Ren Gylden."

"Gesundheit," he quipped.

"It's Swedish."

He smiled an indulgent half smile. "Congratulations."

She held out her gloved hand for him to shake, and, after regarding it in confusion for a bit, he smiled again and shook it gamely. "How do you do?" he said with joking formality. "I'm Fitz."

"Fitz what?"

"Just Fitz."

"Well, Just Fitz." Ren released a laugh at her own joke. "It's nice to meet you."

Fitz blinked, looking past her to the door. "So, uh, Sweden. You transferring from somewhere?"

She straightened, having prepared for this. "I'm not a transfer, no." Her voice came out muffled behind all her layers. "This will be my first experience at a school."

Fitz's gaze jerked back to her. "No shit?"

"Uh, yeah. Correct." Ren's face flushed at the profanity. She'd read every word in the English language—she'd probably read this specific one in multiple languages, but very rarely heard it said aloud. Even the curse words in her movies at home had been edited out. Unfortunately, she wasn't able to pull it off: "No . . . shhi—poop."

Fitz laughed, dropping his gaze to her outfit, drawing attention to the fact that she was still bundled up in her coat, hidden by her hood, wrapped up in a scarf. "You just come in from the Iditarod or something?"

"Idaho, actually." Ren shoved the hood off, unwound the scarf, and then unzipped the heavy parka, shrugging out of it and the beanie to shake her long braid free. A few loose tendrils remained plastered to her face, and she drew them away with a wet, clammy hand, looking up at him.

When their eyes met, Ren felt suddenly naked at the way his expression had gone blank, at the way he stared directly at her face, finally exposed.

He exhaled a quiet "Oh."

"What?" She tried to stand as still as she could under his inspection. Fitz dropped his eyes to take in what she was wearing; she'd chosen her favorites from a recent visit to the consignment store—a red-and-green-striped T-shirt and light blue jeans with beautiful pink and yellow hand-embroidered flowers all down the sides. She'd felt good this morning when she'd put it on, but her confidence was ebbing the longer he stared. "What?" she asked again, finally.

He blinked, clearing the surprised blankness, and his face transformed as she watched. One brow raised, his eyes melted, and lips hitched up in a sideways smile. "What are you doing after this?"

Ren blinked, confused. "After—what? The tour?"

"Yeah. Later. I could answer any questions you have down at the Night Owl." He licked his lips distractingly. Had she ever really noticed a man's mouth before? Were they all so full and soft? "I happen to know a bartender there: me. He makes great cocktails. We could hang for a bit."

Confused, Ren narrowed her eyes at him. "Aren't you already here to answer my questions now?"

"Sure." He took a step closer, and Ren straightened, suddenly feeling flushed and jittery. "But there's probably a lot of stuff you'll think of later, away from campus," he said, shrugging. "Doesn't have to be about classes. We could just get to know each other."

"That's very nice, but—" She glanced wildly around the atrium, wondering what it was about this moment that made her feel like she was already breaking her parents' rules. "I'm not actually supposed to go to bars."

"Don't worry, Sweden. I could get you in."

"It's not that. It's my parents. They forbid it."

He reached forward, drawing a long strand of her wet hair through his fingers. "I wouldn't tell."

Fitz had a very expressive face, and right now, he was looking at her like a wolf sizing up a lamb. The only other time she'd felt this way before—fevered, heart thrumming, goose bumps down her arms—was when she'd read romance novels, hidden away in a dark corner of the barn or under her favorite tree, far out in the eastern pasture. She'd never felt it in someone else's presence before. "Yeah, but *I* would know."

At these words, his gaze slowly cleared, and he dropped her hair. "Seriously?"

"Seriously what?"

"I'm asking you out for drinks, and it's—" He waved a hand in front of his own face. "Nothing? Not even a flutter?"

"I don't know what you mean. Flutter—what?"

Fitz stared at her for a prolonged beat. "This must be an off day for me." There it was again, the half smile that reminded Ren of a vampire, teasing a glimpse of a single fang. Lifting his chin to the stairs, he said, "Let's get your schedule printed."

"Actually, no need. I have it printed already." Ren shifted the big coat in her arms, digging into the side pocket to pull a manila envelope free.

He slowly took it from her, staring down at her coat. "You had this whole folder in there?"

"You bet. I can collect the vegetables I need for dinner, shoot a sage grouse, and tuck it all in here to carry it home."

Fitz's lip curled, and he loosened his grip on the folder so it was pinched only between the tip of his thumb and index finger. "You carried a dead bird around in that pocket?"

"Oh, loads of them," she corrected proudly. "We regularly hunt our dinner. I'd say I'm the best shot in the county." With a laugh, she translated his expression. "I've washed the coat since, silly." Ren took the folder, pulled out the sheet with her course list, and handed it back. "Those are my classes. Don't worry. That paper is dead-bird-free."

He scanned the page once, brow furrowing, and then again. "Homeschooled for every grade? For real?"

Ren thought for a moment how to answer without telling him anything too personal. "I'm sure it's uncommon for you to give a freshman tour to someone older like me who's never been on a college campus before." She swallowed. "I'm twenty-two, and I realize most freshmen here begin at eighteen and have been in school with their peers since kindergarten. But I assure you I have spent a lot of time researching the campus maps and schedules, and I mostly understand what's required of me. What I'm interested in is any advice you might have picked up along the way for how to juggle the demands of different courses, or if there are any small things I should know. Which professors I might need to handle carefully, and the best studying places. Only on campus, of course."

Slowly, he turned his attention back to her. A hundred questions passed through his eyes before he settled on "You've never even been on a college campus?" Ren shook her head. Fitz's jaw cut a sharp angle as he looked back at the course list. "How do you know these are right? This is a pretty intense course load."

Ren leaned over to look, too. "I chose classes from a list the registrar recommended."

"Because you're older," he said. "They probably assumed you're a transfer."

"I don't think so . . ." she hedged. "I took a lot of placement tests."

"Placement tests? Like what?"

She looked up, thinking. "I think they were the fall semester finals for Calculus, French, Mandarin, Microeconomics, Organic Chemistry II, Molecular—"

"And you passed?"

"Yes, of course."

He dragged the tip of his index finger down the list. "Why are you taking Intro Mandarin, then?"

"I can only read and write it," she admitted. "I've never had a conversation with anyone. I don't know if my pronunciation is right because we don't have a CD player, and the textbooks only write phonetic pronunciation."

Silence stretched between them, and he chewed his lip, working through something.

"Is . . . is my schedule okay?" she asked, finally.

Fitz nodded, eyes pinned to the page in his hand. "You're in my immunology seminar."

"That's great!"

He jolted slightly to awareness, his frown replaced with a smile, and there was that shift again, him stepping out of one body and into another. "Yeah, it's *great*." He winked at her, leaning in. "Let's get to that tour."

CHAPTER FOUR

FITZ

In all honesty, Fitz thought everyone on campus was a sucker.

Corona students, faculty, and staff looked at him and saw Fitz: campus playboy, soccer captain, teacher's pet, academic scholarship whiz kid. They saw a soon-to-graduate senior with a 4.0, a rich daddy, and a loving family. They looked at him and saw a golden future.

They assumed he got straight As because he was genetically gifted.

They assumed he grew up playing soccer on the manicured fields of Clyde Hill.

And they assumed he gave tours to new students because Dean Zhou was so charmed by him that he asked Fitz to occasionally welcome incoming students, and he agreed out of the goodness of his heart.

See? Suckers.

In fact, work-study was only one of the many side hustles Fitz needed to keep his head above water and his bank account in the black. He also worked as a bartender at the Night Owl, and, in his free time, helped a group of thick-spectacled octogenarians with their tech issues.

Sweet grannies who got flummoxed when their phone stopped working and didn't realize the battery had simply died. Pun-loving old grandpops who called Fitz up to help them fix a "broken" desktop computer without realizing they'd just turned the monitor on and off over and over. And all Fitz could think while he watched this girl with the Swedish name skip ahead of him down the campus sidewalks, pointing to buildings and calling out the names of architects and trivia about the granite used in this or that statue, was that Judy, Bev, Dick, and Joyce would love the hell out of this kid.

Unfortunately, college was another thing entirely, and if Sweden kept up her brainy-farm-girl thing on campus, she would be eaten alive.

"Whoa, whoa, Speed Racer," Fitz called when she'd managed to skip half a block ahead of him. She turned, arms sticking straight out in that ancient arctic jacket. "Stop and take a look." He pointed to the right. "This is where your music class is."

She jogged back and followed his outstretched arm to the building in front of them. She had to turn her head up nearly to the sky to be able to peer out of that enormous hood. "Oh! The Blackburne Mansion! Did you know this house was built in 1898?"

"Sure did." In fact, he'd had no idea, though the information was likely italicized and underlined somewhere in a training pamphlet Dean Zhou had handed him at some point.

She grinned, bolstered by what she seemed to read as Fitz's enthusiasm. "And in the late 1940s the school bought it, and it became the music conservatory building. Legends say that it was once haunted."

"Cool story." Fitz clapped his hands, relieved that they'd reached the end of their walk around campus and he could head to work. He pulled his phone out of his pocket to check the time. "Well, you have a class here Tuesday and Thursday mornings at ten."

"Would you go into a haunted house?" she asked.

He looked up from his iPhone. "What?"

"A haunted house." She pointed to the mansion again. "The priest who used to teach here would sleep in his office to reassure his students that there were no ghosts."

"And? Was he right?"

"No. He eventually had to perform an exorcism."

Fitz laughed. "An exorcism, huh?"

"I know. I think they're made up, too, but even so, I'm not sure I'd be brave enough to sleep in an empty house that everyone thinks is haunted." She smiled, revealing those perfect teeth and the little dimple low on her cheek, and once again he was lost in the absolute beauty of her face.

She was, without question, the hottest woman Fitz had ever seen. She had these enormous, sparkling green eyes that seemed to take him in all at once, drinking in everything in front of her. Maybe that was what made him so uncomfortable in her presence—that feeling that she might be the first person on this campus who could see straight through him right to his rotten, unending bullshit. She was small, had zero flirtation game, and dressed like her only source of clothing was hand-me-downs from a much older aunt, but when she'd unzipped her coat earlier, he registered that she had a banging body under all those frumpy layers. And then there was the hair. It seemed alive, somehow, a kind of golden that appeared metallic in the rare glimpses of the sun they'd had so far. Even though it was wound up in a heavy braid, some of it had fallen loose, and it was unsettling how many times he'd thought about reaching out and touching it.

The problem was *her*. Fitz was the one doing the campus tour but felt like he was on a field trip led by a golden retriever with a PhD. She sang a song naming all the elements as they passed the science quad; she recited the entire preamble to the US Constitution when he'd pointed out her political science building. She could name every tree, flower, and leaf on the grounds—and, to his dismay, she would, unprompted. Fitz made the mistake of expressing doubt that she was truly fluent in seven languages, and she proceeded to speak only in German, French, Italian, Spanish, and then Dutch to him for the next five minutes. The only time she paused was to remind him in English that she wasn't good yet at conversational Mandarin.

And that wasn't even the worst of it. Nobody liked a know-it-all, but if she'd just been rattling off facts and information, he could've tuned it out. It was the unending questions he couldn't ignore. Where did he grow up, what was his major, what was his favorite class, who was his favorite professor, did he have a roommate, where was his favorite place to eat on campus, where was his favorite place to eat off campus, what was it like being in the athletics program, did he have a car, did he go home on the weekends, did he go home for the holidays, would he have a summer job, how many of the states had he visited, had he ever been out of the country, what did he want to do when he graduated, and on and on.

She was completely irresistible as long as she wasn't speaking, which, unfortunately, was never.

He blinked back into focus just as she was midsentence about, he thought, the exact method of the Blackburne Mansion exorcism.

"Okay, well, Gwen—"

"Ren."

"Great, listen, you'll have a chance to tell your classmates all of this when you take your vocal performance seminar here." He made a show of looking at the time again. "I'm gonna grab a bite before my shift at work."

Ren took a step forward, her palm outstretched. "Well, in that case, *Just Fitz*." She giggled and shook his hand firmly. "It's been very nice meeting you. I hope our paths cross again."

"They likely will, given that we're both in Bio 335."

"That's right." And just as he turned to lead her back toward the quad, she asked, "May I sit by you tomorrow?"

He turned back, finding her gaze uncertain, brows furrowed. The question and the wobble in her voice pulled him up short. It was a woman being vulnerable, and if anything was his weakness, it was that. But it was also this pitiful woman in particular, and even a half hour with her had been too long. Fitz couldn't imagine three class hours and three laboratory hours a week with her beside him, Rensplaining every tiny detail of the course material.

But a deeper truth floated to the surface: She also made him uneasy. Fitz had a perfect record at Corona so far, the top grade in every class he'd ever taken. He got them honestly—well, most of the time—and with charm and wile when the occasion called for it. But he didn't do it to be valedictorian or for any other reason related to pride. He did it because his father, the biggest living donor to the school, made it clear that neither his money nor his reputation was Fitz's to enjoy. And he did it because from the moment he was released from juvenile corrections nearly seven years ago, finishing at the very top was his only path to redemption and revenge. The way Ren came in with perfect scores, shooting to the most advanced courses before she'd even started, was the first real threat to his plan. The last thing he needed was a self-schooled farm girl ruining it in the final semester.

So he left her with the only reply he could muster: "Don't worry, Sweden. Wherever you end up, you'll be just fine."

CHAPTER FIVE

REN

On her first official morning as a college freshman, Ren woke without an alarm. Which was good, she supposed, given that she no longer had one. Miriam was still asleep and almost eerily silent on her side of the room, nothing but a tuft of messy black hair peeking out from beneath her fluffy comforter. Briefly, Ren considered holding a hand mirror under her nose to make sure she was breathing, but she didn't have one of those, either.

After her first meal alone in the overwhelmingly crowded dining hall the night before, she'd walked around campus, learning the paths by heart and planning out her schedule for her first day—when she would need to be up and showered, when she would need to be at the Student Services office to get her student ID, when she would need to be at the dining hall at breakfast to avoid the long and frankly intimidating line like the one at dinner. She felt the yawning chasm between herself and her peers—could sense in their body language how strange she seemed to everyone she tried to speak to—but while wandering, she met Joe, an older man who managed the athletic facilities, when he drove past in a golf cart and asked Ren if she needed any help. She hadn't, but when she'd asked him about what he did at the school, he gave her a full tour in his cart, as well as a schedule for all the upcoming winter sporting events, a T-shirt for basketball games that said CORONA KENNEL CLUB, a stuffed terrier, and a tiny plush basketball.

Giddy with excitement, Ren had crawled into bed at nine, curling up on her side, but slept fitfully her first night ever away from home.

She was missing the settling-down sounds of her animals in the corral, the uneven cadence of Steve's snoring down the hall, and the ever-present tick of her clock. Even so, she knew none of it really explained why she couldn't sleep. Usually when she closed her eyes, she saw sparklers and fireworks exploding in a golden blast overhead. But last night, when she'd closed them, she saw a sprawling campus, and hordes of jeering, impatient students. She saw herself swallowed in a sea of bodies, penned in on every side. Walking too fast or too slow, trying to open the wrong door, asking the wrong questions.

Ren stared up at the textured plaster ceiling; in the bright light of morning, she let her eyes grow unfocused until it became a blank, smooth canvas. She could paint this room, she thought. Paint the sizzle-glow, the bursts of light and color in the deep ocean blue of a sky. Even imagining it soothed her. She reminded herself that friendships would come, that she would learn the routine of school, and that beyond the four walls of this room was the same sky she'd seen every day of her life, the same as back home. It felt different, but she was rooted in exactly the same world, ready for a new adventure.

With that thought, she sprang from bed.

Years ago, Ren had read somewhere that air travelers should plan to be at the airport at least an hour before their scheduled flight, but apparently the same was not true for students and classes. Even twenty minutes before her immunology seminar began, the hallways were empty.

Ren's blood was humming, vibrating with excitement. At the locked classroom door, she cupped her hand around the small window and peered in.

"Let me open that."

Ren turned to find a man in a navy shirt and matching pants with a large set of keys hanging from his belt loop. He sorted through a few before finding the right one.

"Are you a professor?" she asked.

"Oh, God no." The man laughed, shaking his head. "Name's Doug. I'm just the custodian."

"There's no such thing as *just* a custodian," Ren said. "Custody comes from the Latin root *custos*, which means guardian. That means you take care of this building, and everyone in it should be grateful for what you do." She held out her hand. "Ren Gylden, student."

Doug wrapped his thick fingers around her hand and shook, grinning at her. "Nice to meet you, Ren. Have a good class."

When she turned to look inside the room, every thought fell away. Absently, Ren dropped Doug's hand. She'd seen a few films that depicted classrooms as huge lecture halls with steep stadium seating—and had mentally prepared herself for that kind of overwhelming introduction to learning—but Hughes Hall room 205 wasn't like that. Ren hooked the strap of her bag over her shoulder and stepped inside. The room was smaller than she'd expected, with eight long tables organized in a square U shape and all the seats along the outer edge, facing the center. Along one wall was a glimmering sweep of windows looking out on Lake Douglas and the Spokane River beyond. The other three walls were mounted with end-to-end whiteboards, as if the class would collectively be so inspired here that their words and ideas would spill in two hundred and seventy degrees around the room.

Ren wasn't sure how seating worked, whether it would be assigned or open, but she decided to choose a seat as close to the front as she could get, knowing she might not have the luck—or the seniority—to hold on to it. When the first student entered, Ren made sure to explain, "I'm happy to move if this seat isn't available for me."

The woman looked at her and then made a slow show of looking around the rest of the empty room. "I think you're good," she said dryly before choosing her own seat in the back corner.

Much like with Miriam the day before, silence gobbled up the space between them, and Ren worked to strangle down every one of the questions she had about what to expect. So far, she'd felt like a walking chatterbox with her peers. Fitz had been sardonic in his silence; Miriam was still borderline hostile in hers. The other college students seemed surprised at Ren's friendly greetings as they passed on the sidewalk. She was used to others being quiet—Steve was always nonverbal until he'd had at least two full mugs of black coffee, and Gloria was never much of a talker even at her most energetic. Ren might not be street-smart, but she did realize that not everyone was a morning person. But when the other student took her jacket off and revealed two arms covered in the most colorful flowers Ren had ever seen, she couldn't keep quiet.

"Oh my *goodness.*"

The woman looked up, startled.

"Your arms," Ren said, lifting her chin. "They're *beautiful.*"

"Oh." Something hard in the other woman's gaze eased. "Thanks."

"They're the most beautiful tattoos I've ever seen," Ren told her. There were two brothers at the farmers markets with tattoos down their arms and weaving up their necks, but they were nothing like this. "I've never seen color like yours."

"My guy is really good." The woman looked at one arm, sending the opposite hand softly down the length of it. "I gave him the sketches, and he did them perfectly."

Ren gaped at this. "You drew those?"

She nodded, and Ren was left speechless. She'd been drawing since she could hold a pencil, but she'd never considered drawing art for her own body before. The way the other woman created the overlapping flowers and foliage to perfectly fit the curve of her bicep, the crook of her elbow, the narrowing of her forearm into her wrist . . . It was magical.

She broke into Ren's stunned silence. "What's your name? I haven't seen you around before."

"Ren. Today's my first day."

"Transfer?" she asked, and Ren deflected.

"Sort of."

"I'm Britta. Give me your number. I can AirDrop my tattoo artist's info."

With a little grimace, Ren admitted, "I don't have a phone."

Britta took this with the expected amount of shock. "How?"

"I've just never needed one," Ren told her honestly.

"Holy crap, I knew your kind existed, but I've never seen one in the wild."

Ren laughed hard at this, and Britta grinned back just as two other women came in and sat in the back with her. They were soon followed by a hulking blond man, who began to make his way to the back as well before spotting Ren. She smiled politely, and he paused, then redirected, sitting down in the seat just beside her. "Hi."

"Hello. I'm Ren."

She reached her hand out, and he stared at it for a beat before clasping it firmly. "I'm Jeb."

The room was quickly beginning to fill now. Another man came in and Jeb stood, greeting him with a hand-slap-and-hug combination that Ren longed to catalogue in writing because it looked ritualistic and important.

The other man noticed Ren, and a slow grin curled across his mouth. "Who's your friend, Petrolli?"

"Oh, her?" Jeb said and sat down, looping a heavy arm around Ren's shoulders. "Yeah. This is my new friend, Jen."

"Ren," she corrected quietly.

"Ren," the second man said with a seductive depth to his voice. "Where'd you come from, sweetheart?"

Britta called out from across the room: "Don't be gross, Nate."

Nate looked over in feigned shock. "I'm not being gross, Britta, I'm being *friendly*."

"Well, Nate, don't be *too* friendly," Ren warned him with a genuine smile. "I'm new here, so how would you know whether I'm sweet or not?"

She startled when the three women in the back began clapping.

"That was awesome," said Britta.

"Savage," Jeb said.

"I'm savage?" Ren asked, surprised, and he grinned over at her.

"Totally."

A hush fell over the room, and Ren followed everyone's attention to the doorway, expecting the professor.

But it wasn't the professor, it was Fitz, and for a strangled moment, Ren's heart forgot how to function. She understood, on an intellectual level, why everyone fell quiet when he stepped across the threshold and into the room. He was tall without being imposing; his features were beautiful without being too perfect. Ren imagined drawing a portrait of him and knew she wouldn't be able to get the straight line of his nose right, the correct sharpness to his jaw, the paradoxical teasing softness of his brown eyes. No posture she could draw would capture the way time seemed to slow as he moved through the room with confidence and ease. And though it made sense to her heart why it would stutter, it didn't make sense to her brain how she was distracted enough by Fitz to miss the entrance of the world-famous Dr. Michel Audran.

Because when Ren finally pulled her eyes away from Fitz and toward the front of the room, there stood the man himself. Tall, thick browed, and with the firm slash of a mouth Ren had seen in countless textbooks, Dr. Audran looked out at the class, waiting for everyone to settle into quiet. Ren felt something vital and solid turn over in her chest.

For so long she'd wondered whether there would be a crystalline moment of transition, one when Ren would know for certain that her life was truly beginning. And it struck her, as Dr. Audran clapped his hands and greeted them with a simple "Well. Let's begin," that that delicious, perfect, long-awaited moment was right now.

STUDENT PROFILE: CORONA'S GOLDEN GIRL

by Allison Fukimora

with contributions from Corona Press Staff Writers

She's unlike anyone you've ever met before. Someone your age who has never used an iPhone, laptop, iPad. Who has never set foot in a movie theater. Who has never been on an airplane, walked into a Starbucks, heard of Taylor Swift, or gone swimming in a chlorinated pool. And paradoxically, the reason she agreed to this profile at all is also the same reason she's unlikely to ever read it: It can only be found online at the Corona Student and Faculty Portal.

"I know it sounds old-fashioned," she says, "but I don't use the internet unless it's for a class. I made a promise." Her preternaturally enormous green eyes meet mine, and I feel the same visceral protectiveness experienced by many of my peers rocket through me as she very earnestly adds, "Promises mean something, don't they?"

Her anonymity was a requirement for doing this article, but it was also easy to assure because it is irrelevant. Even without a photo to accompany this profile, anyone who's walked on campus in the last month and a half knows who the Golden Girl is. She is the streak of blond hair rushing gleefully across Willow Lawn when the sun finally pushes its way through the clouds. She is the tiny ball of hunched-over determination helping Corona's master landscaper fix the broken irrigation line out near the north shore of Lake Douglas. She is the student with her hand high in the air in every classroom. And she is, without question, one of the most captivating people to ever cast her shadow on the grounds of the school.

Captivating now, but almost universally annoying at first. That's the general consensus, at least. *Uncool, naive, overeager*—these are some of the descriptions given by students when I asked their initial impression of her, and always with a guilty wince, like they were confessing a sin, owning up to a character flaw simply by not adoring her from the start.

But it makes sense, doesn't it? She *would* be uncool—she was born near the debut of the iPhone but has been fully and intentionally unplugged for her entire life. She *would* be naive—she's never been to school of any kind before. She *would* be overeager—it took her months of convincing her parents to let her come to college at all; being here is literally her lifelong dream.

"No, no, *everyone* here has taught themselves!" she protests when I suggest that she's done the impossible by learning subjects such as calculus, organic chemistry, physics, European history, and written Mandarin all on her own. "You all were learning complicated rules and logistics about the world. I have to do all of that now, and I feel about as smart as a brick." That plain vulnerability passes over her face again, but, as always, she's smiling. "I was overwhelmed just getting in line for dinner that first day! I had no idea how to call the elevator in Hughes Hall. My parents would say I'm self-sufficient, but I think my peers would say I'm book-smart, not street-smart, and that's okay, because it's true!" At this, she laughs.

And about those parents. Did they raise her as part of some isolationist cult or religious sect? Are they political extremists, plotting the overthrow of our government? Apparently not; by her own account, Golden Girl's parents simply prefer to make their own way in the world. They built their own house and barn. They have cows and horses, chickens and pigs. A pond full of fish, several fields of crops to harvest three of the four seasons. A house full of books their daughter used to educate herself beyond what most of us could have wrung from our paltry public-school curricula. That's all she'll share about her upbringing, but nothing in what she told me made her parents sound like fringe isolationists. Maybe they just don't like people very much.

But their daughter does.

She's everywhere, and after only six weeks on campus, she's left quite an impression. Ask any student on the quad, and they're likely to have a story. There's the story of the night she found Dean Zhou's cat outside with a broken leg and splinted it until the cat could be taken to a vet the next day. There's the rumor about how she repaired the Admissions Office copy machine with a toothpick, a piece of aluminum foil, and a bobby pin. And, of course, there was the afternoon barely a week ago when she did the impossible and fixed the campus theater popcorn machine that most of the student body assumed was just a piece of vintage art. She's a member of the Corona Women's Choir, the Agricultural Economics Society, Project Climate, School Spirit Council, and several foreign language clubs. So what if it's a little weird that she never steps foot off campus unless it's to leave with her parents every Friday promptly at 5 p.m.? She's allowed to be a little weird because she is otherwise amazing.

And here's the thing: She's also truly, deeply *nice*. Nice in the way that initially makes you worry, like the steel-toed boots of the world will surely stomp it out of her. But when you meet her and spend time with her—good luck finding some; when she's here during the week she's got nearly every waking hour scheduled—you'll realize that in fact she's the kind of nice that saturates every layer. The kind of nice that immediately shares lunch when yours turns out to have a bug on the lettuce. The kind of nice that makes the interview run nearly an hour over because she has as many questions for you as you do for her. The kind of nice that genuinely means it when she asks the ubiquitous throwaway question, "How are you?"

The world might peel away one or two of those layers—and no doubt it will—but what's in there deep down is precisely what's at the surface. "What do I want people to know about me?" she asks, laughing at my final question. "Why would they want to know anything? I'm the least interesting person on this campus! I don't have any stories yet! I want to hear *yours*." She pauses, looking out the window of the dining hall, where it rains, and rains, and rains. Rivers of muddy water make the sidewalks nearly impassable, and the sky hovers overhead a sickly blue-gray. And still, her expression says she's never seen anything more beautiful. Finally, she turns back to me and nods, satisfied. "I'm so happy to be here. I think that's enough."

CHAPTER SIX

FITZ

To Fitz's complete lack of surprise, the article about Ren had the whole campus falling over themselves in fawning adoration. Suddenly every person in his loose social circle had a Ren story to share. She was brilliant, she was selfless, she was just so *fascinating*. To them, unconventional meant inspiring; naive meant idealistic. But in fact, there was only one line in the entire article that Fitz agreed with: *I think my peers would say I'm book-smart, not street-smart.* He couldn't agree more. Despite whatever Allison Fukimora thought, this world was going to eat Ren alive.

Did no one else notice how she held the door to the building open for so many people that she was late to her own class? Did it not irritate anyone else how profusely she overthanked a student when he picked up her pen after it rolled off the table? Did it not make anyone else want to claw their face off how from the moment Dr. Michel Audran began the very first class with a round of trivia, Ren's hand never went down?

Sitting maddeningly close to him, she'd correctly answered everything the rest of the students couldn't: that Dr. Audran did his doctoral work with Wolfgang Banzhaf at Michigan State before running his own lab at Institut de Génomique Fonctionnelle in Lyon. That his "research on nonsynonymous substitutions in SNPs had contributed significantly to the various genotyping technologies that companies were using to provide private users with their DNA-based hereditary information." That he was, in fact, one of the board members for the world's most commercially successful DNA testing kit, HereditarME.

So, of course, it was Ren who correctly guessed today that the next lab project the class would be doing was comparing the findings of the commercial kit with a simpler form of the genotyping assay they'd conduct in class. Necessity meant that Fitz was prelaw, but his joy had always been science. He'd been looking forward to this class as soon as it had been announced last fall. That top spot was his; he wouldn't really even have to try that hard for it. Until Ren Gylden arrived, that is, and quickly outranked even the highest class scores, therefore making his life a living hell.

A hell that was only getting more unbearable, because while a case of the assay kits made its way around the classroom, Audran took a few minutes to hand back the unit one tests the class had taken the previous week. Fitz looked down and, for the first time in his entire college career, stared at a thick, red D.

Before anyone else could see it, he shoved it into his backpack, heart pounding.

Is this when it all started to fall apart? Had he really let her get under his skin this much? What the hell had happened? He'd been distracted by Ren the morning of the test—irritated by the way the entire class had circled around her before Audran appeared, enthralled by her story of helping a cow give birth or something—but he still thought he'd done okay. He thought he'd answered the essay questions completely. But Audran's lengthy scrawled notes in the margins said otherwise. There were only four exams in the entire lecture portion of the course, making up 80 percent of his grade. Even if he scored perfectly on the next three exams, the best he could manage would be a low A.

That wouldn't cut it.

Fitz was vaguely aware of Audran directing them to go grab a kit at the back of the room near what he called the Polaroid Wall, where he had goofy photos of each student to help himself and the TAs remember their names. Fitz was vaguely aware of Ren returning to her seat, of her setting an assay kit in front of him. He was vaguely aware that she'd asked him something. But he ignored her because he was *intensely* aware that this grade was a disaster. Judge Iman—now Governor Amira Iman—had been very clear in the deal in writing she'd made with him the night of his release from juvenile detention seven years ago: If he could finish at the top of every class in college, she would have his record completely expunged and write him a letter of recommendation to any law school he wanted. She knew it would be a challenge, but if he could do it, she promised to be his personal champion.

This assurance had been the foundation of his future, and unfortunately the new, brilliant woman in the class and this stupid, mediocre grade had just unraveled everything.

CHAPTER SEVEN

REN

For an innately self-possessed man—who was regularly greeted by the class like a beloved king walking into his court—Fitz had grown suddenly and weirdly silent. Was he having the same internal debate she was? Because as she held the boxed DNA kit in her hands, Ren knew without having to think about it very hard that Gloria and Steve would never—not in a billion years—allow her to send her DNA off to some giant laboratory in New Jersey.

Around her, students happily opened their kits, read the directions, and laughed as they watched each other spit into the vials.

"Should I?" she said quietly. She knew what her parents would say: an unequivocal *no*. No meals out, no leaving campus, no boys, no alcohol, no makeup, no internet. But Ren had been away from home long enough to have softened some of those fearful boundaries. She'd walked with a professor to get a cup of tea at the café across the street from Davis Hall, and it had felt just as safe as sitting in the dining hall. She'd let Miriam put a small amount of blush on her cheeks for an outdoor concert on campus, and Ren hadn't felt the need to start wearing makeup all the time. She'd had a study session with a group of students at a TA's apartment a block off campus, and none of the males in attendance had tried anything untoward. It was *fine*. The profile in the student portal was perhaps the best example: Her name wasn't searchable anywhere in there. Sure, everyone on campus knew it was about her, but no Google search could bring up her name. There were times when you simply had to trust people to do what they said they would do, and if Dr. Audran said he would protect their anonymity, then he would.

Right?

Ren groaned, scrubbing her hands over her face. Was this a test of her conviction? If so, she worried she would fail; her curiosity raged. "Ugh. I don't know what to do."

Dazed, Fitz turned. "About what?"

"Whether I should do this DNA thing."

"It's optional," he said. "It's all anonymous anyway." He gave her one of those brief sarcastic smirks that she liked despite her better instincts, and said, "You know, just like that *anonymous* fluff piece in the portal."

"Fluff piece?"

"The article about you." He rubbed a finger over his flirty eyebrow.

"You read it?"

He nodded. "It was *glowing*."

"I'm sure you've had one, too."

"I have."

"And yours wasn't glowing?" she asked, ducking to smile at him. "That seems improbable."

"Mine was basically about how I'm smart and my dad is rich," he said with a humorless laugh, and then looked back at his own DNA kit. He gazed at it as if making a wish, before unceremoniously opening it and carrying out the directions. Ren watched while he peeled one label from the instructions and carefully lined it up over his vial. The other he stuck to the inside of his folder and pointed to the sample ID there. "You only link it to your name online if you want to. Otherwise, you're just a number."

Just a number, she repeated in her thoughts. *Not even linked to my name.*

She swallowed down a tiny, nervous flutter in her throat. "I want to do everything while I'm here."

Fitz replied with a disinterested hum and turned to talk to the other students at the table.

"It could be anyone's data," she whispered to herself while Fitz and the other students discussed their plans for spring break in over a week: an Alaskan cruise with parents, road trip to Nashville, flying to Cancún.

Quickly—but carefully—Ren carried out the instructions, then pressed one sticker with her sample ID inside her classroom notebook and the other on the vial. Before she could think better of it, she dropped her package in with the others to be mailed off that day.

The rest of the class flew past in a blur of lecturing, discussion, questions, and exercises. Too soon, Ren was packing up and heading to her international political economy course, and then to introductory Mandarin, and then holing up in the library carrel reading and completing the day's coursework. The next day was the same, but with different courses—vocal performance, chemical engineering, and advanced expository writing—but for these classes came study groups and peers and a whole giant group of students inviting her to sit with them at a big round table in the dining hall, sharing stories of college life with her. College was already everything she'd dreamed of, and by the time Friday rolled around, Ren had all but forgotten about the commercial DNA assay.

So in the end, it was wild how fast it all felt. On Monday, she was spitting into a vial, telling herself that it was a harmless experiment and a good opportunity to learn, and on Friday she was sitting at her table for immunology as Dr. Audran said he had some preliminary results for them.

"We'll do a deep dive after spring break," the professor said as he walked around, passing each student a sheet with a sample of their data. "This is just a taste to whet your appetite. I want you to spend the last ten minutes of class getting familiar with how this data looks and comparing your sequences for these alleles I've pulled. There's nothing intense here, nothing dire—no one is finding out today that they have a rare genetic disease." The class laughed, eyes flickering nervously around. "But for these five sequences, see if you can identify among yourselves which have homology across most humans, and which have the most variance." He handed Ren her sheet and kept walking. "Oh! And a number of you have relatives who've done this kit already. You can see how your data compares on these five genes to your relatives. Those will be at the bottom of your page."

Relatives. The word washed over Ren, irrelevant to her perusal of her data.

But then her eyes froze at the bottom half of her sheet.

"Some of you may not have a relative in there," Audran quickly added. "Don't worry! You were not created in a lab!" More laughter. "Your relatives would have had to do the assay, too, at some point. But some of you will see parents or siblings there and may even be able to tell which parent you inherited these alleles from."

Ren was vaguely aware of Fitz beside her, setting his sheet face down on the table, leaning back in his seat. But she could barely move. For as excited as she'd been to see some sequences from her very own DNA only five days ago, Ren was barely looking at that information now, because there was no way to explain the rest of what was there.

Steve Gylden would never do this test; she knew that with the certainty that she knew the sun would rise in the morning.

So who on earth was the person listed under *Paternal sequences*?

Out of the frying pan and into the fire, she thought, going from this class to the next, and the next, doing her best to stay in the moment and not obsessively worry about what she'd seen on that innocent piece of paper.

Before they'd left the classroom for the weekend, Audran had collected their class folders with the assay sheets tucked inside, locking them in the cabinet. It had been the only place their names were connected to their sample numbers, he'd reassured them, and besides, he didn't trust them not to lose the sheets over the weekend. With laughter, the class had filed out, discussing weekend plans like their worlds remained perfectly intact, unchanged by whatever they'd seen on their sheets.

By contrast, Ren struggled to reconcile a father back on the homestead—who refused to use the soil pH meter Ren had built because it had an LCD display—with one who existed only as a sequence of letters in a database somewhere in New Jersey.

Still in a fog, Ren jogged down to the street at 4:45 p.m., expecting to be early, but finding Gloria and Steve already waiting for her at the curb.

Suddenly, the desire to return to normalcy was overwhelming—to greet them with joy, to reassure herself that she hadn't just tugged at a dangerous thread. But Steve gestured that Ren go ahead and get right in the cab of the truck rather than bother with hugs, and Gloria waved off Ren's exuberance with a "Later, later," so Ren quietly slid onto the bench seat.

On the road, her parents were quiet, like they always were on the drive home. Gloria slept, Steve listened to old Hank Williams cassettes, and Ren was left to her hurricane of thoughts. The excitement of all her courses dissolved into the background as the single looming question ballooned, blocking out everything else: What did it all mean?

Steve had to have done the test, Ren thought. *He must've, at some point. Maybe before we moved to the homestead?* But that was impossible; the technology only came out a handful of years ago, and they'd moved there when Ren was around three. That was nearly twenty years ago—she was turning twenty-three in just over a week. It didn't make sense. The only explanation that made sense was that her results were wrong. Audran must've mixed up her sheet with another student's.

But she couldn't check it—the sheet was locked securely in Audran's classroom, and she'd been in such a daze that it hadn't occurred to her to compare the sample ID there to the number on the sticker in her notebook. Now she was left considering every possibility, looking at her parents with new eyes.

Eyes. Hers were green; both of her parents had brown eyes, dark hair. Ren knew two brown-eyed people could easily have recessive green in there somewhere. The problem was, Ren didn't know how to ask. She couldn't remember the last time Steve or Gloria had mentioned anything about family; it was so long ago, Ren knew instinctively to not even bring it up. How mad would her parents be if, after only a handful of weeks at college, she started asking all sorts of questions about her genetic history and people the Gyldens had long since stopped speaking to?

At home, Gloria pulled dinner from the oven, and they sat down at the table the same way they always had. But suddenly, she felt like she'd been gone for a year, a stranger in her own home. For the first time in her life, Ren truly realized that her parents had stories—so many stories—that she might never know.

Was a secret father out there one of them?

No. There was no way. It didn't matter that both of her parents were tall and muscular, while Ren was petite and lean. It didn't matter that their hair was dark and hers was golden. It didn't matter that, physically, she couldn't be more different than they were. *Genetics are a wonder,* she told herself, poking at her dinner. *I'm jumping to conclusions.*

All the questions floating in her thoughts made unease twist in her chest until it was hard to breathe. Her dorm room was small, but somehow the cabin felt smaller tonight than it ever had, and so dark inside, with all the curtains pulled tight. She used to marvel at the construction of this new home, how much bigger and more modern it was than the old one had been, the cabin they tore down to make room for the barn, but Ren couldn't help but see how rustic it was, really, and for the first time imagined how the small rooms would look through the eyes of everyone back in Spokane. She imagined Miriam with her phone and her frown, lamenting over the lack of Wi-Fi. How her composition study partners would look crowded around the small coffee table in the cloying warmth of the living room. What would her Mandarin professor think if he saw her practicing conversational Mandarin with a pig named Frank?

And, for a bewildering flash, Ren imagined Fitz at the table beside her, sitting in the empty fourth seat. In her mind, he leaned casually in his chair, one arm flung across the back as he gazed at her with that mysterious gleam in his eye. Imaginary Fitz pointed to the food on his plate. *Did you shoot this bird yourself?* he asked, whiskey eyes teasing and warm. He seemed outsized for the chair, outsized for this entire cabin. His feet would hang off the end of her bed—

"Ren?" Steve leaned into her line of sight. "You listening to your mother?"

She blinked hard, clearing her trance. "Yes! Sorry! Just tired."

"Well, you can be tired tomorrow night after you finish your chores. You've been studying on a cushy sofa in a library all week, I expect you to be rested up."

Nodding, she scooped up a forkful of casserole. "I am, sir, absolutely. I had the best week, too. You would not belie—"

"I was saying we need to get the last of the winter greens from the hothouse," Gloria cut in. "The front garden needs to be cleaned out and prepped before we take you back on Sunday. That's on top of your other chores. If you can't handle it then maybe—"

"I can handle it," Ren assured them, nodding at her plate and recalibrating how the weekend would go. If there would be no discussion of school tonight, there would certainly be no discussion of long-lost relatives.

Gloria put a hand on her arm. "I'm just trying to help bring you back home. Mentally. Spiritually. I sense that you're getting more and more tied to that place, but here is what matters."

Ren smiled gratefully and tried to mask any panic before it bled into her expression. And then she forced her attention back to her plate, because the longer she stared at her mother across the table, the more aware Ren became that this new suspicion buzzing in the air had just changed something in her forever.

CHAPTER EIGHT

REN

Sunday night, back in her dorm room bed, Ren stared at the ceiling, hating the gnawing panic that festered in her stomach. Her parents had dropped her off two hours ago, and she'd been immobilized with anxiety. The longer it ate away at her insides, the more she knew it wouldn't go away until she'd seen for herself whether Audran had handed her the correct results.

She couldn't wait until morning. After the profile in the student paper, Ren felt like she was living under a spotlight. She couldn't dig into this with an entire classroom of her peers there to witness her realization that her genetic history wasn't what she thought it was. The last thing she needed was to be a spectacle and for any of this to get back to Gloria and Steve somehow. No, if her world was indeed falling apart, she wanted it to happen under the cloak of darkness, where she'd be completely alone.

She sat up and, without thinking about it too much, pulled on her boots. Moving on instinct, she walked to the door, opened it, headed down the hall and out of the dorm. Every step loosened the tight feeling in her chest.

But as she walked across the quad and her panic eased, her rational mind peered back in. What on earth was she doing? Gloria would be furious. Furious about the test, yes, but Ren was also out after curfew. How many times had her parents said that bad stuff happened to people when they were out doing things they weren't supposed to be doing? The world was full of robbers and murderers, and hadn't Steve and Gloria kept her safe until now? Almost twenty-three years old, and she'd never been robbed or murdered once! What more proof did she need that they were right about everything?

Wispy fog curled around her ankles and sent a shiver up her body. She picked up her pace, speed walking the rest of the way across the wet, dark lawn.

The brick front of Hughes Hall curved gently alongside a wide flower bed. In the day, the sun reflected off the front windows, but at night they seemed to hold shadows at every turn. To give certain students access to labs, the front doors were unlocked, but even so, Ren braced the door carefully until it closed with barely a whisper and tiptoed past the open spaces filled with groups of red, gray, and dark blue modular sofas. A surreptitious peek into classrooms and labs as she passed showed the occasional student hunkered over a desk or lab bench, but otherwise the building seemed mostly empty.

The front doors might have been unlocked, but unfortunately, the handle to Audran's lab wouldn't budge.

If her friend Doug the Custodian had been here now, Ren had zero doubt she could convince him to let her inside. A forgotten worksheet, she could say, or maybe a lost wallet. But with the halls empty and seeming to stretch a mile in either direction, she'd have to rely on a different skill set.

Back home, they couldn't run down the street if they needed a duplicate key, and even if they could, the idea would be so far out of her parents' comfort zone that it almost made Ren laugh into the dark just thinking about it. *An extra key?* Steve would say. *For who? The person who'll rob us blind?* If they lost a master, that was it. Thankfully, the three of them were better lock pickers than any cat burglar you'd find in the movies. Tension wrenches, rakes, screwdrivers, and even nails—all came in handy. She once broke into the locked barn using a hoof pick and some twine from the hay bale.

Unfortunately, Ren had none of those things in her backpack, so the paper clip around her Intro to Mandarin packet and the pin in her hair would have to do.

Straightening the bobby pin, she slipped it into the lock and then slid the straightened paper clip in to find and carefully lift the tiny pins inside. It took some patience, a few stops and starts, but with just the right amount of pressure, the mechanism started to give, and the lock turned over with a satisfying click.

With one last furtive glance up and down the hall, Ren slipped inside and closed the door behind her with a near-silent tick. The lab was near black, illuminated only by fog-obscured moonlight streaming in the windows, and her heart galloped like a wild beast in her chest.

Pushing off the door, she headed to the computer farthest from the window and booted it up. While it loaded, she snuck to the cabinet where their active in-class work was kept.

Again, the door was locked.

"I'll do extra chores over spring break." Ren whispered her penance into the empty room, putting the bobby pin and paper clip to use one more time. The flimsy lock on the cabinet opened easily. Shuffling through the papers in the tray there, Ren found a folder with her name on it and carried it over to the computer to read by the screen's light.

Inside the folder was the piece of paper with the preliminary data linked to her sample ID. Digging into her backpack, she pulled her notebook out, flipping it open to the sticker she'd put there with the ID number. Ren stared down, numb, at the identical sequence of numbers there.

Audran hadn't accidentally handed her someone else's data.

She closed her eyes, trying to explain it away. Maybe her sample had been mixed up before she sealed it, or switched in transit, or replaced with someone else's at the testing lab. But Ren knew the odds of this highly validated system failing in such obvious ways were slim.

After dimming the screen as low as it would go, she loaded the genotyping software and then hesitated, knowing she'd have to create an account to access more information. She wondered if this was a step too far. Did it matter anymore? She'd already committed a handful of crimes and broken twice as many of her family's rules. Stopping now wouldn't change any of that. Besides, Audran would have them do this in class tomorrow anyway.

Carefully, Ren created a profile with her ID number, giving a fake name and her address as the student dorm. The software loaded with an overwhelming number of options: ANCESTRY REPORT, DNA RELATIVES, BLOOD & BIOMARKERS, TRAITS, and RESEARCH. Ren's mouse hovered over the DNA RELATIVES tab; then, with shaking hands, she clicked the link, typing her information when prompted, and checked the box not to allow others to view her profile.

Hopefully whoever her paternal match was had been more generous with his own information.

As expected, there was nothing on the maternal side of the tree, but just beneath her generic pink profile image was a cartoon of a man's profile in blue and the words *99.9999% paternal match*.

Her mouse hovered over the link, and a balloon popped up.

You are approved to view this profile.

Sick with anticipation, Ren clicked, and it felt like the floor opened up beneath her as she began to read.

Name: Christopher Koning
Known relatives: 100133654 (spouse); 100133655 (daughter); 100136482 (brother); 100136485 (sister-in-law); 100137298 (aunt); 100137291 (cousin)

Allergies: Tree nuts, dust mites
Ancestry report: 99.9% Northwestern European (53.6% Scandinavian, 30.3% French & German, 16.1% Broadly Northwestern European)
Hair: Blond
Eyes: Green
Profession: Chemical Engineer
Location: Atlanta, Georgia

At the bottom was a hyperlink reading, simply, *Christopher Koning*. With her fingers trembling on the computer mouse, Ren clicked the link, and a new window opened, filling the screen with a full-color photo.

Ren didn't realize she had her hand pressed to her mouth until a sob broke free.

Staring back at her was a face that was so familiar it felt almost like a photo filter comically turning her into an older, male version of herself.

Ren pushed away from the chair, taking a few stumbling steps back from the computer.

Her eyes, her chin, the color of her hair—everything was the same.

Maybe he was an uncle. A cousin. *Something*. It didn't mean he was her father. Her brain scratched around wildly for understanding. There had to be an explanation.

But no matter what it might be, her detective work tonight confirmed one thing: She had more family out there. She had people she belonged to who she'd never known existed. Who might not even know *she* existed.

Her heart twisted painfully, and she stepped closer again, staring at the face of the man on the screen. She wanted to memorize him, to see him in motion, longed to tunnel down into the part of her most primitive self that whispered, *I know you*. When Ren closed her eyes, breathing deeply and working to steady her rocketing pulse, sparklers popped behind her eyelids, and she felt a pull, a desperate ache in her chest. She wanted to see him.

No . . . she *needed* to see him, to understand who he was to her. But Georgia was so far away. Ren couldn't think of a single scenario that would put her in Atlanta.

A tiny creak in the building startled her back to herself, and Ren jerked to attention, trying to pull it together. She quickly wiped her eyes, sucked in a jagged breath. She could freak out back in the dorm, under the covers. Not here.

Still stunned, Ren carefully returned the assay sheet to the folder and shut down the computer. But when she moved across the room to put her file away, a light from under the connecting door to Dr. Audran's office caught her attention. Her heart launched into her throat; a million horrifying scenarios raced through her thoughts—where security caught her in the lab after-hours, where she was disciplined, where she lost her scholarship and was sent home for good.

In a panic she turned to quickly leave . . . but then stopped. This didn't look like the sweeping cone of a security flashlight. It was dimmer, like the concentrated glow of Miriam's phone from beneath the covers.

Ren had been told time and time again that she was too curious for her own good. She'd been kicked in the gut when she got a little too close to Callie during calving season. She'd tried to fix a tractor tire with gasoline and a lighter like she'd read in an ancient copy of *Popular Mechanics* and nearly gotten her head blown off when a fireball erupted in front of her. It took six months for her eyebrows to look normal again.

She knew she should slip out and get back to her room, but something itched in her thoughts, some sense of Not Right. And there was relief in this distraction, in this delay of thinking about that other, enormous thing.

Moonlight cut through the blinds in stabs of light across the floor as she crept closer and peered through the small rectangular window cut into the door. She immediately recognized the slope of those shoulders, knew the strength in that back and the imposing presence that made goose bumps erupt along her skin.

He turned his face into the light of the computer monitor, and Ren knew that she was right; Fitz was on the other side of the door, hunched over in the dark as he furtively typed something into Dr. Audran's computer.

CHAPTER NINE

FITZ

Fitz had done a lot of questionable things for an A grade.

He'd worn a tour T-shirt of a professor's favorite band to class, pretending to also be a huge fan. He'd organized fundraisers, joined jog-a-thons, picketed, and canvassed for signatures to benefit their favorite causes. He'd rounded up groups of students to fill the auditorium for guest speakers and helped students who were struggling with the material. He'd flirted with professors—he'd done far more than flirt with their TAs. He'd made sure the dean loved him, leveraged his father's reputation at every possible opportunity, and never regretted it, not once, because he was so close to the finish line he could taste it.

He knew in his heart he wouldn't have regretted this, either, if Ren hadn't shown up.

It was the tiny creak of the door that gave her away. Just the smallest sound of metal on metal, a hinge shifting a fraction of an inch. It was enough to pull his attention away from the screen and to the inch-wide expanse of darkness leading into the lab. There, in the shadow, was a face.

And there, in the flesh, was Ren Gylden, with her big green eyes and spools of golden hair and round, shocked mouth, shoving the door wide open. "What are you doing here?"

"I'm—" Panic rose like a violent tide as consequences scrolled out in his mind: academic dishonesty, the loss of Judge Iman's letter, maybe even no shot at graduating, ever. He'd been so sure of this plan, he'd never bothered to make another.

And then he paused, narrowing his eyes. "What are *you* doing here?"

"I asked you first." She pointed to the computer, stammering, "That's—that's Audran's grade book."

"He asked me to come in and check something for him."

"You?"

His heart hammered so hard he wondered if she could hear it. "Yeah."

"Why?"

"Because he trusts me."

She stared at him, frowning. "Why didn't he ask one of the new TAs?"

"How am I supposed to know? He just asked me."

She chewed on this for a beat. "So why didn't you turn on the lights?"

"I'm lazy."

"But not so lazy that you won't come into the lab at midnight on a Sunday?"

"Just a quick in and out," he said with a sideways grin, "and then I'm done."

Before he realized what Ren was doing, she'd moved in a blur, stepping forward and reaching above him for something on the shelf. He was about to tell her to let him wrap up and head home when a bursting flash filled the room, temporarily blinding him.

"If you're here on his instruction, I'm sure you won't mind if I verify it with Dr. Audran."

He grasped for the table. When his vision started to clear, he could just make out the way she gently waved something in the air near her head. Fitz's stomach bottomed out. She'd taken a Polaroid photo of him with Audran's grade book open on the screen in the background.

"Ren," he said, low and steadying, moving just a little closer. He put on his trademark sultry half smile. "I swear it isn't what you think."

But, as ever, Ren was immune to his flirtation. "It isn't you panicking about your test score and breaking in here to change it in Audran's computer?"

He swallowed. "I can explain."

"I can't wait to hear it."

Fitz took a closer look at her. Gone was the affable golden retriever energy. This Ren was shaken, rattled. Whether it was the anger over finding him here or something else, she wasn't going to budge. Dread filled him with a cold blackness, and he slumped back into the chair. Was this how it would all fall apart? Eight years of hard work and the occasional con, and it was gone in the flash of a Polaroid? Fitz couldn't believe he was going to be buried by long-dead technology. He had so much riding on this, more than Ren could even fathom.

"My father will cut off my inheritance if he finds out I cheated," he lied, doing his best to sound terrified. Honestly, it wasn't much of a stretch, and if there was one thing Corona students knew about Fitz, it was that his father was loaded. "After graduation, I have plans to create a charitable organization for clean energy research, but all of that will be lost if this gets out."

She took a deep breath before blowing it out in a burst. Fitz had always been able to read people. He'd gone a little overboard with this story, but she was buying it, he could tell.

Ren shook her head. "You're lying."

Dammit. "Why would you say that?"

"Your voice got all garbled, you gave way too much information, and there's not a charitable bone in your body." She pointed. "And you're jiggling your leg. An obvious tell."

He placed a steadying hand on his thigh. "Well, it's the truth."

Ren crossed her arms over her chest and stared down at him. She looked worked up, those giant green eyes a little wild. Something was happening in that big brain of hers, and Fitz could only wait to see what she was going to do with the Polaroid in her hand. "You know what, Just Fitz," she said finally, jaw tightening in determination, "I don't actually care what your reason is. I just want to know what this photo is worth to you."

"What it's wor—?" He broke off as awareness landed. "You're *blackmailing* me?"

"Call it whatever you want. I overheard you last week. You're going to Nashville for spring break, aren't you?"

"Nashville?" He pretended to think. "You must have me confused with someone else."

She huffed out a laugh. "If you want me to keep this photo a secret, you're going to take me with you."

Stunned, he gaped at her. He was completely unaccustomed to being on this side of a negotiation, and honestly, it sucked. "You can't be serious."

"Serious as a sleep attack."

Whatever he was going to say next evaporated from his thoughts. "A sleep attack?"

"When one gets an uncontrollable urge to sleep. A common symptom of narcolepsy."

"Why not just say 'serious as a heart attack'?"

"Because heart attacks kill people! I don't want to make light of that!"

"But if someone has a sleep attack while driving," he argued, "couldn't that also be leth—"

"Fitz! Listen to what I'm telling you! If you want to keep this a secret, you're taking me with you. Yes or no?"

A flush of vulnerability passed over her face, and he felt a subtle shift in power. It wasn't quite enough to get the ball back in his court; he needed to leverage everything he could. "I think you need to tell me what had *you* breaking into the lab at midnight on a Sunday."

"No way," she said, resolutely shaking her head.

"Then go ahead and show Audran the photo. I'll just tell him I was changing things back after busting you fixing your score in here."

She gasped, long and horrified. "You wouldn't dare."

This made him laugh. "Of course I would. If you're going to take me down, I'm taking you down with me."

"Audran wouldn't believe it. And . . ." She looked around, desperately searching for something, before setting her steely gaze back on him. "Listen, mister. Everyone else here might be fooled by your charm and looks and voice, but not me."

He leaned in, giving her his best, teasing smile. This is what he was good at. He could flirt his way out of anything. "My charm and looks and voice, huh?"

She flushed. Bingo. "What I'm saying," she started, for once visibly flustered, "is that I'm guessing this isn't the first time you've cheated, and the last thing you want is the dean looking closer into your past here."

She was grasping at straws, but it was too close to the truth for his comfort. Fitz closed his eyes, trying to weigh the situation objectively. A handful of days with Ren jabbering his ear off in the car versus potentially having academic dishonesty on his permanent record, losing his recommendation letter, and—most importantly—ruining any chance at having his criminal record expunged. Basically, if she exposed him, he could lose everything.

There was no question. He'd come too far.

Fitz bent, cupping his forehead in his palm. He could get her to Nashville and dump her wherever she needed to be before he went to Mary's, before his interview, before Ren learned anything else about his life. "I planned on leaving Tuesday, before spring break starts. It means I'm missing half a week of classes."

"That's fine," she said, nodding. "I can make it up, no problem."

Jaw clenched, he stared at the wall for a few deep breaths. Finally, he looked squarely at her, trying to infuse some menace into his voice: "If you're coming with me, there will be rules."

Her face cleared, eyes round in relief. "Anything you say."

"Number one, I'm in charge."

"One hundred percent!"

"And . . ." He dug around, trying to find more ground rules, but all he could focus on was how much this was going to suck.

"And?"

"And I'll tell you the rest when we leave."

She lifted her arm in a dorky salute. "Yes, sir!"

"Rule two: No saluting."

Ren dropped her hand, bowing instead.

"Rule two continued: No bowing."

She straightened, rigid. "I'm so relieved. Thank you, Fitz. I promise I won't show anyone the photo, and you can count on me, because—"

"No talking, either."

She motioned to zip her mouth closed and he pushed away from the desk, standing. With a sigh, Fitz turned, making sure Audran's computer reflected his doctored score before shutting it down and checking that all the items on the desk were the way he found them. When he turned back, Ren was still standing at attention, waiting.

From behind her pinned lips she mumbled, "Ahrarehrooree ruhrehrohrihrarhrrharhar!"

He stared, finally relenting. "What."

She mimed unzipping her lips. "I promise to be the best road trip partner ever!"

"Sure, whatever," he said. "Meet me outside of Davis Hall at six on Tuesday evening. Don't be late."

CHAPTER TEN

REN

Ren had never seen an airplane from anything closer than tens of thousands of feet overhead, but her parents had. They used to fly all over, apparently, until the greed and corruption of the world got to be too much, and they sold everything they owned and moved onto the land Steve inherited from his grandparents that became their homestead. But even though they wouldn't step foot in an airport again, her parents would humor her when she was smaller and wanted to hear all about it. They'd tell her about the ticketing agents and the fancy uniforms they'd wear, about the security lines and how it used to stress them out something awful. Ren would ask over and over again to hear about how big the planes were up close, about walking down the jetway and getting to their seat and being given little bags of peanuts or crackers and a whole can of ginger ale just for themselves, and about getting to the airport hours early to get through it all.

Ren didn't expect a road trip to be anything like a trip on a plane, but just in case more preparation was required than she expected, she was ready and at the curb in front of Davis Hall by five on Tuesday evening. By five fifteen, she was pretty sure road trips worked nothing like air travel. There were plenty of people walking around, plenty of cars pulling to the curb, but no Fitz.

It gave her time to sit with the thoughts she'd done her best to outrun for the past forty or so hours. What was she doing? Was she really thinking about leaving? For the past five days, she'd felt unfamiliar in her skin—frantic, anxious, suspicious. She'd been frustrated with her parents before, of course, but only in small ways. Things like when they wouldn't let her try something new to help with the harvest, or they didn't want to branch out and add a new farmers market to their monthly rotation. But nothing like this, when the confusion and hurt seemed to tangle into a ball of ache she wasn't sure how to look at straight on.

But was she really doing *this*? This, as in getting in a car with a virtual stranger and driving for days? What choice did she have? She *had* to meet Christopher Koning. The curiosity had transitioned overnight into a burning, desperate necessity. Unfortunately, she only had sixty-three dollars to her name. Not nearly enough for a bus ticket, let alone a plane trip to Atlanta and back. But if Fitz could get her to Nashville, she figured she'd be able to afford a bus to Atlanta from there.

The bigger issue was her parents. This wasn't sneaking off campus to grab a sandwich or buy a new alarm clock. This was *leaving* leaving. Today was Tuesday; Steve and Gloria would be there Friday evening to pick Ren up, expecting her home for the entirety of spring break next week. She had to delay them but hadn't figured out *how* yet. What if they showed up early, before she'd thought of a good excuse for them to stay home? Would they go to her room and ask Miriam where Ren was? Would she tell them she hadn't seen Ren in three days? And then what? What would she do if she actually managed to find Christopher Koning? Was finding him really worth the chance that her parents wouldn't let her return to school?

Panic clawed its way up Ren's throat at the possibilities that spiraled from there, and she blinked hard, trying to clear it. Behind her lids, she imagined a highway passing beneath her, the skyline of Atlanta coming into view, and the soothing relief of fireworks popping all around everything. The jittery adrenaline cleared from her blood when her mind went unfocused and she felt the safety of a big, warm hand holding hers, when she saw the sparkling lights glowing just in front of her.

The truth was, this trip was only partly about finding Christopher Koning. There had always been something inside Ren that knew there was more out there—more to learn, more to see, more people to meet, and more to her story. She knew, each time she imagined the fireworks, that the fantasy somehow took her off the homestead. Ren's entwined dread and hope that this was a clue to all of that made her feel like she was a boulder balanced precariously at the lip of a cliff.

She reached down, absently winding her watch, before pulling her sleeve back to peek at the time. Five thirty.

The coffee shop across the street was open. Inside, it looked cozy, with soft lighting and a pastry case full of baked goods she could practically smell from her place on the curb. Digging into her pocket, she felt the small wad of cash there. It had to last her the next week at least. But if Fitz was driving her across the county, the least she could do was spare a dollar for a nice coffee for him, right?

When she stepped out of the small shop, the *four-dollar* coffee in hand, Fitz was bent over the hood of a rusty white Ford Mustang parked at the curb. "I might have to take her," he mumbled as she stepped up behind him, "but I don't have to be nice about it." A loud ping sounded from somewhere inside the engine. Fitz slammed the hood closed, and the sound was echoed by a pop. "Bet she doesn't make it to Missoula. We'll see who breaks first."

"Who's breaking before Missoula?"

He turned, startled. "Hey. Oh. No one." He scowled, and a tiny corner of her attention was pulled to the sight of his hair sticking up sweetly on the side, mussed from his fingers running through it, she guessed. She straightened. The appearance might be cute, but the man was grumpy: "I told you to be here at six."

"It's five forty-five."

"Exactly my point," he said. "I don't need more time with you than I already have."

She reminded herself that what he'd said was true: He didn't have to be nice. He only had to get her closer to Atlanta. "Who were you talking to?" she asked.

"My car. Max."

"You named your car?" she asked, delighted. "We named our tractor!"

Fitz had that look he'd worn around her a few times already, the one that said he wasn't sure whether he was supposed to find something funny. "Sure, I'll bite. What's your tractor named, Ren?"

Her chest tightened, and she wished she hadn't brought it up. "Steve."

"Steve, huh? Wow. Cool." Fitz walked to the curb for his bag.

Ren swallowed, following him. "Yeah, Gloria—uh, my mom, she named it after my dad." She could hear how the word *dad* came out thin, like her throat didn't want to let it out. For the thousandth time, Ren felt heavily aware that the man she'd been raised to think was her biological father might not be, after all.

Grief felt like a hand wrapped around her windpipe, and she didn't know what to do but shove the coffee toward Fitz. "Here. I got you this."

"What is it?"

She pointed to the coffee shop back over her shoulder. "From there. It's their special today. White chocolate something. It's to thank you for taking me."

"I'm not taking you because I chose to."

"I know. But I feel bad about blackmailing you."

"Well, by all means, a coffee makes things right." He set his duffel down to take the coffee, but before he could take a sip, Ren grabbed his forearm and pointed to the cup. "No, no, look first! She made a *leaf* with the *foam*!"

Fitz pried off the lid, significantly less impressed than she'd been, saying flatly, "Wow, look at that." He took a sip, his entire body jerking in a shudder. "Oh, my God that's sweet."

Ren laughed. "It was four whole dollars, so maybe she wanted to give you your money's worth of sugar?"

With a playful smirk, Fitz opened his mouth to say something and then snapped it closed, reaching with his free hand to pinch the bridge of his nose. "Look, Sweden. Let's—let's just go over the ground rules."

She was ready for this. "Rule one: You're in charge. Rule two: No saluting or bowing."

"Right," he said, "and no—"

"Oh!" She remembered something she wanted to show him first and dug into her backpack. "I made sandwiches!"

Fitz's lip curled, and she followed his gaze to the seven plastic-wrapped PB&Js she'd made this afternoon at the dining hall. "They're a little smashed," she admitted, "but I make them every Monday for the week, and trust me, they get better over time. If we ration it, this could get us to Nashville."

Delicately, he plucked the bundle from her hand and dropped it in a trash can near the curb. "No."

"Why'd you do that?" She walked to the can and peered in, but they'd already been swallowed by the random mess of banana peels, coffee cups, and other detritus. "What are we going to ea—"

"Rule three: No eating in the car."

"Isn't that what road trips are for? Snacking and driving and singing—"

"Rules four through six, I'm in charge of the music, no singing, and no being annoying."

Her mood dropped. "These aren't very fun rules."

Fitz barked out a laugh. "You're blackmailing me. I'm not going to make this trip *enjoyable*."

She lowered her voice to a whisper. "I told you I feel bad about that. It's why I got you the coffee."

"Rule seven," he said, "no backseat driving."

Ren bent to look in the back window. "I have to sit in the backseat?"

"Rule *eight*." He ignored her and placed a gentle hand on the top of the car. "Treat Max with respect. Rule nine: No talking."

"At all?"

"Remember rule six?"

Deflated, she nodded. "No being annoying."

"What are you even going to Nashville for?" he asked. "If it's so important that you're willing to *extort* me, why not just take a bus or, better yet, fly?"

She lifted her chin, steeling herself against the wave of nausea that rolled through her. "It's none of your business."

"Well, fine, but here's rule ten: I hope you have a way home, because I'm not sure what day I'm leaving to head back, and I'm not working around your schedule."

Her brain hiccupped. She hadn't even figured out how she was getting to Atlanta from Nashville, let alone that she might have to find her way back to Spokane afterward.

Perhaps sensing something in her reaction, Fitz bent to catch her eye. "You *do* have a plan for how you're getting home, right?"

She nodded vaguely.

He leaned closer. "Sweden?"

"Yes," she said with more conviction. It was too late to turn back now. "I do—or, at least, I will by the time I need to come back. But either way, it's not your problem."

Fitz turned, opening the trunk to put their bags inside. "We got ourselves a fly-by-the-seat-of-her-pants girl here, Max." He paused before closing the trunk. "Do you need anything out of here before we go? We won't stop until Missoula."

With her mouth closed tight, she quickly shook her head.

"Good." He closed the trunk with a nod of finality.

"ButIwantedtosay," she whispered in a rush, shrinking under his glare. "I just wanted to tell you thank you. I know you're doing this under duress, but it's very important to me." Digging into her coat pocket, she pulled an envelope free and thrust it toward him. "I also made you a card. Okay, now I'll try to stick to rule six."

He took the envelope, unceremoniously ripping it open. Inside was a hand-drawn card with the words THANK YOU "JUST FITZ" in bright block letters surrounded by a vibrant field of tiny, intricate fireworks. Yellow and orange, green and blue, red and purple. The precision, up close, was impressive, she knew. But when viewed from a little bit of a distance, it would look like stained glass. She'd made it last night—had spent nearly two hours on it, in fact—and she was proud of how it turned out.

For a beat, Fitz's grumpy forehead smoothed as he stared down. "*You* made this?"

"Yeah."

He exhaled a defeated breath and squeezed his eyes closed for a beat before shoving the card into his pocket and pointing to the passenger door. "Get in."

Excitement rolled up inside her, bubbling free with a tiny clap-and-jump combo.

"Knock it off," he said, rounding the car.

"I'm just so exci—"
"Shh."

CHAPTER ELEVEN

FITZ

Even the click of her buckle was too exuberant.

"Calm down," he muttered.

"I'm just getting in the car!"

"Just—" He exhaled a gusting breath. "Do it with more chill."

She nodded firmly, and he could swear she tamped down the urge to salute.

He pulled away from the curb, and they were off. He watched as the lights of Corona College grew smaller and smaller in the rear-view mirror . . . along with his enthusiasm for this trip.

This was not how he imagined making the drive from Spokane to Nashville. He'd imagined himself, Max, a giant mug of coffee in the cupholder, and some music blasting, windows down. He imagined having the freedom to let his thoughts run wild with the first *What's Next* he'd ever relished. He was three months from graduating college, three months from getting everything he'd been promised, three months from beginning his revenge and starting fresh, alone.

Except he wasn't alone. He had the world's most annoying tagalong, who was furiously writing something in the notebook in her lap.

Maybe that's what she'd do the entire time?

Maybe she'd write and draw, and Fitz could just pretend she wasn't—

Ren raised her hand, and he tightened his grip around the steering wheel. "Yes?"

"Do you have a map?"

"You mean GPS? Yes, of course."

"Not a paper map?" she asked.

"People don't really use those anymore."

"Well, as you probably know, I don't have a ph—"

"Rule nine," he reminded her.

"I'd be less inclined to *speak*," she said pointedly, "if I could follow our progress on the road."

"Then you should have brought a map yourself."

"Oh!" She clapped, delighted. "I couldn't sleep last night, so I borrowed Miriam's laptop to look up some road trip games!" She opened her notebook again, where, a quick glance told him, she'd been writing down his stated rules for the road trip. She flipped back a page. "There's the license plate game, where we can—"

"No."

"—try to find a license plate from every state, and—"

"No."

"—the alphabet game, where we find signs that start with each letter of the—"

"No games. Just—here." He growled, reaching for his phone and, with his eyes on the road, holding it up to his face to unlock it. "Open Google Maps, but don't touch anything else."

She squealed, holding it up at arm's length.

"Don't read my texts."

"I won't."

"Or emails."

"Why would I read your emails?"

"I don't know, just don't."

After about five minutes of blissful silence, Fitz felt his shoulders loosen in relief. Maybe she was capable of being quiet. Ren was transfixed watching their little blue circle bob along on the interstate, which allowed Fitz to return to the absorbing relief of the *What's Next*. He mentally listed the overarching path: finish school, secure a letter of recommendation from Judge Iman, complete his law internship, take the LSATs, enter law school. And then ruthlessly take down his father.

Finishing school wouldn't be an issue; securing the letter from Judge Iman might be, but there was nothing he could do about that right now. Now he should focus only on nailing the interview for a yearlong paid internship at the law offices of Fellows, Wing, and Greenleaf. Not only was it the best corporate law firm in the country but it was in Nashville . . . where he could be near Mary again. Where he could finally keep an eye on her.

A shrieking giggle ripped through the car, and Fitz barely managed to keep from slamming down hard on the brakes. "Holy sh—*what*! What is going on?"

"There's a place called Sex Peak about sixty miles down that way!"

He took a beat to gape at her before turning back to the road. "What in the hell is Sex Peak?"

"I don't know! But it's on the *map*!" She turned to him. "Fitz, may I use your browser to google it?"

He sighed, resigned. "Fine. But don't look at the other tabs."

She was quiet for a second and then hummed. "Oh," she said, frowning down at the screen. "That name is misleading. It's a lookout point and camping area. I don't see anything about sex happening here."

"A lookout? Yeah, for sure people have sex there."

"They *do*?"

"I mean, I assume so. It's called Sex Peak."

"I guess you would know."

"What's that supposed to mean?"

She ignored this, whispering in awe, "The internet is magic."

He quickly glanced to see what she was looking up. "What are you googling?"

"Whether people have sex at Sex Peak."

"Okay there, Sweden, let's just . . ." He reached for the phone and tucked it into the center console. "Maybe let's take a break from Google. I don't want you getting carsick."

"Oh, good point." She looked out at the slowly darkening view ahead of them for a few minutes and cleared her throat before turning to look at him. She didn't speak, but he felt the pressure of her attention on the side of his face like a finger gently tapping there.

Finally, he couldn't take it anymore. "God. *What.*"

"I wanted to apologize if that was rude just now when I said 'You would know.' You might not be a lothario at all, I don't want to assume."

"A *lothario*? Seriously, Ren, where did you learn to speak?"

She ignored this. "When I first arrived, before I met you for the tour? Miriam—that's my roommate—said you were always in everyone's pants and warned me not to let you in mine."

Fitz swore Max's engine stuttered beneath him, and he gripped the steering wheel tighter. "Rule eleven. No discussion about whose pants anyone's been in."

With a nod, she pulled the pencil from the spiral ring of her notebook, turned back the page, and added number eleven to the list of rules.

He sensed a change in Ren the second they reached the border to Idaho. As they passed the sign indicating that they'd crossed the state line, her shoulders hunched up to her ears and she pulled her knees up, hugging herself.

"You all right there, Sweden?"

"Yes."

He wasn't so sure. For the entire forty-five minutes through the panhandle, she appeared to be going through an existential crisis. Mumbling quietly to herself, she argued with an invisible voice. He thought he caught an "If they found out, this would kill them!"

Ignoring her, he turned the music up.

Finally, she raised her hand to speak.

He lowered the music again. "Yes?"

And then she dropped a bombshell: "Fitz, can we—can we turn around?"

Beneath them, Max swerved on the road. "What?"

Ren quickly waved her hands. "Never mind. *No*," she said with more force. "Ignore me. I do not want to turn around."

He weighed the relative bummer of losing three hours round trip with the even greater bummer of continuing with her for the next few days. "We're only a couple hours out. If you want to turn around, tell me now."

"No. Keep going." But then she groaned, leaning her head back against the seat. "What they don't know won't hurt them, right?"

"Look . . . I know this is stressful for you, okay? No harm, no foul. Tell me now, and I can take you back."

"No. *No*." And then she released a tight "I'm just a terrible daughter, that's all" and dropped her head into her hands.

"Let me ask you something," he said, then attempted another sip of the now-cold sugar bomb she'd bought him. "Does anyone other than me know that you left?"

She reached down to fidget with the notebook on her lap. "Of course."

An obvious lie.

"Does that seem like a safe choice?" he asked her, holding up a hand when she started to protest. "Come on, kid."

"I'm almost twenty-three, Fitz, I'm not a kid."

He huffed out a laugh. "I'm just saying, you barely know me."

"You?" She turned those giant green eyes on him. "I think under that cocky shell, you're a big softie."

He laughed, incredulous. "I assure you, no female has ever called me that before."

She smiled, sweetly. Too sweetly. "Fine," she said. "You're a *little* softie."

"Oh my God. That's not—"

"Anyway," she said, putting on that tough face again. "I told you, it's not your business where I'm going or who knows."

"You shouldn't trust me just because we go to school together."

Beaming like she had him cornered, she said, "The fact that you're worried about this tells me you're a good guy."

A good guy? She had no idea. "Just— You'll get your own hotel room, okay? And keep the door locked."

"A hotel?"

He did a double take over at her. "Yes . . . ?"

"We're not staying in hotels, are we?"

Fitz coughed in disbelief. "You want to sleep on the street?"

"Not in the street, but I thought we'd be sleeping in the car."

A laugh burst free. "*Hell* no."

"I don't have money for a hotel, Fitz. I only have some money for food."

"What do you mean?" Panic rose in his throat. "How did you expect to get across the country?"

"Well, you threw out my sandwiches, which is definitely unfortunate because—"

"Wait." Alarm bells sounded. Somehow, he suspected their definition of *some money for food* didn't align. "How much money do you have in your bank account?"

She laughed like this was a silly question. "I don't have a bank account."

For several long beats he stared blankly at the dark road vanishing beneath his car. Finally, he managed, "Okay, how much cash did you bring?"

"I have about sixty dollars."

Exasperation exploded in his chest. These were all things he should have asked before they left: Does anyone know you're leaving, do you have enough money to take this trip, how are you getting home? Fitz had put aside enough money from his paychecks to cover his own way and maybe a little extra, but certainly not enough for two hotel rooms in every city, two meals at every stop. This was insanity. "Ren, seriously? Even if we're frugal, you only have enough for maybe six meals, and you're planning to be gone for a *week*!"

"I'll—we'll figure it out. I'll make it up to you!" She widened those green eyes at him, and he looked back to the road. "I promise." She paused and then spoke with such deep sincerity, he found himself turning to her again: "I *promise*, Fitz."

Sincere or not, this was absurd. "How are you going to make it up to me? Are you planning on setting up a table selling pickling spices in the quad when we get back?"

Excited for a beat, she opened her mouth to respond and then clamped her lips shut, narrowing her eyes. He ignored the way this cute frustration sent a tiny thrill down the back of his neck.

"I think you're teasing me," she said.

"Of course I'm teasing you. But what else are you going to do? Get a job at Starbucks? Maybe you'll be a cashier at Target?" He studied her in tiny glances away from the road, genuinely curious now. "Everyone knows you don't even leave campus except when you get picked up by your parents on Fridays."

Ren turned her face forward, expression crashing at the sneer in his tone. "I didn't think I stood out so much."

"Are you kidding me?" He coughed out a sharp laugh. "Sweden, did you even read the profile about you? You came in halfway through the year. You have seventeen acres of blond hair, if your eyes were any larger you'd be a lemur, and you greet every mammal on campus as you walk past. You've never been to school before but know more than most of the professors, you can fix a rocket engine with duct tape and a shoelace, and you fooled everyone but me into thinking you're a gift from God. Yeah, I'd say you stick out a bit."

A worm of regret moved through him, but he shoved it aside, seeing the opening in her insecurity about being a fish out of water. "You've barely been off campus but think you can handle yourself on a cross-country trip with a stranger?" He laughed. "You really are so naive."

He felt like a jerk, but at least it worked. She didn't say anything else for the rest of the drive to Missoula.

CHAPTER TWELVE

REN

A real dilemma landed at her feet when it was time to stop for the night: She'd resolved to keep quiet for the rest of the day's drive, and then they pulled up in front of what had to be the most beautiful hotel she'd ever seen. The building itself was sand colored, with an entrance that was five sliding doors wide and a giant well-lit white archway. Behind them was a wide paved path bracketed by manicured grounds with flowers and grass and beautifully placed rocks.

They climbed out of the car, stretched in the waning light, and stared at their home for the night.

Ren lasted all of ten seconds before it burst out of her: "It's so beautiful!"

Fitz followed her attention to the entrance, his gaze sweeping, unimpressed, across the sight before them, then coming back to her. "It's a Holiday Inn."

She exhaled, awed. "Even the name sounds magical."

He stared at her for another beat before wordlessly walking to the back of the Mustang and retrieving their bags, slinging one around each of his broad shoulders. His was an unblemished leather duffel. Hers was an old ratty backpack. Together, they looked so funny she couldn't help but laugh.

"You don't have to carry my stuff, Fitz," she called, jogging after him.

"It's fine."

The automatic doors slid open, and they were hit with a wall of cool air smelling of industrial cleaner. She'd expected temperatures to be warmer the farther south they drove so she hadn't bothered to pack her winter coat, but the early April air in Missoula still had a real bite to it and the air-conditioning didn't help. She rubbed her arms, following Fitz into a lobby with shiny brass light fixtures, a stacked stone fireplace, and wood floors everywhere.

"Wow," she murmured.

At the reception desk, a girl appeared from the back, coming to an abrupt stop when she spotted Fitz.

Setting their bags at his feet, he leaned his folded arms across the Formica counter. "Hey," he said, voice low and deep. Even behind him, Ren could hear his trademark smile in the sound, and she looked up in time to catch the woman's visible swoon.

"Hey—hi." She swallowed. "Good eve— Welcome. To the Missoula . . . Checking in?"

Smoothly, he reached into his back pocket and pulled his wallet out. "I have a reservation." He handed her his ID. "But was wondering if we could add a second room?"

The woman pushed a cloud of frizzy curls from her face and typed in his name. "Hmm. I do see your reservation here . . . one night, in a double?" She glanced sidelong at Ren and then quickly away. "But you want a second room?"

"That's right."

She pressed a few more keys and winced. "It looks like we're fully booked because of the rodeo and won't be able to add another room tonight."

He lowered his voice further, dripping honey. "You sure?"

The girl stared at him for a long, silent beat. Ren looked from Fitz, to the girl, and back to Fitz again, wondering what was supposed to happen. Finally, he cleared his throat, and the girl jolted back into awareness. "Um . . . y-yes. Unless you want a room on the club level."

"How much are those?"

She swallowed thickly. "Those are two fifty."

"Two hundred and fifty dollars?"

"Yes."

"Per night?" he asked.

"Yes."

"In Missoula?"

"Yes."

"On a Tuesday?"

She swallowed again, eyes flickering away. "Yes."

Fitz deflated, turning to Ren. "You can take the room. I'll sleep in the car."

"No!" she yelled, startling them all. "No *way*. If anyone sleeps in the car, it's me."

He shook his head. "We're not doing that."

"Then I won't even walk upstairs to the room," she said. "I mean it, Fitz."

After a moment of jaw-clenching contemplation, he turned back to the girl at the counter, resigned. "Fine. I guess we're doing the one room. Is there a rollaway you can send up?"

She nodded, then stopped. "I—no, sorry. Unfortunately, this size room doesn't accommodate one."

"Don't worry," Ren told him in a whisper, "it's not like there will be any hanky-panky."

The girl smothered a laugh, and Fitz glanced at Ren with a smirk. "Hanky-panky?"

"You know. Like kissing and canoo—"

"Yeah, Ren, I know what hanky-panky is." With a quiet laugh, he handed over his credit card, signed a screen when prompted, took the key card, and wordlessly picked up their bags again. "Thanks," he said over his shoulder, charm turned off.

Ren smiled at the other woman, saying a quick "Thank you very much" before jogging after Fitz to the elevators. In silence, they stepped in when the doors opened, and Fitz hit the button for the fifth floor.

"I really don't mind sleeping on the rug," Ren told him.

He exhaled through his nose, eyes up as he watched the numbers climb, and then exited without answering. Ren fully intended to keep arguing, but when he unlocked the door and indicated that she should go in ahead of him, she pulled up short in shock.

She'd never even been in a hotel, let alone slept in one, and simply didn't have the words for how stunning it was. The room itself was as big as half of her cabin back home, and when Fitz stepped through a door and turned on a light in a bathroom, Ren let out a cry, covering her mouth with her hand. "A bathroom *in the room*? For real?"

When Fitz emerged, Ren would have sworn he was fighting a smile. "Well, at least you're easy to please."

"I've never slept in a hotel before."

One dark brow lifted. "Never?"

"I'd never even spent a night away from my own bed before Corona."

"No shit?"

"Not even a little shhhhh . . . it," she told him.

Fitz looked playfully shocked. "One day on the road, Sweden, and you've already got a mouth on you."

While he stepped out to put the parking tag in the car, Ren looked around, opening drawers and exploring what the room had to offer. A dresser with room for clothes, an empty fridge that didn't appear to be plugged in. The view wasn't much—a street, empty hills in the distance—but even if Fitz was unimpressed, Ren couldn't get past the luxury of having everything at their fingertips.

Fitz came back and dropped the car keys on the dresser. "I'm gonna grab a shower."

With a distracted wave, Ren resumed her snooping. She found a nightstand drawer with a Bible and a Book of Mormon, a desk drawer with a small notepad and a Holiday Inn pen, a binder on the dresser with information about all kinds of things to do in Missoula, and a closet with enough pillows and blankets to make a bed fit for a queen.

Getting to work, Ren folded the thicker blanket on the floor for a mattress and then the second for a cover, dropping a couple pillows at the top and staring down in satisfaction. "Perfect," she said just as the bathroom door opened and Fitz exited in a plume of steam.

"Don't look," he said immediately, but it was too late, because she'd already gotten an eyeful of bare, wet torso and the dark line of hair just above the towel he had clutched around his waist. Ren slapped a hand over her eyes. "I forgot my bag," he explained.

The door closed again, and the thought of her perfect makeshift bed and the excitement of being in a hotel room for the first time were eclipsed by a rush of adrenaline so intense she practically stumbled into the desk chair, feeling hot and jittery and stunned. She'd seen men without shirts; during the harvest it got hot, and Steve and any other neighbors who showed up to help often took their shirts off at the end of the day or even while working, but they didn't look anything like *that*. Like smooth, warm, sculpted skin. Both soft and hard. Her palms felt fevered just from thinking about touching him.

Wait. Why was she thinking about touching him?

Linda down at the library would save any book for Ren that happened to come across her desk, and many of those were romance, which Ren of course gobbled up voraciously. But last summer she'd registered while reading one that she'd only ever experienced those feelings as a reader: the heart racing, the prickles at the back of the neck, the feeling of being inarticulate in someone's presence, the sensation of being engulfed in heat, heavy with it. And here she was in real life, reacting just like that after seeing Fitz in only a towel.

Ren had *told* him no hanky-panky. She was already a burden to him. The last thing he needed was one more female staring with moon eyes when he was just trying to get to Nashville for whatever it was he was doing there. So when he came out, blessedly dressed and avoiding eye contact, Ren ducked in right after him, leaving the water as cool as she could handle to flush away any ridiculous romantic notions.

CHAPTER THIRTEEN

FITZ

The last thing Fitz needed at the end of this nightmare of a day was Ren singing her face off in the shower. Even if she was singing Dolly Parton—and even if she was actually doing a pretty good job of it—he'd been looking forward to ten blissful minutes of pretending he was alone in the room.

Though . . . if he'd taken her up on her offer to sleep in the car, he *could've been* alone right now. That was on him. She was little but scrappy, and probably would have been just fine sleeping in a Holiday Inn parking lot. Unfortunately, Fitz knew better than most what kind of human trash was out there. No matter how much she annoyed him, he wouldn't have slept for a minute knowing she was out there alone.

And look. She'd made a bed for him out of extra blankets. She was *trying* to be useful. He could give partial credit for that.

Taking his bag to the makeshift bed, he pulled out his chargers and searched the walls, finally locating an outlet jammed behind a table leg, and plugged in his phone. He'd avoid his parents' calls until the end of time but at least tried to check in with Mary every few days.

The line rang once, then again, before she picked up. "Hey, baby."

At the sound of her soft, smoke-weathered voice, Fitz felt his muscles unwinding. He settled back on the makeshift bed. "Hi, Mare."

"It's late. You make it to Missoula all right?" she asked.

"Yeah. Easy drive."

"Still gettin' here this weekend?"

"That's the plan." He winced as Ren started belting "My Tennessee Mountain Home," and the sound echoed around the bathroom and out to where he was sitting. Fitz raised his voice, suddenly desperate to get off the line. "Not much else to report, so I guess—"

"Who's that?"

He squeezed his eyes closed. "Who's what?"

Mary laughed, husky and thick. "I hear a girl singing in your room, child, don't play the fool with me."

"Must be the housekeeping in the hall."

Her silence communicated the skepticism he could easily imagine on her face. But when she spoke, he heard only her smile: "Are you bringing someone when you visit?"

"No," he said, too fast, too sharply. Relenting, he admitted, "She's a classmate who needed a ride. It's not like that between us." For some bewildering reason, he added, "She couldn't afford the bus or plane."

"That's nice of you, sweet boy."

"Nah, it's fine," he said.

A silence lingered on the other end. "But if it's just the two of you, you know what that means, don't you? Means it's your job to look after her whether you like her or not."

A tiny ache flared in his ribs at the idea of Mary at this age at the mercy of a stranger the way Ren was right now. If anyone understood that Fitz's life had been hard, it was Mary—because hers had been hard, too.

This, right here, was why he'd never let Ren sleep in the car.

"Of course I will, Mare, you know me."

"You're a good boy."

I'm not, he thought. But to the only woman who mattered to him, he said, "I'm trying."

By the time the door to the bathroom opened, Fitz was off the call and contemplating whether he wanted to Postmates some late-night burgers or burritos. He was starving. He was also resigned to the fact that he'd be floating Ren for this trip. Despite what everyone assumed, Fitz wasn't flush with cash, but he worked hard and didn't spend much; he wasn't strapped, either. Later, he'd worry about how she'd pay him back. For now, hunger took priority.

"Burgers or burritos?" he asked without looking up.

"Fitz! That's my bed!"

Now he did look up. All that hair was somehow wrapped up in a towel. She was wearing a too-big T-shirt that he hoped was covering sleep shorts, but the only thing that extended past the hem of the shirt was her long, smooth legs. In her arms was a bundle of clothing; a thin white bra strap dangled from the pile, and he immediately looked away, unwilling to put bras and Ren in the same thought.

"What are you talking about?" he asked, his eyes back on his phone.

"The bed," she said, and stepped into view so he was looking down at her bare feet. "I made that for myself. You paid for the room, you get to sleep in the real bed."

"It's fine."

"Fitz—"

"Ren." He cut her off, looking up again. "I'm not arguing about this. I'm too hungry. Just tell me if you prefer burgers or burritos."

A brief pause, and then: "I've never had a burrito before. Are they good?"

He sat up. "Are they *good*? Is that a serious question?" He was going to have to stop being surprised every time they ran into something Ren hadn't experienced, but some things were beyond his comprehension. He couldn't imagine life without burritos, and despite hours of annoyance today he felt a buzz of excitement for her to experience this. "Burritos it is. Trust me, you're going to flip."

She walked to her backpack and then approached, handing him a five-dollar bill. He pushed it away. "Let's figure that out later, okay? I'll keep receipts."

"Okay, but please take the big bed."

Fitz fell back again, rubbing himself all over the pile of blankets on the floor, rolling from his stomach to his back before sitting up again. "There," he said. "I've marked it. It's mine."

"Please, if you think that will deter me, you clearly don't know that I've slept in a pen with pigs before."

"Gross." That was hardly worse than some of the places he'd slept, but he didn't bother mentioning it. He pushed to his knees to find the TV remote. "Why don't you pick something for us to watch?"

Ren took the remote like he was handing her a magic wand. "Really?"

"With great power comes great responsibility," he told her absently, scrolling through the menu of a local Mexican joint. "Choose wisely."

"There are so many buttons."

"Push the red one."

She did, and let out a gasp when the screen came to life. "Amazing."

He submitted their food order and then watched in amusement

as, through a process of trial and error that inadvertently took them to the adult movie section and quickly back out, Ren navigated to the free movie options.

"What's good?" She paused on *Clueless*. "A retelling of *Emma*? This looks fun!"

"It's pretty good. Hit it."

She fell back to the bed, starfishing her arms and legs like she was making a snow angel. "I'm sure you know what I'm about to say!" she called loudly, as if he was in the other room and not eight feet away from her.

"That you've never been on a bed that big?"

The opening credits started, and Ren bolted up at the sound, sitting cross-legged on the mattress. Fitz dug around inside to find that kernel of annoyance at every little thing she did, but at least for tonight, it seemed to be taking a break. Their food showed up quickly, and Ren patted the mattress beside her, laying down some towels and insisting they set up a little burrito picnic on the bed. At her first bite, she let out a moan so suggestive, Fitz had to bite his cheek to keep from reacting with a laugh, a joke, something to diffuse the way his brain went haywire at the sound. One look at her, and he knew she had no idea what she'd just done.

He blinked away, back to the TV, uneasy with how quickly he found himself softening to someone who, only hours ago, was deep on his shit list.

And as if some power in the universe knew he needed to remember how annoying she could be, she hit play on the movie and peppered him with constant questions.

"Have you ever been to Beverly Hills?"

"Do you skateboard?"

"Was your high school like that?"

"Does anyone really have a closet like Cher's?"

"What do people do at parties?"

When she asked Fitz to explain the joke about balls flying toward faces, he grabbed a pillow and pretended to smother her with it. "All right," he said, laughing in spite of himself, "let's just watch the movie."

Thankfully after that Ren fell quiet, grabbing the pillow and hugging it to her chest as she watched with wide, absorbing eyes until the credits finished rolling.

Fitz walked into the bathroom, pulling his toothbrush out of the toiletry bag and running it under the water. In the other room, the TV turned off, and footsteps padded across the tiled entryway floor.

"That movie was so good," she said, walking into the bathroom with him and running her own toothbrush under the water. "But as an adaptation of *Emma*?" She jammed her toothbrush in her cheek, speaking around it. "I found it a little lacking."

Fitz raised his brows, watching her begin to brush, her mouth turning foamy. "By all means, join me," he said wryly. He'd never even had a girlfriend long enough to create a bedtime routine with, and here Ren was, standing with him at the sink in her pajamas, unselfconsciously opening her mouth wide to reach her molars.

"Shher ish sho cwearwy bootiful an schpecial," she garbled out, and then bent to spit.

"I caught none of that," he said.

"Cher is so clearly beautiful and special," Ren repeated.

"So?"

"So," she said, leaning back against the counter to face him, "*Emma* is a book about a girl who is considered prized and special relative to everyone in the tiny, isolated town around her, but who is otherwise completely average."

"Okay," he said around his toothbrush.

"It was a cute movie but makes me think whoever wrote that

missed one of Jane Austen's most important messages."

He bent, spitting his toothpaste into the sink. "Go write about it in your notebook, Ren, I honestly don't care this much about *Emma* or *Clueless*."

She followed him back into the bedroom with a brush in her hand. He hadn't noticed during the movie when she took the towel off to let her hair air-dry, but it fell down to her butt now in gleaming metallic waves that she began to painstakingly brush through.

"I may be the first to mention it," he said, sitting in the desk chair and spinning back and forth in a slow arc, "but your hair is super long."

She laughed a playful *har-har* sound. "You don't say."

He watched her work through a small tangle. It was mesmerizing. And then he realized he was staring. Blinking away, he looked down at his feet instead. "Brushing it looks like a lot of work."

"It is."

"You ever cut it short?"

"No, but I trim it a couple times a year to keep it healthy."

"Did you ever *want* to chop it off?"

She hummed, considering this, and then smiled over at him. "I never really thought about it like that. Isn't that weird? Gloria—my mom—always had strong opinions about not cutting it, so I just went along with whatever." Ren sighed. "I knew there would be ways that I'm different from other girls, but there are so many things I didn't realize were weird about me until I got to school."

The words were out before he could consider where the impulse came from: "Your hair isn't weird. It's just different, but not in a bad way."

Fitz didn't miss the way her cheeks went pink.

"I guess when I was little it was so blond it was almost white," she said. "As I got older and read more about symbolism and the types of tokens humans in various cultures and backgrounds carry with them through life, I began to understand that my parents equate my hair with how unspoiled our lives are on the homestead." When he looked up, he found her staring in contemplation at the wall. "They can't go back and perfect their pasts, but they can make my upbringing perfect, you know? They took a lot of pride in raising me in the way they think everyone should be raised: without the influence of pop culture or the internet and with the ability to be completely self-sufficient."

"Seems like your parents still have a lot of say in what you do."

Ren sighed, breaking her trance to look over at him. In that moment, she looked so much older than she had even three hours ago. "Not as much as they'd like." She began the complicated process of braiding her hair, and he fell silent, watching her fingers capably wind strands around and around until she had a thick, tidy braid draped across one shoulder. He noticed the heaviness in her eyes, and she yawned suddenly, then clapped a hand over her mouth. "Wow, sorry. The sleepies hit me hard all of a sudden."

"I'm wiped, too." Standing, he moved to turn out the lights. The room was washed in darkness, and he bumped into the side of the bed and tripped over a shoe as he made his way back across the room.

Ren laughed. "You okay?"

"I'm good." He settled on his little bed, pulling the blanket up to his waist. They both fell into silence, and in the blackness the room seemed to shrink. He thought about what Mary had said earlier and wanted to reassure Ren in some way that although they barely knew each other and the circumstances of this trip were weird, she was safe. She could sleep.

"This is like a sleepover," she whispered, her voice giddy even with exhaustion shading it. Fitz realized she really wasn't nervous around him at all. "I've only ever seen a sleepover in *Grease*."

"Wanna pierce our ears?"

She burst out laughing. "You've seen *Grease*?"

"Everyone has seen *Grease*, kid. It's a classic."

He could hear her shifting in bed, could hear her legs kicking away the covers. God, he was just so *aware* of her.

"Have you had a sleepover?" she asked.

"Sure."

"What do boys do at them?"

"Mostly we eat junk food and play video games." He looked toward the bed in the darkness, wondering for the first time what her life had really been like for the past twenty-two years. "You really never had a sleepover?"

"No."

A car passed outside the room, the tires crunching on the asphalt outside.

"Were there just no kids your age nearby?" he asked.

"Oh, there were a few," she said. "But Gloria always said kids should sleep in their own beds at night. She didn't like me going over to other people's houses very much."

He closed his eyes, marveling at how different their lives had been from each other. Ren's overprotective mother ensured she never spent a night away from her own bed. For many years, Fitz had no mother and was grateful when he had a bed to sleep in. They were both sort of broken, just in totally different ways.

"I don't know," he said. "I think being away from home is how kids learn to be polite in front of other people, how to be a guest."

A long stretch of silence followed. He was beginning to wonder if she was asleep when her voice rose out of the darkness, tinged with sadness. "I'm starting to think Gloria was wrong about some things."

He had no idea what to say to this, so he let it pass, and they fell back into silence.

"Do you snore?" she asked finally.

“No one has ever told me I snore.”

“I don’t, either.”

“How would you know?” he asked. “You’ve never had a sleepover before.”

“Good point.” She laughed self-consciously, and the sound hit him in a new tender spot in his chest. “Good night, Fitz.”

“Night, Ren.”

CHAPTER FOURTEEN

REN

Ren didn't remember falling asleep. She remembered the gentle rumble of Fitz's voice and then nothing, not even the relief of letting go of the day. After a few hours of deep, dreamless slumber, her eyes drifted open, and in the darkness of the hotel room with only the even rhythm of Fitz's breathing and the occasional rattle and drone of the heater, she was trapped completely alone with her thoughts.

Sometimes, at the most grueling points of the planting or harvesting seasons, Ren would tell herself to shut off all musing and keep moving forward. *Don't think about the relief of being done, or the bounty at the other end. Just complete one task, then the next, and the next.* Yesterday was a little like that. She was moving toward a goal, not thinking about the possibility of a father somewhere ahead of her, or of the two worried parents back in Idaho.

But once consciousness opened the spigot on her thoughts, she couldn't turn it off. Worry rose like a salty tide, guilt and doubt and regret close on its heels. She was foolish to have left the way she did, impulsive. In two and a half days Gloria and Steve would drive to campus looking for their daughter, and she would be all the way across the country. She had to keep them from coming to campus on Friday. No matter how angry she was at whatever lie the DNA test might have unearthed, she couldn't just vanish.

A letter wouldn't get there in time, and there was no landline on the homestead so there wasn't a way to call—

Her eyes widened, the nightstand taking shape in the dim light. It was early Wednesday, the day her parents went to town. If Gloria and Steve stuck to their routine, they'd be at the Hill Valley Five and Dime at seven, right when it opened.

At six, she got up and used the restroom, brushed her teeth, and climbed back into bed. Fitz was still out cold. At six fifteen, she opened a couple of drawers, closing them softly at first, and then less softly. He was still out. At six thirty, she feigned a coughing attack, and he slept through the entire thing. And at six forty-five, she said his name three times—nothing.

But even so, when the clock on the nightstand turned to seven, she glanced over at him, silently studying him for any movement. All she noticed were slow, steady breaths and tiny muscle twitches as he slept. Carefully, she slipped his phone out from beneath the corner of his floor bed and tapped the screen. A digital keypad appeared, and Ren stared at it, unsure what to do. She tapped zero. Waited. Nothing happened. She tapped one-two-three-four-five. Nothing.

Releasing a quiet growl of frustration, Ren tried to remember how he'd accessed his phone for her in the car. With a hopeful wince, Ren held the phone up to Fitz's face and let out a tiny squeak of victory when it unlocked. Opening the browser, she googled the number for the Hill Valley Five and Dime, writing it down on a piece of notebook paper from the desk.

Number in hand, she tucked Fitz's phone back under his bed and took the cordless room phone into the bathroom, carefully shutting the door. After only two rings, the call connected, and she sent a silent wish to the universe. *Please let them be there.*

She'd recognize old Jesse's voice anywhere. Years of smoking unfiltered Marlboros had left tracks through his words, dragging them each through gravel and smoke and ash. "Hill Valley," he said. "How can I help you?"

She cupped a hand over the receiver, careful to keep her voice down. "Jesse?"

"Yes'm?"

"Hello . . . it's—it's Ren."

A pause and then, "Ren? Ren Gylden? Girlie, what're you doin' callin' me on the phone for?"

"I'm not sure if you heard, but I'm away at college now."

"I did hear that," he said, and her heart squeezed at the communal pride that filtered through the line. "That's really somethin'."

"It is, yeah, thank you." She cleared her throat. "So, the thing is, I don't have any way of reaching my folks, but I got the date wrong for my spring break next week and need to let them know."

"Why're you whispering, hon?"

"Oh." She glanced at the thin door separating her from the silent bedroom. She could only hope he was as dead to the world as he'd been a few minutes ago. "My roommate is still asleep, but I wanted to call the store early, knowing that Steve and Gloria might be coming in for supplies soon."

"Ah," he said, "I got you. You want to give me your number, and I'll have them call you from here?"

"I don't mind staying on the line if it's all right with you. I expect they'll be there soon."

Jesse's laugh was a rumble that tightened into a cough. "Well, all right, hon, if that's what you want. I'll put them on when they get here."

His receiver thumped against the counter, and she listened as he explained to his wife, Tammy, in the background. Anxiety churned, acidic, in her stomach at the sound of Jesse helping a customer in the background, the ding of the cash register and the slam of the drawer.

Stepping into the empty tub, she sat and pulled her knees to her chest, throwing a towel over her head for added insulation.

She startled when the phone scraped across the counter and her mother's voice, so unfamiliar this way, carried through the phone line. "Ren? Is that you?"

Cupping a hand over the receiver, she whispered, "Hi, yes. It's me."

"Everything okay?"

"Yeah, everything's fine. I just wanted—"

"Why're you whispering?"

Wincing, she lied. "Miriam is asleep still."

"It's seven in the morning," her mother said in disbelief. "Light as day outside."

Squeezing her eyes closed, she tried to think of the fastest way to get through the conversation. "I know. College kids sleep in late, I guess. Listen, I got the dates wrong for spring break next week."

"You what? I can barely hear you."

She glanced nervously toward the door again, ears on alert for any sound. "I got the dates wrong for spring break."

"Now how'd you do that?"

"I don't know. I'm sorry. It's actually midterm exams next week." The lie felt oily and wrong in her mouth, but she swallowed it down and pushed on. "And I was hoping to use this weekend to study."

"You're saying you want to stay in the dorm over the weekend? And that you won't be home next week, but the week after instead?"

Ren grimaced, wondering how she'd make up missing an entire week of classes after spring break. But she swallowed thickly, saying, "That's right, ma'am."

"I don't know, Ren."

"Please? I set up a drip system in the cold frames so you won't have to water, and I can work extra hard the week after to catch up on everything I miss. I don't think it would be too disruptive for me to stay just this one weekend before exams. I'll only be in my room or the library." She swallowed, wincing past the lie: "I promise."

She heard Gloria's muffled voice, then Steve's, and Ren's stomach crawled into her windpipe while they discussed it in the background. Finally, Gloria was back. "Just this one weekend, Ren. I mean it. We'll be there the Friday after next, like usual."

Relief was a blast of sunlight across her skin. "Of course! Thank you!"

"But you'll need to earn this free time you're getting. We'll have a list for you when you come home."

Ren nodded, elated. "Absolutely."

"No leaving campus, nothing we wouldn't approve of."

"Of course, ma'am. I understand."

Steve's voice came closer, like he was leaning toward the phone. "We're letting you do this one time, Ren. You get one free ticket, that's it."

A spike of panic stabbed through her, but she swallowed past it. "Tell him I understand and am so grateful." Wincing, she lowered her voice again. "I'll see you in a week and a half."

Her mother gave a reluctant "All right, then."

"I love you, Gloria!" Ren said, waiting to hear it back. "Hello?"

Her mother had already hung up.

Ren sat in silence for a long moment, trying to find relief in all of it but mostly feeling sick to her stomach. Gloria hadn't said anything out of the ordinary, but Ren felt the distance yawning between them already anyway, and she hated it. For better or worse, they were all Ren had in the world . . . even if what she was doing secretly widened that distance even more.

Pushing out of her little cave, she stepped out of the tub, hung up the towel, and walked across the bathroom floor. Hesitating at the threshold, she listened. Still quiet. With a calming breath, she gently turned the knob and swung open the door. Dread slithered, slimy and cold, into her veins. There, standing on the other side of the threshold waiting for her, was Fitz.

"Before we go one more mile today," he said, "you'd better tell me what the hell is going on."

CHAPTER FIFTEEN

FITZ

Fitz stood and walked past her into the bathroom. "How much did you hear?" she said behind him.

"Enough." He ran water over his toothbrush and jabbed it into his cheek, brushing vigorously. "I was right, wasn't I? No one has any idea where you are."

She grabbed her own toothbrush. "I told you yesterday, this is none of your business."

"Who goes off on a twenty-three-hundred-mile road trip without telling anyone?"

"Does anyone know where *you* are?" she fired back, and, yeah, she had him there. Other than telling Mary and confirming with the HR team at Fellows, Wing, and Greenleaf, he'd left town without making much noise.

"It's different," he told her.

"How?"

"I'm a guy, for one."

Her eyes went wide. "Oho, well in *that* case, you big, invincible—"

"I don't mean it like that," he cut in, bending to spit and rinse. "I mean, there are fifty podcasts a week about missing women that start just like this."

"I'm not missing, Fitz. I'm with you," she said, searching his face. "And I know you well enough already to know you're not going to let anything happen to me."

He threw down the hand towel he'd used to wipe his face. "I don't want that responsibility. Don't you get it? I don't want to be responsible for your well-being, I never asked for that."

"Then just give me a ride and stop worrying about it!"

"How can I do that?" he asked, seething. "I don't even know what your plans are once we get to Nashville."

"I'm taking a bus to Atlanta."

Fitz went lightheaded with disbelief. "What? What are you doing in *Atlanta*?"

"It. Is. Not. Your. Business."

"But you're planning to go back to school eventually, aren't you?"

"Of course!"

"Of cour—?" He cut off, incredulous. "Sweden, *nothing* about your plan is obvious."

She threw up her hands. "It doesn't need to be!"

Fitz erupted. "I don't want to be the last person who saw you alive if you don't show up at school again!"

This last sentence reverberated off the bathroom tile, and they found themselves in a staring match. Ren's jaw ticked, nostrils flaring, and the baser part of him liked seeing her worked up, the intense emotions behind her happy Golden Girl image. Tearing his eyes away, he sent a frustrated hand into his hair. "Tell me what's got you running across the country with no money and no safety net or I'm not driving you one more mile."

She exhaled a long, hard breath. "Fine," she said, at last. "But I need food first. I can't do drama on an empty stomach."

They dressed and packed up in tense silence, then trudged across the blustery parking lot to a brick building labeled only MARKET. Inside, a long line was visible through the foggy glass windows, but what they could smell just from the sidewalk promised it'd be worth the wait. Fitz held the door for Ren, who ducked inside with her shabby backpack, and he couldn't help but feel a pang of sympathy. Ren was beautiful and brilliant, with her hair up in two braided buns and lips as naturally red as the raspberries leaking from the jelly doughnuts behind the glass, but anyone looking would see poverty and innocence all over her. It stuck to her like gum on a shoe.

Poverty he got. He couldn't fault her for being poor when he'd had to scrape for every penny, too. It was the innocence that got under his skin. How on earth did she think she could cross the country without someone conning her, robbing her, exploiting her—or worse? If she wanted to get out in the world so badly, the street rat in him thought she should have to face it head-on, without his help. But even as he thought it, he used his body to shelter hers, shifting their positions so she was next to the pastry case and wasn't being jostled by customers coming in and out of the front door. Ugh, Ren was right. He wasn't going to let anything happen to her, which meant he had to find a way to ensure she got back to Spokane.

At the counter, she ordered a giant pink doughnut and a cup for water—refusing money when he offered to pay. He got two breakfast sandwiches and a cup of black coffee before gesturing that she lead them to an empty table in the back.

It took no time for him to shovel down his breakfast, but when he came up for air, he realized Ren had only taken a few bites of hers. After wiping his hands on a napkin, he dropped it to his empty plate. "Was the doughnut stale or something?"

"No, it's really good. I just have no appetite." She pushed the plate toward him. "Want some?"

Fitz had never said no to free food in his life and took down half the doughnut in a single bite. "All right," he said. He'd let her put this off long enough. "Let's hear it."

She exhaled and looked past him, eyes unfocused, out the window. "Do you remember that DNA test Audran had us do?"

He answered around another bite. "Uh, yeah. That was only like a week ago."

"When we got our result printouts," she said, cupping her hands around her water, "mine indicated a paternal match."

"Yeah?" he asked, popping the last bite into his mouth. *Lucky you,* he thought.

She turned her eyes back to him. "Yeah."

He could tell she was waiting for something to click, but he shrugged. "What?"

"My parents live on a homestead," she said, slowly. "We don't have a telephone. We use a pump for our water. My mother and father think that the outside world is poison. That technology is poison." She pointed to her now-empty plate, a few rainbow sprinkles the only remains. "That food we don't make or grow ourselves is tainted."

"But are they wrong?" he asked, wiping his mouth. "It was delicious, but that pink frosting alone probably had fifteen things in it that could kill me."

This made Ren laugh, but sadly. "I think you're missing the point."

"Then explain it to me like I'm a toddler."

"My dad—or whoever Steve is—would never give his DNA to a company. He would never, not in a million years, spit into a vial and mail it off like that. There's no way he's the paternal match on my printout."

Fitz sat back in his chair like he'd been shoved. He'd been so wrapped up in his own family problems, so determined to push forward with his own plan, that he hadn't stopped to consider someone else might get a bombshell from that DNA assignment. "You think he's not your real dad?"

"I don't know." She reached into her backpack and pulled out a piece of paper she'd carefully folded. When she spread it on the table between them, he glanced down. It was a photo of a man, printed on computer paper. He had light hair, big, friendly light eyes, and the smile of an optimist. He looked polished and—Fitz was familiar with the type—rich.

And he looked *exactly* like Ren.

"Oh," he said on an exhale. "I'm guessing that isn't the guy back at your homestead."

Ren shook her head. "That's the guy in Atlanta. I think he might be my dad."

"You *think*?" Fitz reached up, pinching the bridge of his nose while he thought this through. "Did you contact him before leaving town yesterday?"

She frowned. "Of course not."

"So you're going to drive all the way to Atlanta and just—what? Stand outside his door and wait for him to come out so you can ask him if he had a daughter twenty-two years ago?"

"What? *No*."

Bracing his elbows on the table, Fitz leaned in. "I'm asking what your plan is, Sunshine."

For a beat, he froze. He wasn't sure where the new nickname came from. But if she noticed it—or the gentle tone—she didn't react. "I'm going to talk to him," she said. "I just—haven't figured out what I'm going to say yet."

"Okay. Listen." He held his hands out in front of him. "Call me insane, but driving all the way to Atlanta to meet someone who may or may not be your father seems like a lot of trouble when you could just ask your mom about him instead."

"You don't understand," Ren said, and she began tearing her

napkin into small pieces. "My parents—well, Steve and Gloria—they barely let me go away to college. They have strict rules about what I can and can't do while I'm away. They want me home every weekend. They don't want to hear about school. They don't want to talk about it. They're just looking for a reason to tell me I can't go back in the fall. If, after only a few weeks at college, I came home and started grilling Gloria about the possibility of a secret biological father being out there somewhere, they'd lock me down so fast I'd be on the homestead forever."

"You're an adult. They can't keep you there against your will."

"I know. And I shouldn't say it like that. I mean, I do plan to return to the homestead. I *want* to, after college. But with all of this . . . it's hard to not wonder, what else did they keep from me? Or keep me *from*?" She dropped her head into her hands, groaning. "But, no, I love them. I mean, whatever their reason is for keeping this from me—if this is even true—I'm sure it's a good one."

"How can you say that?" he asked, as heat seeped under his skin. What she was experiencing—the emergence of blood relatives from this technology? That was his dream. She had no idea. He wanted nothing more from that assay than to find family. "If this is true, your mom kept you from your dad."

"Maybe he's a criminal."

He pointed at the photo. "This guy? He looks about as dangerous as a guide dog." Fitz leaned back, gusting out a breath as understanding hit him. "That's why you broke into the lab."

"I was making sure my results hadn't been mixed up with someone else's."

"Why don't you just call him?" he asked. "Or—I don't know—email?"

"I need to see him for myself. And yes, okay, it was impulsive of me to leave, but I was upset and confused."

"You have sixty dollars in that coin purse of yours and nine states to cross," he said as gently as his lingering annoyance would allow. "It wasn't just impulsive, it was stupid."

"Actually, I have fifty-five dollars and seventy-two cents. Doughnuts are expensive."

"Still enough money for a bus ticket back to Spokane. If you left now, you could get back to your dorm room and be on the phone with this"—he sat up again, squinting down at the name in the lower corner—"this Chris Koning within a few hours."

Ren nodded, and then kept nodding. For a minute, he was elated, thinking she agreed.

But then she said, "I know you're trying to get rid of me—"

"Of course I am."

"—but you have secrets, too, Fitz. And not just that I caught you cheating." She leaned in. "Your turn. Tell me what's in Nashville."

He laughed and sat back. "Nope. I don't do backstory." She stared at him and her eyes softened, as if she was trying to be appealing. Honestly, it worked, but not enough. "Don't bother trying to charm it out of me. It's not happening."

Ren frowned. "Why? I just told you all this stuff about me."

"This isn't a quid pro quo moment. Am I taking you to the bus station or not?"

"Not."

"You're really going ahead with this?"

"I have to get to Christopher Koning and find out the truth."

"You might not like the answer," he told her.

"I have to try, right?"

Standing, he collected their plates. "That's what everyone says before they do something really stupid." She was so naive; she didn't even know what she didn't know.

And it was precisely that realization that made him think he had a shot at convincing her to give up on this wild-goose chase.

CHAPTER SIXTEEN

REN

Ren had never studied animal behavior in any official capacity, but she could confidently say she was an expert anyway. She knew the second she saw Steve's grouchy old mare whether she was in a kicking mood and how to read the different squeals and grunts of each of their pigs. She knew when their milk cow was going from impatient to pained, when a fight was about to break out in the chicken coop, and how to lure their shyest cat out from the shadows.

She also knew that while Fitz didn't necessarily like having her tag along, he wouldn't abandon her in the middle of nowhere, either. He'd hovered close, protecting her in line at the restaurant. He carried her bag to the trunk and unlocked her car door first. Once they were seated inside, he looked over at her, saying simply, gruffly, "Put your seat belt on," before falling into silence.

But the silence wasn't tense, at least not for Ren. With her secret out in the open, a weight was lifted. She felt like herself for the first time in days.

Eventually Fitz turned on some music, and they rolled over the next couple hundred miles in easy quiet. Ren wondered what he was thinking, wondered what she'd be thinking in his place. She'd bet he grew up in a giant house, perched high on a rolling hill, with manicured lawns, polished hardwood floors, and some variety of servants milling around. From the way he was so unimpressed with their hotel room last night, she imagined his bedroom as this high-ceilinged space stretching bright and glossy as far as the eye could see. She wondered if his family had a ten-car garage full of luxury automobiles buffed to a gleaming shine. Max was pretty banged up, but Steve loved clipping old magazine photos of classic cars and would be proud to know she'd spotted the 1970 Wimbledon White Ford Mustang right away.

"Tell me about your homestead," Fitz said out of the blue, reaching to turn the music down.

Ren grinned over at him. "Here we are, both thinking about where the other one lives."

He let out a short laugh. "Oh yeah? Where do you think I live?" She described it to him, and he laughed, harder now. "That does sound like my father's house. Though my room isn't that huge."

"It must've been amazing to grow up there."

He exhaled another short laugh through his nose. "I'm sure. Now you tell me about your homestead."

She turned in her seat, excited to try to describe the beauty of the land. "It's the prettiest place you've ever seen," she gushed. "You turn off Corey Cove and, in my head, it's what the Shire must've looked like. Have you read *The Hobbit*?"

"I've seen the movies."

"More than one movie? Like, just for that one book?"

He laughed at this. "Right?"

"Maybe we can watch them together at the hotel tonight?"

Fitz's smile faded, and he didn't answer.

She went on to tell him about the cottonwoods that lined the dirt road, with a stream just on the other side. She told him about their cabin and how they rocked the chimney with their own hands, about the big red barn and the picket fence around the little vegetable garden where they grew their own food. "We grow all kinds of things—wheat and potatoes and corn. Beets, asparagus, all kinds of lettuce. We have so many fruit trees: pear and apple, peach and nectarine."

"For real?" he asked, awed.

She nodded. "We have three horses, two cows, a ton of chickens, seven pigs. There are cats that hang around, and my favorite is Pascal. We have beehives that make more honey than they can use, so we jar the extra and sell it at markets. Steve even raises carrier pigeons."

"Do you grow things to sell mostly?"

"A few people around us have farmsteads, which means they're more like working farms, a business that grows things specifically to sell. We only sell what we don't need." She fidgeted with the hem of her T-shirt, feeling a pang of homesickness. "Gloria doesn't like it when we buy something we can make, so we do a lot of trading with our neighbors and at the market. And since we don't have Wi-Fi or a landline or anything, we can't just order something online if we need it."

"Wait," he said, steering off the highway toward a gas station. "If you don't have Wi-Fi or a landline, how did you talk to your mom earlier?"

"I knew she'd be at the five-and-dime when it opened this morning. We go—they go—every Wednesday."

She felt him watch her at a stoplight, really studying. Finally, she looked over, meeting his eyes. "What?"

"I've just been thinking about what you told me," he said. "How you said they'd keep you home if you brought up this guy in Atlanta." He turned back to the road. "I mean, they probably lived out in the real world for a lot of their lives, right?"

"Yeah," she said. "I'm not totally sure what they each did for work because they don't like to talk about it, but I think Steve was in construction and Gloria worked in an office or something."

"At least they know how the world works, right?" He smiled sweetly. "Here I am worried about you all alone in a big city at some point, but I'm sure they helped you learn how to fend for yourself and whatnot."

She swallowed. "Well, *fend* is a strong word. They focused on self-suffi—"

He waved off the wobble in her voice. "I just mean they taught you some basic self-defense moves, right? Like if someone approaches you on the street, how to protect yourself. Or, like, in a restaurant."

"A restaurant?"

"You know. Because in the city it's very different from the small towns. Someone'll pick a fight because they feel like it."

Blinking, she asked, "That happens?"

Fitz shrugged easily. "Sure. I mean, it probably won't happen more than once or twice a week. Listen, ignore me, I'm just babbling about boring stuff. My point is this: At the end of the day, your parents must love you a lot if they let you go to school. Especially if it scares them so much."

"Yeah . . . you're right." The light turned green, and she was grateful because it meant his attention was off her and she could wipe her sweaty palms on her pants.

They were truly in the middle of nowhere, she realized, looking around as they pulled into a tiny gas station with one pump. It wasn't a big city, but still, anything could happen. Was he right? Did people just randomly attack in places like this? Was everything Steve and Gloria said right, after all? Ren imagined someone approaching Fitz right now and him pulling out a combination of karate kicks and punches, taking down the attacker. Maybe Ren would have to jump out of the car, and they'd have to take on the attacker together like a real team.

A knock on the window startled her, and she looked to see Fitz right there, so close on the other side. She rolled it down, letting a blast of spring air fill the car.

"You hungry?" he asked with a sideways grin.

Her stomach rumbled, reminding her of the doughnut she barely touched. "Starving."

"Great." He stepped to the side, revealing a weatherworn wooden building about a quarter mile down the empty road. A sign out front read THE SCREAMING EAGLE SALOON, and rows of motorcycles filled the dusty parking lot. "Bet they've got great barbecue, don't you think?"

CHAPTER SEVENTEEN

FITZ

Fitz could not have been happier. As Ren stared up at the outside of the Screaming Eagle, he could practically see her brain spinning through a mental encyclopedia of shady characters. Did she even realize she was still clutching Max's door handle?

Behind them, the car shuddered once, engine still ticking. Fitz covertly kicked the tire with the heel of his sneaker.

"Is this really a restaurant?" she asked.

He pointed to a sign in a dusty window. "That sign says tacos are fifty cents apiece every Thursday from three to six. And that one," he said, moving his finger just to the right, indicating the next window, which was somehow grimier, "says it's 'Wing Wednesday.'" He rubbed his stomach. "I don't know about you, but I could use a few chicken wings right about now."

With a reluctant nod, she let go of the handle and followed a half step behind, nearly glued to his side. In front of them, the front door burst open and an enormous man wearing a dingy apron reading THE SCREAMING EAGLE: BIKES, BEER, BABES stepped out and poured a giant bucket of what appeared to be biohazardous waste onto the dead bushes nearby.

"Oh good," Fitz said, smiling over at her. "They're open! Let's go."

They were temporarily sightless when they stepped into the dark interior, and it felt like sound fell away, too. When his eyes adjusted, Fitz realized the sudden hush was the result of every head in the place swinging in their direction.

A crowd of what looked to be a very well-attended meeting of very large motorcycle riders parted as they passed through the middle of the room, aiming for a table, the bar, any stretch of open space. Whispers followed as they went, quiet whistles and catcalls, a couple mutters of "Whatd'ya got there, kid?" and "Did somebody get lost on the way to the mall?"

Fitz placed a reassuring hand low on Ren's back and leaned in to whisper, "Don't worry. If one of them challenges me to a fight to claim you, I'm pretty sure I can win." He paused. "Unless they have a weapon."

She turned her round eyes on him, exhaling a terrified "What?" before her attention was drawn over her shoulder. Following her gaze, he spotted a piece of paper that looked to be a failed health inspection pinned to the wall with a knife. All around them, the decor theme seemed to be *rustic*, with wood everywhere, sawdust on the floor, and dozens of deer antlers mounted on the walls.

"This is so cozy!" he crowed, ushering her forward. They found a pair of empty stools at the bar, and Ren reached forward to steady herself with a palm on the bar top as she sat.

"You look like a young lady who'd like a root beer," he said.

Grimacing, Ren turned her hand over, palm up. It was wet with some sort of thick, brown liquid.

"Yeah, bar muck," he said, nodding. He tried to hide his own revulsion. "You'll get used to it."

Ren dry heaved a little before finally moving to stand. "I'm just going to use the restroom. Order me whatever looks the safest."

"You got it, Sunshine!"

A man approximately one and a half times Fitz's body mass approached, swiping a filthy rag over the bar in front of him. "What'll it be?"

"Two root beers, please."

The man stilled, drawing his eyes from his rag slowly up to Fitz's face.

"Did I say 'root'? I meant 'beers,'" Fitz said, grinning. "Regular, American, manly beers."

With a hint of a nod, the man reached into a fridge behind the counter and popped the top off two cold ones. "Eight bucks."

Reaching for his wallet, Fitz said, "Can I ask a favor?"

Another heavy-browed stare.

"When that blond girl comes back from the bathroom, could you pretend to be a little scary?" Fitz said as he set a ten down on the bar.

The bartender blinked, impassive.

"It goes against type, I know," Fitz added.

More silence.

"Fine." With a sigh, Fitz reached into his wallet and pulled out another ten. "How's that?" The man grunted, taking the money and crumpling it in his fist. "And a couple menus, please."

Reaching below, the man grabbed a pair of laminated menus and slammed them down so hard a few bottles shook on the bar, the music screeched to a stop, and everyone looked over again.

Into the yawning silence, Fitz's "Thanks!" seemed to reverberate. Quickly scanning the menu, Fitz guessed it would be smart to keep things simple. More to the point, he would not be having the niçoise salad.

A minute later, Ren returned, looking shell-shocked as she slipped onto the stool beside him, her cheeks flushed a bright pink.

Giddily, Fitz leaned in to get a better look. "You okay there, Sunshine?"

"Yeah." She blinked rapidly, composing herself. "I'm good."

"I must admit, that wasn't very convincing."

"It's nothing." Absently picking up her bottle, she took a sip of the beer in front of her, grimaced, and then took another sip. When she spoke again, her tone was a little too casual. "There were some photos of naked men on the wall in the bathroom."

"I'm sorry, what?"

"I mean, more like wallpaper. As in the whole room was wallpapered with photos of naked men."

Fitz coughed a laugh into his fist, managing, "Yeah, that's pretty standard for a restaurant restroom."

"And then someone opened the men's room as I came out, and first, the smell coming from inside was *awful*, but also, there were photos of naked women in there."

Fitz pretended to get off his stool. "Now this I've got to see."

"Don't leave me." Ren jerked him back by his collar, gripping his shirt even after he'd settled again. "I've never seen a naked man before." She had a thousand-yard stare. "I mean, I've studied anatomy textbooks, and of course we see all kinds of things with barnyard animals, but . . ." She swallowed and took another long sip. "I saw David Sparrow changing at the state fair after he spent the whole day in the dunk tank, but not . . . he did not look like *that*."

"Listen, Sunshine, it's a bathroom in a bar, just like every other bar bathroom in the world. If it's too much for you, you really should reconsider this trip."

The bartender materialized again, leaning two meaty fists on the counter in front of them. The wood groaned in protest. "What do you want?" he growled.

"Apologies, barkeep," Fitz said, wincing. "My friend here hasn't had a chance to peek at the menu. Maybe another couple of minutes."

He leaned in menacingly. "Should I give you a little bell that you can ring when you're ready?"

"Oh," Ren said, smiling sweetly at him, "that would be amazing. Thank you!"

Something softened in his gaze before he flickered it back to

Fitz and looked homicidal again.

"You know what," Fitz cut in, hoping the man was just a better actor than ten dollars in a run-down biker bar in Middle of Nowhere, Montana, warranted. "We'll have two of your Char-Spangled Burgers."

The man peeled their menus off the bar with an audible squelch and pushed through the swinging doors to the kitchen in the back.

"Lovely place," Fitz said, inhaling deeply and looking around. "I always figured if I was going to open a saloon, I'd go with peanuts in bowls and let the peanut shells litter the ground, but the sawdust and bullet casings are a nice touch."

Ren stared at her beer before lifting it and finishing it in a series of long gulps.

"Easy there, Sweden."

She let out a satisfied "Ahhhh" and set the bottle down. "I've never had one of these before, but it's pretty good."

"You've never had beer?" Fitz bumped her shoulder. "I figured that was a staple on the homestead."

"I've had alcohol," she clarified, looking at the label. "Just not a Coors."

"No kidding? Y'all make moonshine on that farm?"

"We have some neighbors who make moonshine—I've had it. . . ." She looked at him and grimaced comically. "I prefer our wines and ciders."

"You're telling me you get to live on a big piece of land with wild cats, don't have to speak to anyone if you don't want to, and you make your own booze?" He tilted his bottle to his lips, speaking against it. "Homesteading is sounding better by the minute."

They looked over at a crash of glass to the right, where a fight was breaking out near the jukebox. The crowd backed up to give the fighters space, jostling Fitz and Ren against the bar. On instinct,

Fitz put an arm around her shoulders, shielding her. The furor reached a crescendo, and they looked at each other and then to the kitchen doors when they swung open and a leathered woman in a greasy apron stepped through, held up a shotgun, and fired it twice into the ceiling. Ren and Fitz slapped their hands over their ears, hunching for the impact of the ceiling raining down, but other than a spray of dust, it seemed to remain intact.

"Knock it off!" the woman yelled, and returned, Fitz hoped, to making their lunch.

"Is this normal?" Ren whispered.

Slowly, he lowered his hands. Trying to hide his own panic, he muttered, "Define *normal*."

"Shotguns at every meal?"

"Maybe not *every* meal."

Their bartender friend appeared from the kitchen with two plates he dropped down with a clatter in front of them. "Twenty-two bucks," he said, and waited.

Fitz reached back for his wallet and—

His fingers scrambled over his back pocket. "Where—?" Panic clutched him. "Where's my wallet?"

He looked to Ren, who was performing a similar scouring of her pockets and backpack. "Fitz, my money is gone!"

"Mine, too. I think someone took it."

Ren yelped, clapping a palm over her mouth. "Are you telling me we've been *robbed*?"

"This is life out in the real world!" he cried, sending a hand into his hair. He'd have to call his bank, the credit card company, his *father*—God, no, this was the worst—

The bartender rapped two knuckles on the bar. "And are you telling me you can't pay?"

Gulping, Fitz stared at him. The man could easily crush Fitz's windpipe with the gentle pinch of a thumb and forefinger. "Sir, I believe someone took our wallets."

The bartender laughed at this and lifted his chin, indicating the rowdy mob behind them. "Why don't you go ask 'em to fess up?"

"I—" Fitz began, but realized the man wasn't looking at Fitz anymore. Fitz followed the man's attention up, up, up to where Ren had climbed onto the bar.

"What the—" Fitz scrambled to hold her legs so she wouldn't fall and take a header onto the disgusting floor. "Sweden! What are you *doing*?"

Ren ignored him and clapped lightly. "Everyone? Can I get your attention, please?"

No one reacted, not even a glance.

God, this was mortifying.

"Ren," Fitz whispered, gently cupping her ankles. He tried cajoling. "Come on, Sunshine. Get down."

A piercing whistle cut through the room, and Ren slipped her index finger and pinkie from her mouth. "I *said*," she repeated, louder now, no-nonsense, *"can I get your attention?"*

Voices faded out, and the only sound in the room was that of fifty menacing bodies turning to face them. Someone cleared their throat. Knuckles cracked.

Fitz laughed jovially. "Oh boy! This one, am I right? She's a lightweight. Please, friends, go back to your meals and beers and darts and fisticuffs."

But when he slid his hands higher to the back of her calves, urging her forward, the muscles tensed under his hands. She was strong, and she wasn't budging.

"It seems that our wallets have disappeared," Ren told the room.

A man with an eye patch, a hook for a hand, and twin tattoos on each of his bare biceps reading BORN TO RIDE and BORN TO DIE stepped forward. “Are you suggesting one of us took ’em?”

“No, of course not,” she said with an innocent smile. “But maybe somebody was traveling just like we are and found themselves in a tough situation. Maybe someone made a bad decision.” Ren shrugged, sincere. “I’ve been there. I’ve stolen before.”

“Stealing Lip Smackers and nail polish at the drugstore don’t count, hon,” a husky female voice yelled from the back of the room.

“Actually, I stole from honest, hardworking people like yourselves. I was thirteen and wanted new paints for Christmas.”

Groaning, Fitz mumbled, “Here we go.”

The roomful of hit men seemed undecided about whether to bury them alive or eat them for dinner, but she did have their attention.

“I begged Gloria—that’s my mother. I did my chores, I did *extra* chores, I did all my studies, and wrote Santa about a dozen letters.” Fitz didn’t know how, but Ren’s smile appeared, and it was like watching her hand a lollipop to everyone in the room. “But Christmas morning I woke up, and there weren’t any paints for me under the tree. Gloria said I didn’t need them.”

“Gloria sounds like a dick!” someone yelled.

“I mean, you might be right,” Ren said, “but that doesn’t excuse what I did.” She paused. “I went into town the next day and stole some paints from the five-and-dime. Gloria saw me painting that night and knew what I’d done. She made me go back and tell the owners.”

“Kill the narc!” another voice yelled.

“No, come on, we all know she was right,” Ren said, looking out over the room. “I shouldn’t have taken them. Jesse and Tammy are just trying to make a living, same as everyone else out there. I told them what I did, and Jesse let me work stocking shelves for a few hours a day for a week or two to work off the cost of the paints. And when I was done, he even gave me a new set of brushes. My point is that we all make mistakes, but if we're lucky someone gives us the chance to make it right."

Fitz truly, deeply wanted the floor to open up and swallow them both.

"Ren," he whispered. "Cool story. Let's go." But she wasn't done.

"I don't have much to my name." Shaking him off, she pulled her belongings from her backpack—some clothes, some paints, a few brushes, a notebook, and a scarf—and bent to set them on the bar. "So I'm gonna send this empty bag around the room," she said, "and maybe someone will put our wallets back in here. And since I've interrupted all your conversations, I'll tell you a few jokes while you pass it around."

Oh, good God.

Bending, Ren handed the bag to the man closest to Fitz, who laughed and passed it along without putting anything inside it. This was a nightmare.

"Why did the pig dump her boyfriend?" Ren asked, and got absolutely zero reaction whatsoever. Somewhere behind them, Fitz heard a gun cock. "Because he was a real boar. Get it? Boar? It's a type of pig!" She laughed at her own joke.

"Sweden," Fitz urged, feeling nauseated. "Let's go."

"Okay, here's one: What do you call a sleeping bull?"

He was about to lift her bodily off the bar and carry her out to the parking lot when she pointed to the crowd. "Do we have a guess?"

A towering man in a Budweiser hat and with a nose that had probably been broken a dozen times guessed, "A bulldozer?"

"Yes!" Ren crowed, and a few people in the crowd actually laughed. "Okay," she said, brushing some strands of hair out of her face, "let me try something a little harder. You're too smart for me.

What did the ocean say to the beach?" Around them, people murmured, trying to guess without calling anything out. "Nothing, silly," she said, laughing. "It just waved."

There was a collective groan throughout the room, but it was carried on laughter. In the back, someone let out a loud whistle. "Keep it going, kid!"

When Fitz looked back up at her, Ren was backlit from the bar lights, and for a breathless pulse, she looked like a figment from a dream he once had. "I asked my dog what two minus two is. Do you know what he said?" She planted her fists on her hips. "Absolutely nothing!"

More people cheered now, and a woman in the back yelled, "These are terrible! Do more!"

"Why can't a nose be twelve inches long?" Ren said, and a chorus of bawdy catcalls rose from around the bar. "No, not that, you rascals! A nose can't be twelve inches long because then it would be a foot!" She took a couple steps down the bar. "That car seems nice—"

And a voice to the side called out, "But the muffler is exhausted!"

The whole bar was laughing now, even the bartender.

"What did the Zero say to the Eight?" she asked, just as the bag made its way back to her feet. "Nice belt!" She glanced down at Fitz when he squeezed her calves. "Knock knock!"

The entire bar yelled, "Who's there!"

"Tank."

"TANK WHO?" the room shouted in unison.

"You're welcome." Ren did a little curtsy to their roaring applause, losing her balance and managing to fall directly into Fitz's arms.

She stared up at him, wide green eyes shining. "Well, look at that. There's something in my bag."

"Bet there's some great trash in there," Fitz said, but as he put her down, he couldn't help but let her go slowly, keeping her close even as her feet touched the floor. Hunger flashed warm inside his chest, and he pulled her a little closer, feeling her go soft against him. "That was really something."

"Not bad, huh?" She lingered, arms draped around his neck.

"Correct. It was *terrible.*" He reached up, drawing a long strand of hair away from her flushed cheek, and, with his other hand against her delicate shoulder blade, Fitz could feel her wildly beating heart. *What a surprising thing you are,* he thought.

"You laughed," she said, grinning up at him. He felt her fingertips toying with the hair at the nape of his neck. "I saw you."

He stared down at her, soaking her in as it seemed every synapse in his brain rewired. She was such a paradox: delicate but unbreakable; modest but intrepid; innocent but electrifying. Fitz found his eyes dipping to her full, pink lips and back up to those assured, sparkling eyes. He'd wanted to touch many women in his life. But he'd never so badly wanted to deserve one before.

"Kiss her!" someone yelled, breaking the spell.

Startling, Ren stepped back and pushed loose strands of hair out of her eyes. "We should go."

"Yeah," Fitz said, bending to take one bite of his burger, "let's get out of here while they still like us."

While Ren ate as much of her burger as she could, the bartender gave Fitz what he desperately hoped was a smile. "On the house," the man growled.

Then they moved through the crowd, being patted and hugged and fist-bumped until they reached the door where they burst outside, squinting at the brilliant daylight. Fitz let them into the car, where they collapsed, stunned.

"What the hell just happened?" he asked her.

Ren dug into her bag and pressed a hand over her mouth. One

by one, she pulled items out: a watch, a wad of assorted crumpled bills, their wallets with everything still inside, a Subway gift card, a roll of quarters, some sunglasses, a pack of gum, a business card for a motorcycle shop, a whole bunch of loose change, a burner phone, and a fat wad of twenties secured with a rubber band.

Fitz took the twenties, unbinding the roll, and counted out nearly a thousand dollars. "This money is definitely not clean," he murmured.

Ren slid the sunglasses on, looked over at him, and grinned. "Looks like pizza's on me tonight."

CHAPTER EIGHTEEN

FITZ

Billings, Montana, offered up a motel room with twin beds, which was both a blessing and a curse. The upside, of course, was that Fitz wouldn't be on the floor, waking up with a sore back. The downside, unfortunately, was that he could lie there, turn his head to the side, and pretend that the four feet of space between their beds had disappeared. Not that he wanted that, of course.

Ren was on her stomach over on her bed, wearing the sleep shorts he was relieved to see existed and the roomy T-shirt, with a pizza box splayed open in front of her, legs kicking behind her in delight as she watched the first movie in the Hobbit trilogy.

He wanted to go back to the Fitz of twelve hours ago, the one who felt determined to put this tiny, blond obstacle on a bus headed west. He didn't want to keep thinking about the scene back at the saloon, where she was fearless and beautiful and naive and irresistible all at once. He didn't want feelings of warm spring wind passing over his arm from an open window, and Ren's pretty voice singing absently along to an oldies station they'd found when his Spotify dropped out of cell range. He didn't want to see the world through the eyes of someone who was experiencing the most basic of things for the very first time: delivery pizza, on-demand post-1990 movies with decent CGI, the apparent splendor of a run-down lobby in a Motel 6. Everything Ren did, she did with enthusiasm, and without any ego or pretense whatsoever.

He had a vague uneasiness settling in his chest, like something huge had shifted inside, a boulder rolled over to reveal a secret opening. He worried he would never be the same again.

He *wanted* to be the same. This was a skin he'd worked hard to become comfortable wearing: Fitz, who could insinuate himself into any world to get what he needed; Fitz, who was at his best when he only pretended to care what other people thought; Fitz, who had one—and only one—path forward. But the only thought he had tonight wasn't compatible with any of that: *Why was I in such a rush to get rid of her?*

Don't talk to her, he told himself now. *Zone out. Scroll Instagram. Catch up on baseball scores. Stare at the ceiling.*

It was like being carbonated and sealed in an aluminum vessel. Every time she laughed or gasped or made a sound of awe, he wanted to look over and see what it was that caught her attention.

He wanted her attention.

What the hell was happening to him?

"I didn't know you like to paint," he said out of absolutely nowhere.

She glanced away from the movie and reached for the remote, pausing it. "What's that?"

"I knew you drew, I guess. The card, I mean, from before we left," he stammered, as he remembered the card. That amazing, intricate card she must have spent hours drawing. He cleared his throat. "But today at the bar, your story about the paints. Then, when you emptied your bag, you had some paintbrushes in there. A science whiz, a petty criminal, *and* a painter. Who knew?"

She laughed. "Gloria says I started painting the second we arrived at the homestead. She says it's how she knew I was supposed to be there."

"How old were you when you moved there?"

"I think I was around three."

"Where did you live before?"

She frowned down at the bedspread. "I don't know, actually."

"What kinds of things do you usually paint?"

Ren hopped off the bed to walk over to her bag. Digging around, she grabbed her notebook, and before he realized what was happening, she settled down beside him. Shoulder to shoulder, with their backs against the narrow headboard, she flipped through the pages, showing him what was there. There were a few sketches of people—including her roommate, Miriam—a pig, a cat, a view out the door of her bedroom back home, and her cabin from the outside. But those weren't the main event, not even close. Because surrounding every object and taking up all the remaining space on every page were the same tiny explosions she'd drawn all over his thank-you card: the most detailed fireworks he'd ever seen. In the world of Ren's imagination, the air was made of playful fire, mischievous sparklers, sensual licks of color.

"These are insane," he said, slowly flipping through them. "The fireworks—they're really good."

"Thank you." She reached over, tracing her finger around a swirl of fiery yellow.

"I like how you choose colors for them based on the subject." He pointed to one of a pig in which the sparklers were green, brown, and purple. "It's just a pig eating from a trough, but the way the page is filled with color feels so playful and . . . beautiful, actually."

"That's a really nice thing to say, Fitz."

"I've never seen fireworks drawn with so much detail before."

"When I was little I thought they were called flowerworks. I thought they were magical flowers in the sky."

He laughed. "That's cute."

Fitz wasn't sure who was more shocked that he'd said it. She turned to look at him, and he couldn't help it, the way his attention dipped to her mouth again. When he forced his gaze back up, she was slow to follow. She'd been doing the same thing.

He needed her off his bed.

"I was thinking we could take a little detour tomorrow," he said, standing, walking away from the bed, needing something else to do with himself.

Ren followed and dropped her notebook back into her bag. "A detour?"

"We'll be passing by Mount Rushmore, and I thought maybe we could go. If you wanted."

"You're not in a hurry to get to Nashville?"

"I mean . . . if it was just me, yeah, I'd power through. But you haven't seen any of the country yet, have you?"

"No." Before he had time to react, she stepped forward and wrapped her arms around his waist. "I do want to go. Oh my gosh, thank you, Fitz."

Frozen, he stared blankly at the wall over her shoulder for a few stunned seconds before he lifted his arms and closed them around her shoulders. She exhaled into the hug, molding to him. Holy shit, it felt so good. He gave himself five seconds to enjoy it. He closed his eyes, inhaling the sweet honey scent of her hair. And then he released her, stepping back. "You didn't have to hug me, we're just going to see some old white dudes on a rock."

"I was excited. Sorry. I've read so much about it."

"Does that mean you're going to talk my ear off in the car?"

She was too smart for him. She read the lie in his voice, saw it all over his face. Fitz didn't know why, but he was finding it impossible to maintain his façade with her. "Yes," she said, grinning, "and you'll love it, don't lie."

"We can't take *too* long."

She lifted her arm in a salute and then winced. "Whoops. Rule number two. Sorry."

Ren skipped back to her bed and launched herself onto it,

hitting play again on the remote. Fitz did a terrible job of focusing on the movie, the wall, anything but her, his own thoughts screaming at him that these were not emotions he should be having. The idea of being attracted to Ren was a shock; the idea of being tender toward her was unacceptable. Although it was different, of course, with Mary, Fitz knew his brand of tenderness was fierce. He would move mountains for Mary; would spend his life ensuring that hers was comfortable and safe. Fitz didn't have room for someone else to worry over. He'd make time for flings; he did not have time for fondness.

The movie ended, and they met at the bathroom sink, standing side by side while they brushed their teeth. Ren made a face in the mirror, eyes crossed, and lip curled goofily.

"You're weird," he told her.

"You're weirder." She bent, spitting and rinsing, and he went next.

In the dark, he heard her fluffing her pillow and letting out a long, happy sigh. He wondered what today was like for her, whether she'd look back and see it as a turning point the same way he was starting to. He wondered if that moment when he'd caught her in the Screaming Eagle Saloon changed everything for her, too.

"Sunshine?"

She paused a beat before answering, and he heard it, too, how different this new nickname sounded in the dark. How adoring. "Yeah?"

"Your mom's wrong, you know."

"What do you mean?"

"You don't need your parents to keep you safe. You're scrappy."

Her voice sounded bubbly with pride. "I am?"

"Yep." He rolled over and willed his heart to stop beating so fast. "You can absolutely take care of yourself."

CHAPTER NINETEEN

REN

Ren was up, dressed, and packed before Fitz had even rolled over in bed. She'd slept fitfully, thinking about Mount Rushmore as she closed her eyes, feeling content and excited and grateful. But when she finally managed to succumb to sleep, it wasn't the faces of four past presidents she saw, it was Gloria on every facet of the monument. Four Glorias, staring down at her in anger and judgment, in sadness and betrayal. It was a twisty dream, and Ren woke tangled in her sheets, sweaty and heart racing.

But even the lingering memory of her mother's stony face wasn't enough to ruin Ren's mood once she swept the curtains open and let in the bright Montana sunshine. She was lying to her parents, traveling across the country with a man she barely knew to see someone who may or may not be her father, she spent yesterday in a biker saloon, and her entire life could be a lie, but somehow Ren was still having more fun than she'd ever had before.

With Fitz.

Fitz, that confusing, guarded, funny, protective, hot softie asleep in the bed over there. Fitz, who'd been trying to get rid of her for the last two days but for a flash last night looked at her like she was something to be treasured. Fitz, who was quickly becoming her favorite part of this trip.

Speaking of the trip . . . Ren set her backpack by the door and walked over to his bed, lifting his heavy arm and using all her strength to roll him over.

He clung to his pillow. "No."

"Yes! Adventure awaits!"

"The mountain isn't going anywhere."

"That's right, but we are." Ren tugged, harder. "Come on! Don't we have a schedule to keep?"

Grumbling, he slid from the bed and then stood, stretching with a long, rough groan.

Ren's gaze shot to the ceiling, where there was plaster and paint and texture and so very many things to examine that weren't Fitz's body. It was only once he was safely sealed in the bathroom with the shower running that Ren let herself think about the slice of torso she'd seen for only a second—how warm and hard it looked, about Fitz's legs in his basketball shorts, so long and muscular and tan—and about how the photos in the bathroom at the Screaming Eagle didn't look half as good as she imagined he would.

Not that she would ever see him naked.

Not that she *wanted* to see him naked.

Blowing out a breath, she sat down on her bed and pressed the heels of her hands to her eyes. Maybe Gloria was right about a few things, because before Ren started breaking all these rules, she'd never spent much time at all contemplating naked men, and here she was, wondering if she'd ever stop thinking about them.

Or one specific man, at least.

They must have driven across the border into the twilight zone, because for once Fitz agreed to road games while they drove. They tried to find license plates from every single state and played Twenty Questions with items in the car. It was good that he'd become a willing companion because Ren honestly didn't know how else they would have spent the hours on the road; even for someone who'd never been through this part of the country, the scenery wasn't very stimulating. Hills to flat to hills to flat. By the time they reached their hotel in Rapid City, they were both ready to stretch their legs, and Ren was practically vibrating with excitement over the upcoming day trip.

Fitz's relief was palpable when the man confirmed that the room had two beds, and Ren was glad to finally be able to pay for something. She covertly peeled a few twenties off her thick stack and slid them across to the man in exchange for two keys and a pamphlet.

Beside her, Fitz let out a small whimper, and Ren tracked his attention to where the glossy front page read *WELCOME TO RAPID CITY, THE CITY OF PRESIDENTS!* And just beneath it: *Embark on our famous Scavenger Hunt to find all forty of the presidential bronze statues!*

"Oh boy," he mumbled, already laughing in defeat.

Ren shook the pamphlet in his wake as he turned to walk toward the elevators. "We have to do this."

"No."

"Fitz, you don't understand. A scavenger hunt! For statues!"

He groaned, pushing the up button. "No, Sunshine."

But even when he said it, he was fighting a smile. And no matter how hard he tried to smash it down, it lit his eyes up, sent those sweet lines crinkling the corners, and it was that struggle that set a tiny, vibrating firefly loose inside her chest. Fitz was having fun. With *her.*

"Do you know," she said as they met at Max's hood in the Mount Rushmore parking lot, "it took four hundred workers to finish this, and not a single one died?"

Fitz hummed, sliding on his sunglasses and peering up at the mountain, backlit by the overcast sky.

"And also," she said, falling into step with him as he headed toward the entrance, "there's a cave behind the sculptures called the Hall of Records, and it contains a vault with sixteen enamel panels with the Declaration of Independence carved into them?"

"You don't say."

"Also, the four presidents were chosen by the chief sculptor, and not the US government." Another noncommittal hum. "And the original plan was to have the presidents shown from the waist up, but the project ran out of funding."

Finally, he looked at her, smashing down that smile again. "Is that right?"

"It is." They climbed a set of cement stairs, passed under the stone structure of the information center, and finally reached a long cement walkway lined with flagpoles. "This is the Avenue of Flags," Ren whispered reverently.

"I guessed that," he whispered back, "based on the huge letters right there that read 'Avenue of Flags.'"

"Well," she said, whispering again, "did you know that there are fifty-six flags here, one for every state and territory? Let's find ours."

With that, she took off, spotting the Idaho flag in the distance. It was blue, with the state seal in the center and a red-and-gold banner with the words STATE OF IDAHO just beneath it.

Fitz strolled closer, smiling when Ren hopped up onto the stone ledge beside the flagpole. "You want a picture?" He waved his phone, and it took her a beat to realize he meant a picture of *her*.

"Sure." But Ren had so rarely had her photo taken, she felt immediately self-conscious. For Steve and Gloria, posing for photos was a sign of vanity. There had never been a camera on the homestead. Ren had seen cameras before, of course, in books and real life—Tammy took a picture of her once with a disposable Kodak, she'd taken a photo at the DMV, and Dr. Audran had used his Polaroid in class—but this felt different. This was a picture to create a memory, to capture the moment. She wanted to get it right.

Straightening, she crossed her arms. "No, wait, that looks angry." She uncrossed them, but then they hung uselessly at her sides. Ren planted her fists on her hips, but that felt stupid. She dropped one arm, leaving one fist on her hip, and felt even more ridiculous. Finally, she gave up, admitting, "Fitz. I don't know how to pose."

"Just be you," he said, and Ren let instinct take over. Fitz burst out laughing when she hugged the flagpole. "Okay, yes, that's the right vibe." Lifting the phone, he tapped the screen a few times. "Got it."

"Let's find yours now." She looked down the long line of flags flapping in the chilly wind. "Your dad is the real estate mogul Robert Fitzsimmons, right? Isn't he originally from New York?" Her jaw dropped in realization. "Fitz, were you born in *New York*?"

He squinted into the distance, his expression shuttering. "No, I was born and raised in Spokane."

Reaching for Fitz's arm, she tugged him down to the green Washington state flag. "Stand there." She held out her hand for his phone. "Let me get your picture now."

He unlocked it, setting it in her palm.

"Do something cute," she told him from behind the phone.

Fitz scowled at this. "Cute?"

"Oh, I'm *sorry*. I meant do something rough and masculine."

He stared at her. "Just take the photo, Sunshine."

"You look mad!" She peeked around the phone at him. "Do that sweet smile where your eyes crinkle and you look so handsome."

As soon as the words were out of her mouth, Ren wanted to suck them right back in. Heat engulfed her cheeks as a wolfish grin spread over his lips. "The sweet smile where my eyes do what now?"

Ren quickly snapped a photo. "Okay. That one works, too." Fitz laughed, and she took a few more, staring down at them. She'd captured the eye-crinkly smile after all, but she'd also captured that smoldering first expression. It wasn't the fake enticement he used on everyone, and which she'd seen on his face countless times. This was the direct tether between his gaze and hers, the seductive curl of his full lips that carried what felt like a promise.

Ren's blood heated, her pulse accelerating. But with a sinking sensation in her gut, she remembered Miriam's warning: *Don't let him seduce you. He'll only break your heart.* Was this what her roommate meant? That Fitz knew how to captivate every kind of woman, especially one as inexperienced and naive as her? Was she simply a game to him? A sort of conquest he'd never made before?

She tried to shake away the longing, to look away from those penetrating eyes, but she couldn't. For the first time ever, Ren wished she had a phone so she could send herself these pictures.

"Okay, weirdo," he said, standing and taking his phone back, "stop falling in love with me, let's go see that mountain."

It took a few seconds for his words to penetrate, and when they did, he was already several steps away. Ren jogged after him. "I wasn't falling in love with you."

"You were."

"Was not!"

"Staring at my photo with horny eyes."

Mortified, she burst out, "Oh my God, I was *not*!"

Fitz stopped walking and nudged her with his elbow. "Will you stop arguing with me and look?"

She followed his attention up, up, up to the monument. "Huh."

"Huh?" he repeated. "That's it?"

"It's smaller than I expected."

"Some will say that it's not the size that matters, but what you do with it."

Ren slid her eyes to him, frowning. "I think you're making a dirty joke."

He laughed. "I might be."

Taking a deep breath, she redirected. "Seeing this gives me mixed feelings, though. This land was stolen from the Lakota." She gazed up at it. "I feel sort of guilty being excited to see it."

"I know," he said, and gently bumped his shoulder against hers. "But the way to handle problematic things isn't to just pretend they aren't there. It's good to see it and feel this way. Also, you can still be impressed with the artistry. Both things can be true."

This time Ren nudged his shoulder with hers. She liked the contact a little too much, but pushed the thought away. "That sounds very wise for someone who pretends to not care about anything."

He laughed. "I'm not pretending."

"Yes, you are," she said. "You care a lot."

When he looked over at her, Ren turned her eyes back up to the monument, unwilling to show how much it meant to her that he did.

CHAPTER TWENTY

FITZ

Morning found Fitz staring at the ceiling. He was eating into his schedule for these detours with Ren, but for the life of him he couldn't remember why he'd been in a hurry in the first place. His interview at the law firm wasn't until the following Thursday. Even a couple days with Mary would be plenty; he just needed to get eyes on her and make sure she was as fine as she sounded on the phone. Fitz knew most of his urgency was a driving need to get as far away from Spokane as possible, but being with Ren and seeing her experience so many things for the first time made him want to be leisurely for once. When had he ever slowed down enough to just . . . enjoy something?

Never.

Not that he should be enjoying *her*, he reminded himself as they woke and moved easily around each other in their morning routines. It was a miracle they made it through dinner and bedtime the night before without Fitz crumbling under the weight of his attraction and kissing her. He fell asleep to the sound of her soft, even breaths and the knowledge that she was only a few feet away, curled on her side, warm and soft. And he woke to the awareness that he'd never slept as soundly as he did when she was nearby.

It was a realization that was, frankly, terrifying. It made Fitz feel vulnerable: an animal on its back, belly exposed. He realized as she sat cross-legged on her bed, brushing out her hair and causing longing to spiral through him like a wild vine, that it wasn't only that he didn't have time for fondness. He didn't like the powerlessness of it. Didn't like the feeling that he was just handing over keys to a castle he had protected for so long. He imagined the pages of a calendar flying away, tried to relish the thought of a time next week when he wouldn't be so close to her all the time, sent a steel door slamming shut on whatever these feelings were.

But once they were back on the road with the windows down, fresh air flowing inside, all he could smell was the honeyed sweetness of her hair. He lifted his to-go coffee and brought it to his lips, needing distraction. Luckily, the once-scalding drink was finally cool enough to sip.

But the moment his senses cleared, her cheerful voice filled the car: "How many miles are we driving today?"

"About seven hundred." He set the cup back in the cupholder. "We're aiming for Kansas City."

Ren clapped. "Kansas City! That sounds amazing."

"You've really never done anything if Kansas City gets that reaction." He glanced in amusement over at her excitement as she gazed out the window. "If you could have gone anywhere growing up, where would it be?"

She hummed, thinking. "You know what's weird? You don't know what you're missing until you see it," she said. "I knew there were things to see out there, but I didn't think anything could possibly be more beautiful than our land. So, actually . . . I don't know where I'd have wanted to go. The idea is almost overwhelming. I have so much to catch up on." She fidgeted with the rubber seal around her open window. "I wonder if going to school and on this trip with you has ruined me."

"Ruined you?"

She laughed self-consciously. "I mean whether I'll ever be happy just living on the homestead again."

He hated how much hope he felt hearing her say that. For as much as Fitz had avoided thinking about it, he didn't like the idea of Ren disappearing from the world again at some point. "Don't you plan to go back eventually?"

She stared out the window, lost in thought, saying only an absent "Yeah."

Fitz was about to remind her that she was an adult and could make whatever choice felt right for her when she seemed to snap out of it and turned to him with a bright smile. "Let's play a game."

"No."

"This is a fun one," she insisted. "I'll answer your questions if you answer mine."

"You'll answer mine anyway."

"Come on, Fitz, you want to just sit here in silence?"

"Yes, actually."

Only . . . he wasn't sure that was true anymore. The problem was he knew he couldn't answer her questions with his usual smooth evasions and cover stories. The backstory he'd painstakingly constructed at school—about his rich parents, his life of luxuriant happiness in Spokane, his easy ambition—wouldn't work with Ren. He didn't know how he knew this, but he did: She would see right through him. And the second Fitz let her in even a little, he worried that every secret about his past he'd kept wrapped up from the moment he stepped foot in the marbled atrium of the Fitzsimmons home would come tumbling out.

"How about I teach you how to make some bird calls?" she asked, pulling him out of his spiraling thoughts. "Technically that's not speaking or singing, so I wouldn't be breaking any rules."

"I'm good." Fitz glanced over his shoulder to change lanes and pass a slow truck.

She ignored this, folding one hand over the other. "So first you want to overlap your hands with your palms facing upward."

"Ren."

"Then you cup them, lifting them to your mouth, and—" She blew, letting out a sound like a dying loon.

"Okay," he cut in, fighting a laugh when he caught a glimpse of her expression and realized she'd done this terrible call on purpose. Holy shit, she looked so proud of herself for making a joke. "God, fine, let's play your game. But I'm skipping anything I don't want to answer."

She turned in her seat, pulling one leg under her to face him. "What are three things you'd take from your house in the zombie apocalypse?"

This pulled the laugh free. "That is not what I expected."

"Want me to ask about girlfriends instead?"

"Definitely not." Fitz wiped a hand across his face, feeling his smile crack open like a fault line. "Okay, I need a minute to think. Tell me yours first."

"Duct tape, a pocketknife, and a cast-iron frying pan."

"That came out of you so fast, I'm impressed and worried."

"I'm prepared."

"But God, Ren, those are boring options. Duct tape? A frying pan?"

"How is duct tape boring? It's the most useful tool on the planet. It can be used in the place of nails, or for waterproofing. I assume, since this is an imaginary apocalypse where I can only have three things, that this roll of duct tape would be never-ending. And a cast-iron frying pan can be used to boil water, for cooking, as a shovel, or to bash in a zombie's brain. What about you?"

"I guess I'd take my phone—"

"Are you expecting there to be power in this apocalypse?"

"Don't you get never-ending duct tape? Why don't I get power?"

"Okay, sure."

He thought on the other two. "My pillow and a gun."

"I hope you're planning to use that gun to bludgeon people, because if you get power you don't also get unlimited bullets, and after about a week, with no bullets that's all a gun will be good for anyway."

"The rules of this game aren't very clear."

She grinned at him. "Should've picked a frying pan."

"I'll just make sure I still have you with me in any apocalyptic scenario," he said before the wording had time to bake. Ren went still, and then slowly turned her body, facing forward. "Okay, my turn," Fitz said, quickly changing the subject. "I want you to answer my question from before. If you could go anywhere right now—except Atlanta, that is—where would you go?"

"I'm still thinking. Where would you go?"

He shook his head. "I asked you."

She pointed out the window at one of the ubiquitous billboards they'd passed over the last hundred miles. "I want to go there."

"Wall Drug? Not, like, Paris or Istanbul?"

"I've got no idea what could possibly be so exciting it needs this many giant billboards, but I think I need to find out."

He glanced at the fuel gauge. They'd need to fill up again before Kansas City, but not quite yet. Two days ago, it would have been a quick no—he had a schedule he'd wanted to keep, and besides, this trip hadn't been for fun. But as he'd already realized this morning, the original plan was crumbling; Fitz hadn't been able to deny her any adventure, no matter how small.

So right then, he made a deal with himself: He would give Ren her adventures, but that's it. No more of this unfamiliar, perseverating attraction.

Without overthinking it more, Fitz exited, parking in front of a long metal-sided business with giant signs that informed them Wall Drug had been open since 1931.

Turned out it wasn't a single building but dozens in a long line, interconnected so that from the inside it felt like one giant store. And it was enormous, absurdly so. Ren went quiet and tense, and Fitz slung an arm around her shoulders, playfully warning her, "Stick with me, Sunshine, this place might be more dangerous than the Screaming Eagle." But at the feel of her small frame pressed into his side, he no longer cared that he'd left his jacket in the car; warmth spread up his fingertips and down into his chest.

They wandered, browsing the merchandise, pointing to silly hats and T-shirts they joked about getting, and after about five minutes he realized he still had her pinned comfortably to his side.

Pathetic, he chided himself. *Your resolve from the parking lot lasted barely two minutes.*

Unease spread in his chest at how easy and comfortable this was all starting to feel. Instinct was a kick to his gut: *Don't get too comfortable. That's when things fall apart.*

When she reached up to touch his hand on her shoulder, drawing his attention to a T-shirt that read FARM GIRLS HAVE GREAT CALVES, and her hand lingered on his, Fitz abruptly dropped his arm. Ren startled, taking a step away from him. "Sorry, I didn't realize—"

"Meet me in the café," he said, rolling past this before realizing how harsh it had sounded. With a weak smile, he pointed to the café sign. "I'm going to use the restroom."

At the sink, Fitz stared at his reflection. A tremble began in his chest and worked its way up his throat until he jabbed a finger under the collar of his shirt, pulling it away as if it was keeping him from drawing in enough air. When was the last time he'd looked at himself in the mirror? The last two or three days he'd been standing beside Ren at the bathroom sink, looking only at her.

He liked her. Too much, in fact. And she liked him, too. He knew she did. But God, this would be so much easier if she didn't.

He had an interview for an internship in a matter of days and, beyond that, a clear sight to his endgame. Internship near Mary, law school, takedown of Fitzsimmons Development. Revenge wasn't imminent, but it was out there, hovering patiently in the future. Truly the last thing he should be doing was flirting with a woman who was so naive and only knew how to take things sincerely, talking with a woman who could get all his secrets to pour out of him like water from a pitcher, falling for a woman who would put her unscarred heart in his broken hands.

"You're not her boyfriend," he said to the man in the mirror. His jaw tensed, and the worst truths slipped out unimpeded. "She's too naive to know how to handle herself. She's work you don't have time for." Fitz stared at his own reflection, expression hardening. "And more importantly, she's way too good for you, so don't even bother."

When he found Ren a few minutes later, she'd already ordered food for them both and glanced up as he approached, smiling. "I hope you like sandwiches."

"Who the hell doesn't like sandwiches?" He sat across from her and, as casually as possible, tried to slide the bag across the table.

Ren stared at it and then up at him. "What's this?"

"Just something I got you." *A preemptive apology,* he thought.

"A gift from the men's room?" she asked, grinning. "Is it a photo from the wall?"

"And she acts surprised when *I* make a dirty joke."

She giggled, reaching for the bag. "You didn't have to get me something. You've already done so much."

"It's not that big a deal." Fitz reached up, rubbing his neck, hating the way his ears grew hot. When Ren pulled out the book, she let out a tiny, delighted squeak.

"My Adventure Journal?" she read.

He focused on unwrapping his sandwich. "There are maps and stuff inside," he said, waving it off. "I figured you could mark off all the places you've been to on the trip . . . and in the future."

She opened to the first page, where there was a map of the United States, and flipped through to see individual states with monuments, parks, and various famous roads. Fitz watched her flip to the back, to South Dakota, where she drew a finger around Mount Rushmore and the little checkbox next to it.

Emotion pooled inexplicably in his chest. "There's a pen in the bag, too. So you can . . ." He gestured awkwardly. "For checking things off."

Ren dug back into the bag and pulled out the green-and-yellow Wall Drug souvenir pen, placing a careful check mark next to the monument. "This is so sweet of you."

"It's not sweet," he was quick to clarify. "It's just something to keep you busy so you'll stop with the dying bird calls."

She laughed. "Okay, fine." She flipped another page. "I haven't been to the Badlands, but we passed it. Does that count?"

"No, but is the Screaming Eagle in there?" He pretended to stretch and look. "Because you definitely earned that check mark."

Ren grinned proudly, quickly flipping through the pages.

"Come on, let's eat so we can get back on the road," he said, pulling his eyes away from the full, smiling curve of her lower lip and slamming the emotional steel door shut for good this time. "You can go through it in the car and see if there's anything close enough to visit."

He didn't look up but felt her watching him for a beat before turning down to her own sandwich. "Thanks, Fitz."

CHAPTER TWENTY-ONE

REN

Ren was grateful for their detour early in the day—as well as the activity book Fitz got her—because the day's drive to Kansas City was the longest so far, nearly ten hours on the road. Normally she was fine being in her own head about things, but not today. Today she was all tangled up about Fitz.

Gloria once said that some people are dogs, and other people are cats. At the time, Ren didn't have a clue what her mother meant; both dogs and cats are cuddly, cute, and furry. But then one Christmas she and Gloria took a plate of cookies down the road to Widow Dawson's, and after five minutes of Gloria trying to make conversation and Widow Dawson answering in as few words as she pleased, they left. On the drive back, Gloria had said with begrudging respect, "Now that woman? She's a cat."

She meant that Widow Dawson never went out of her way to make friends, that she did things on her terms, that she never felt pressed to fall in line with social niceties. In other words, she was not a pleaser.

But Ren was. And she understood it now: Ren was a dog, and Fitz was absolutely a cat.

He'd ask her one tiny question, and confidences would come pouring out of her. Ren knew other kids growing up but never spent condensed time in their presence, had never truly gotten to know anyone her age before. The thought of having someone in her life, someone who chose to know her, who cared what she was thinking, who sought her out because he wanted to, not because they happened to occupy the same space all day, every day, made her feel dizzy with longing. And after the past three and a half days together, Fitz was the first person she could truly call *friend*.

The need to know more about him—to know *him*—was an ever-expanding presence inside her. But getting to know who Fitz really was felt like two steps forward, one step back. He would warm up to her and then close off again in a snap, making her analyze everything she'd done that could have shut him down. She saw the way he never directly answered her questions, never volunteered anything. Getting information out of him was like bravely sticking a hand into a thorny blackberry bramble and coming out with a single, shriveled berry.

But why was he still holding her at arm's length? Even a brick wall would be able to surmise that they were getting closer, and Ren knew in her bones that what she felt for Fitz was becoming more than gratitude and fondness. There was a new presence inside her, something warm and with its own erratic, animalistic heartbeat. She loved when he teased her, loved his low rumbling laugh. She loved the way he took care of her and pretended it was no big deal; she craved their brief moments of physical contact.

It meant that she studied him the way she'd studied her animals, trying to read his moods and thoughts through his actions. Ren collected evidence like a forensic psychologist, piecing together who this person really was.

For example, she found it odd that Fitz was so friendly the dean asked him personally to show Ren around campus that first day, yet with her Fitz did everything he could to shut down questions about himself, his family, his background. Miriam had acted like everyone knew Fitz, but to her he'd never said anything about his parents or lifestyle. In fact, if anything, he was frugal with his spending, even though his father was such a successful real estate developer that she'd read an old *Time* article about him a handful of years ago down at Jesse and Tammy's store.

Books made Ren believe that men like Fitz loved to brag about their conquests, but despite Miriam warning her about his reputation, Fitz had only ever been a gentleman with her. And he'd never once mentioned having someone back in Spokane.

Also? For the entire trip Fitz had their route up on the GPS, but he never really seemed to look at it. Had he done this drive before? What was in Nashville? Why was he going there?

As the sun was setting and they entered the city limits of Kansas City, Fitz signaled for the exit and navigated Max to the hotel without even once glancing down at his phone.

They stepped out, gathering their bags from the trunk, and Ren couldn't help but try to tease him open, just a little. "How many times have you done this trip?"

"A few."

"A few, like three? Or a few like fifteen?"

He smiled like he knew exactly what she was doing and handed over her bag. "I try to come home for most school breaks."

"I thought home was Spokane?"

His step faltered, but it was quick enough that Ren thought she might've imagined it. "It is. I have extended family in Nashville."

This felt like a jewel he'd set in her palm. Extended family! In another state! "Like cousins, you mean?"

"Something like that."

Questions lined up single file when he said this, but Ren was immediately distracted the moment they stepped foot into the hotel. It was like walking into a small town. The main building was open from the lobby clear to the top, with a glass elevator visible as it stopped on each floor. The floor of the lobby was cobblestone, with little tables encircling a massive four-tiered fountain in the center. There were flower beds filled with ferns, and lampposts. Above the sound of splashing water, the hotel was noisy. People in suits sat around in groups talking, while families moved through the lobby in smiling clusters. The bar was packed; the restaurant, too, looked full, with a handful of people waiting to be seated.

Ren had to spin in a circle to take it all in. "This would be like living in a shopping mall."

"You ever been to a shopping mall, Sunshine?"

"I've seen them in movies. There was one in *Clueless*, remember? And they all have fountains and big open atriums."

Laughing at this, Fitz stepped up to the reception desk, handing over his ID and credit card.

The woman—her name tag read Rita—typed for a few seconds. "I have you in a classic king, on the twelfth floor. Free continental breakfast is down here from six to ni—"

"Sorry," Fitz cut in gently, using what Ren had begun to recognize as his flirty voice. "I emailed yesterday to request two beds. Is that possible?"

Rita scrolled through her screen. "Ah, yes. I do see that in your reservation notes. So you'd like to add a room?"

Fitz shook his head. "One room is fine, but two beds?"

"The only options we have available are junior suites." She glanced at him, and then to Ren, where her eyes lingered. Ren reached up, covering a coffee stain on her T-shirt, before moving her hand to her hair, aware of the way her braid had loosened in the car with the windows down. She must be a mess given the way this woman was looking at her. "Would you like me to book you in one of those?"

Fitz looked over at Ren, and then at the woman, straightening. "How much do those run?" Ren noticed how he took a step to the side, closer to her.

Rita typed a few keystrokes. "With tax, five hundred and eighty-six dollars."

He deflated a little, sighing. "This again."

"I can get my own room," she said quietly. She could understand Fitz wanting some distance, even a night alone. He'd been patient with all her questions and enthusiasm, but since they'd left Wall Drug, his mysterious wall had been up again, and guilt throbbed in the back of her skull, a headache forming. "Let's do it," she said.

She bent to unzip her backpack, but Fitz stilled her with a hand on her arm. "It's too much. You still have to get to Atlanta, and then home. Save your money." Looking back at Rita, he said, "We'll keep the room with the king."

Fitz stared at the wall, mute, while they waited for the elevator to reach the lobby.

"I'm sorry," Ren said into the tense silence. "I owe you so much, and I realize I'm cramping your style."

"You're not cramping my style," he mumbled, unconvincingly.

"If it makes you feel better," Ren said, "we'll have plenty of space. I hear king-size beds are very big."

"That's not the problem. I know how big they are."

Oh. Right. "Duh. I bet you have one."

He didn't answer, and it meant that the pounding echo—*king bed king bed king bed*—returned full force inside her cranium. Actually, she decided, she would sleep on the floor. And if he didn't let her, then too bad. She would insist.

"Maybe I'll go sleep in Max," he blurted once they were sealed up in the elevator car.

"What? No! If anyone sleeps in Max, it's me."

Fitz shook his head. "You're not doing that."

She hated returning to this conversation. It signified all the ways they were going backward; no matter what she suggested, he would say no to anything but her being in the bed, and *she* would say no to anything but *him* being in the bed, and they'd be at an impasse.

Which meant this: Ren was possibly, probably, maybe going to be sleeping in the same bed as Fitz. She might be sharing a bed with him, and his basketball shorts and those strong thighs she tried her very hardest not to look at when he walked to and from the bathroom.

"Okay, then it's settled," Ren said. "If there's a couch, it's an easy solution. If there's space on the floor, it's my turn for a floor bed. If not, I bet we'll be farther apart than we were last night in the twin beds. It's fine." It was so not fine. "This is our fourth night sharing a room. We're practically pros by this point. It's just a sleepover. We can—"

"Ren," he cut in, gently. "Breathe."

She took a deep, steadying breath as the elevator dinged on the twelfth floor. Why did this suddenly feel so different? They'd shared a room for three nights now, and approaching each of those had never felt like they were heading toward a room that might catch fire the second they walked in.

Fitz swiped his key at the door, gesturing her inside, and Ren swore they deflated in unison: no couch, just a chair and a desk, and a bed that seemed to eat up more of the floor every second she continued to stare at it. Truly, it swallowed the entire floorplan. They set their things down and looked at each other across the expanse of the mattress.

Ren tried to smile. "It's very nice."

Fitz shrugged stiffly. "It's just a bed."

"I know it's just a bed," she said. "I'm just saying it's a nice one."

"Doesn't matter if it's nice, it's just for sleeping."

"Of course it is."

Silence yawned between them.

He reached up, scratching the back of his neck. "Should we get some dinn—"

"Yes, absolutely, let's get dinner."

They made the short walk through downtown, stopping at a white brick Art Deco building with a large sign proclaiming it to be Winstead's Steakburger. Fitz had barely spoken the entire walk over, and the silence was starting to feel like a third person on the sidewalk between them.

"Is it a steak or is it a burger?" Ren joked, expecting Fitz to give her the standard smile-fighting, eye-rolling routine.

But instead, he didn't say anything at all, walking toward the door and holding it open for her. So distant, so formal.

Ren came to a full stop just inside, forgetting about Fitz's mood as she gaped at the room around them. With pink neon on the ceiling, pink tables, turquoise booths, and a jukebox in the corner, Winstead's Steakburger looked like a diner right out of *Grease*.

The hostess led them to their table and Ren sat down, unable to stop staring at the decor. "Holy cow. I bet I could order almost the same thing Danny orders at the Frosty Palace."

Fitz glanced up from his menu perusal. "Should I know what that is?"

"Hello, Just Fitz! It's the malt shop in *Grease!* He orders a double polar burger with a cherry soda and chocolate ice cream."

"Exactly how many times have you seen that movie?"

"At least a hundred."

He looked at her, baffled. "It's funny, because your parents don't really sound like the park-your-kids-in-front-of-the-television types."

"They weren't, but I didn't grow up watching all kinds of movies and TV shows. We only had a handful of video tapes and an old VCR. Over years, even once a week, it adds up."

"It also doesn't seem like the kind of movie they'd approve of, either." He laughed. "It's, like, horny teenagers, gangs, premarital sex, and drag races."

Ren hoped her expression didn't betray exactly how much she liked hearing him say the word *sex*. She cleared her throat. "Gloria probably felt safe because we had the edited-for-TV version."

"Oh, God. With commercials and everything?"

She nodded. "I probably asked for Captain Crunch seven hundred times after I first watched it."

Fitz made a sad *womp-womp* sound. "I'm guessing Steve and Gloria didn't give in."

Ren laughed. "You guess correctly. Anyway, imagine how confused I was when our old tape finally gave out, and I borrowed a copy from the library and heard Rizzo ask Danny if he was going to 'flog' his 'log.'" Across from her, Fitz choked on a sip of water. "I didn't even know what that meant, until one day it hit me." She looked around and then leaned in, whispering, "It means masturbation."

He appeared to lose the fight with the water, lifting his fist to his mouth as he coughed harder. Ren quickly grabbed a handful of napkins from a dispenser and shoved them at him. Her delight at having broken his stoic façade was overshadowed by guilt over the brief coughing fit. "Oh my God, I'm sorry."

"Don't be sorry," he said, wiping his mouth. "You just surprised me. Didn't expect you to say that word aloud."

The waitress came to take their order, and Fitz's words rolled around in her head until a streak of irritated rebellion flashed through her. The moment the waitress left, Ren leaned in again. "For the record, I'm not that innocent, even if I haven't done certain things."

One dark eyebrow lifted. "You haven't done *that*?"

Heat exploded across her cheeks and down her neck. His eyes tracked her flush. "What I mean is that I grew up on a farm. With *animals*," she said meaningfully. "You know what animals do, I imagine." Ren pressed a hand to the side of her mouth, stage whispering, "I know what sex is, Fitz."

With a smile in his eyes, Fitz leaned in, pressing a hand to the side of his mouth, too. "Hopefully you aren't basing your entire sexual education on the breeding of barn animals, Ren."

"Of course not," she said primly. "In fact, there is a lot of valuable sex education to be found in romantic literature."

"I'm sure there is."

She grinned at him. "But you probably know a lot more about romance than I do. You could give me some real-life examples from your past."

His smile faded, and he straightened. "Nice try, Sunshine."

Ren glared down at her menu.

Throughout dinner, Ren noticed him doing it time and time again: distracting her from asking questions by pointing to something interesting nearby, asking her about her past, making jokes.

After dinner, they bought ice cream and walked around the downtown area. It was beautiful, with trees and a mix of newer buildings and older architecture. They passed an art museum and block after block after block of shopping and restaurants. Fitz led her into a busy park and pointed to a fountain ahead with four life-size bronze horses and an empty bench nearby.

"Those horses represent what were thought of as the four

mightiest rivers," Ren told him as they sat.

A soft laugh came out on his exhale. "Of course you know all about this."

"The Mississippi, the Volga, the Seine, and the Rhine."

Fitz squinted at the fountain. "That's actually pretty cool."

"Here's the *really* cool part," she said. "It was originally commissioned for a private estate in France, but it was sold as salvage after a huge fire and moved all the way here. Imagine seeing something like that when you look out your window at breakfast."

"Rich people are so weird," he agreed.

She bumped his shoulder. "Okay, rich kid."

"Right." He frowned, leaning forward and bracing his forearms on his thighs. "Well, be sure to check the fountain off your list when we get back to the hotel."

She mentally logged this reaction. Back at Corona, Fitz seemed to proudly play the part of the son of the school's most generous benefactor. Away from school, Fitz lived simply, lacked bravado, and hated being referred to as wealthy. "Thank you," she said. "I might not have remembered. You're sweet, Fitz."

He huffed a soft laugh through his nose, looking down at the ground. "It's not sweet, Ren, it's just a reminder."

"Why do you work so hard to insist you're not a nice guy?"

"Because I'm *not* a nice guy. I'm just—" He exhaled a frustrated breath, looking over at her and then away. "You want me to be something I'm not."

"I don't want you to *be* anything," she said, bewildered. "I like who you *are*."

"You barely know me."

"I like what I've seen so far." Her shoulders hitched up in a tiny shrug. "I only want to know you better."

"Well, don't try too hard. We're almost to Nashville."

Ren stared at his profile and then looked out at the fountain, at a loss. "Okay. I won't."

Fitz stood. "Should we head back? We have a long day of driving tomorrow."

"Sure." An ache passed through her. It was whiplash with him. Ren didn't know what she'd done to make him want to wedge all this distance between them, but she knew better than to ask him about it.

He finished off his ice cream and tossed the wrapper into a garbage can as they passed. It was dark out; in a city like this, Ren could barely see any stars. All of a sudden, she missed them desperately.

She dug around inside, searching for something else to think about. His words echoed back to her. "Would you like me to do some of the driving tomorrow?"

Beside her, Fitz laughed and maneuvered around a couple of kids with skateboards. "No, it's fine."

"I know it can be draining," she said. "I really don't mind."

"Are you even legal behind the wheel?"

"Excuse me." She went to playfully shove him before remembering that the mood wasn't in that place anymore. "I grew up in Idaho. State of the best drivers in the nation."

"Interesting." He slid an amused smile her way. "I've never heard that statistic."

"I got my driver's license when I was sixteen, I'll have you know, and am a very capable operator of motor vehicles of all kinds, including stick shifts."

"No one drives Max but me." Fitz reached over and tweaked her ear, and she had to fight the urge to lean into the contact.

"I would take very good care of him, I promise."

Fitz took a long look at her. "I'll think about it."

"You do that."

Their hands bumped as they walked through the hotel lobby, and Ren could feel the tension brewing between them, feel her own relief that whatever friction had risen seemed to have dissolved infinitesimally. Maybe it was her turn to initiate contact. Maybe he'd just been waiting for her to reciprocate. With her heart hammering in her windpipe, she stepped closer to him in the elevator, near enough to press her arm to his.

But Fitz moved away, a big side step, and began hacking into his fist, racked by a sudden coughing bout.

Surprised, Ren carefully patted his back. "Are you okay?"

He nodded, eyes watering as he croaked out, "Good." He pointed to his throat, letting out a wheezing "Just a—dust or—something." Fitz recovered with a clearing of his throat before shoving his hand into the pocket of his jeans and leaning against the far side of the elevator car.

Ren's stomach flipped over. *Oh God.* Had he just faked a coughing fit? Had he been avoiding physical contact with her? Silence yawned between them, and in that mortifying moment of understanding, Ren wished the elevator would plummet to the basement and put her out of her misery. Every time he'd touched her before had been in public. Of *course* it had. He had simply been getting her attention with a nudge to her side or keeping track of her with his arm around her shoulders. Like one would with a pet or an errant child.

Mercifully, the elevator doors opened on their floor, and Fitz hesitated while Ren rushed out. The walk down the hall with him only a few steps behind her felt like a silent death march. At the door, Ren swiped her key and walked inside.

"Still only one bed," she blurted, and it landed in a deep pool of silence. She immediately wanted to hit rewind or—even better—to vanish into thin air. "I'm gonna—" She pointed over her shoulder, grabbing her backpack and disappearing into the bathroom.

CHAPTER TWENTY-TWO

FITZ

Fitz was an enormous asshole.

He knew it. She knew it. Even this giant bed they were going to share knew it.

For a few seconds after Ren disappeared into the bathroom, Fitz stood on the other side of the door, fist raised, trying to find the nerve to knock. He didn't hear water running, didn't hear teeth brushing. There was only silence, and his mind filled with all the potential images on the other side: Ren glaring at herself in the mirror. Ren crying. Ren burying her embarrassed face in her hands. He stepped away, walking over to the bed and sitting down.

Fitz could remember his first Thanksgiving at the Fitzsimmons table. It was only two weeks after the adoption had been finalized, and in the previous ten years he'd gone from Mary's to homeless to juvie to this; he knew it would be a long time before he stopped feeling like a vagabond in the pristine hallways, if ever. At the dinner, there'd been three forks at each place setting, servants bringing out food, clearing plates. He didn't know to put his napkin in his lap, didn't know which bread plate was his. When the food arrived, he reached for it, not knowing that they were supposed to say grace first, and after grace they were supposed to go around and say what they were thankful for, one at a time. Fitz didn't know that his new father, Robert, expected Fitz to thank him and only him for bringing him into the Fitzsimmons home, that Robert would be sullen and withdrawn for the entire rest of the meal because Fitz had thanked Robert's wife, Rose, first and longer.

But Fitz learned, quickly. He learned how to put on the mask, how to shower Robert with awe and deference whenever he was home. Fitz learned how to play Robert's game, by Robert's rules. It never brought them the true bond of a father and a son, but it brought them a delicate sort of peace. His father started taking Fitz to fundraisers, ball games, charity appearances, and staged photo ops out shopping in Seattle or Portland or Vancouver. No matter how often Robert screamed at his wife and kids, no matter what Fitz heard going on behind closed doors, Robert cared only that, in public, he came off as the perfect parent, and Fitz let him. He could be patient.

Even though Ren wasn't patient—grabbing at life with both fists was more her style—Fitz wouldn't expect her to know how to navigate everything on the first try either, and was amazed how fast she was learning. Whereas he'd spent his first year in his new world quietly observing, Ren was running forward, arms outstretched. He wanted to tell her how impressed he was, how hard and disorienting and intimidating he knew it must be. Most of all he wanted to tell her just how desperately he wanted to hold her hand—and much, much more.

But every time the instinct yawned awake in him, self-preservation slammed it shut. Ren didn't need to know Fitz better. She didn't need to be someone—the first someone in years—who he opened up to. Ren didn't need all the baggage Fitz brought to the table. As much as he wanted to sit her down and tell her everything, it wasn't smart. Their lives could not be more different. Ren had barely seen anything in the world, and Fitz had already seen too much.

He'd learned too many times that when you think life is going the right direction, you were probably only inches from a blind turn.

The worst thing about it all wasn't even the effort it took to keep her emotionally at arm's length; it was keeping her physically distant, too. It was obvious to them both that there was attraction here. Fitz had felt this often enough to know what it was: the adrenaline-flooded limbs, the heat in his blood, the desire to drink in her features like a heavy, sweet brandy. He'd look at her across the console, the table, the sidewalk, and all he wanted to do was touch her. He wanted to tug her hand at night and pull her over him, letting her figure out how her body worked. And if Ren had been anybody else, he would have done it already.

But Ren wasn't *anybody else*; she didn't even speak that language. Everything he wanted to do with her would be her first: first kiss, first touch, first time. Only the worst of men would take those firsts knowing he'd vanish right after.

Shit, but her sweet openness was the exact thing that was making him crazy, turning him into a turbulent sea: high tide, low tide, high tide. He couldn't find a way to be normal with her anymore. And when it came down to it, why *not* open that door? What did he care if this was her first or one thousandth experience? What difference would it make? He could take, and take, and take, and what did he care if it messed with her head? Ren was an adult. She'd figure it out.

The problem was, he *did* care. And worse, maybe, was this: What if she wasn't the only one who got hurt? Fitz had never known this kind of attraction before—one that was entwined with curiosity and amusement and a sense of companionship that felt too, too comfortable. Turned out, he hated it. Sexual chemistry in isolation was so much easier. His dream was to be a free man unbeholden to anyone. He didn't want or need feelings.

They'd be arriving in Nashville soon—could easily make it tomorrow, if they wanted—and from there Ren was going to Atlanta.

He'd drop her at the bus depot, and for all he knew, he might never see her again. Maybe she'd stay in Atlanta with her dad, maybe she'd head back to her homestead. Maybe she'd come back to school, and they'd awkwardly orbit each other for a few months before he graduated. He had no idea. But what he did know was that it'd only been four days, and this level of attachment was stupid. It was dangerous, even. This was when kids like him got hurt. The last thing he ever wanted to be again was the sucker who fell for the promise of more.

But when she came out of the bathroom, hair long and soft over one shoulder and cheeks so flushed she looked fevered, some resolve in him cracked. He could keep her at arm's length physically, could keep his emotions in check, too. But he didn't ever want to bruise hers.

"The bed is plenty big for us to share," he said, silently begging her to look at him.

She glanced up and then quickly away. "Okay. If you're sure."

"I'll stay on my side." He'd wanted it to sound playful, but instead it came out tight, like a warning.

"Of course. I will, too."

"That's not—" He faltered because words about feelings and shortcomings and fears were not in his working vocabulary. "I wasn't—"

"Good night, Fitz." She cut him off gently, walking around the bed to climb in on the other side. The air stirred, and it smelled like honey. He wanted to press his nose to her skin, breathe her in. "I know it's weird for two people who barely know each other to share a room, let alone a bed. I'll never stop being grateful."

Two people who barely know each other.

He'd said something similar to her, he knew it was true, so why did it sting when she said it back?

Ren reached up, turning out the lamp beside her bed, so he did the same, lying there in miserable silence.

"Ren?"

He caught the tiny, frustrated sigh that preceded her amiable "Yes?"

"If you want to drive tomorrow," he said, "I'm cool with it."

He was such a liar. Cool with it? Not even close. It went against every instinct, but he'd kept his word and handed her the keys on Saturday morning, watching begrudgingly as she unlocked the door and settled into the driver's seat. She'd been quiet as they'd gotten ready to leave, but her subdued vibe transitioned to elation as he directed her out of the hotel parking lot. Ren opened up Max's speed on the frontage road, letting out a giddy whoop.

"Ease him in gently," he said, leaning forward and feeling oddly jealous from where he'd been banished to the passenger seat. "You don't need a brick foot right off the line."

Ren adjusted her grip on the steering wheel. "I told you I drive all the time on the farm. I know how to handle an old car."

"An *old*—" The words sent him back against the seat, insulted on Max's behalf. "This Mustang is a finely tuned machine. A classic." He reached out and put a consoling hand on the dashboard. "Don't worry, Max. She didn't mean it." The engine rumbled in reply.

"His model is from the 1970s," Ren said, matter-of-factly, in that know-it-all voice that had always set his teeth on edge. "He's beautiful and you've kept him in great shape, but objectively he's an old car." She pursed her lips, thinking. "He's the same year as our manure spreader, I think."

Wow, the insults kept coming. "He's also getting your butt to

Nashville, so a little respect, please." Fitz looked at the map and glanced up ahead. "Take this left turn."

She flicked on the turn signal, and a twinge of irritation colored her voice when she asked, "Is the plan to stay on surface streets the entire drive?"

"It wouldn't be if you stopped taking the turns so wide. He's a Mustang, not a school bus."

"Why'd you let me drive if you were just going to grumble at me the whole time?"

Fitz didn't need the years of mandatory child-services therapy under his belt to get that he was being a backseat driver and, frankly, sort of a dick. They were already in a weird place with each other after his mental meltdown last night. Unfortunately, he liked being in the driver's seat—literally and metaphorically—and knew it was unlikely he'd be able to shut that down over something as enormous as another person driving the car he'd saved up for years to buy.

But Ren was right: He either trusted her to do this or he didn't. Yes, there had been the car she'd cut off in the parking lot, and she'd sped up instead of conservatively slowing down for two consecutive yellow lights. She had a lead foot and tended to hover on the right side of her lane, but they'd been on the road for more than twenty minutes and it had been fine, hadn't it?

With a glance down at his phone, he propped it in the empty ashtray where she could see the map and sat back in his seat.

"Get in the right lane and merge up ahead."

"We're getting on the freeway?" she asked with a hopeful lift to her voice.

"Sure. You're right, you don't need me babysitting you. Just go where the GPS tells you."

"I'll watch the speed and keep Max safe," she insisted, smoothly shifting lanes and guiding Max up the on-ramp. "You won't regret it,

Fitz, I promise."

"I know, Sunshine. You're doing great."

The freeway was blessedly empty, and as the miles rolled seamlessly beneath them, Fitz felt the muscles in his shoulders loosen, felt his worries ease.

And after three consecutive nights of crappy sleep, exhaustion started to settle in.

Max's engine rumbled comfortingly all around him, lulling him into a heavy trance. Traffic was light, it was an easy route. Ren could handle herself, and they'd be in St. Louis before he knew it.

He yawned. It would be fine.

A truck horn blared so loudly it sounded like it was inside his cranium, and Fitz startled into consciousness, bolting up as the semi barreled past them, sending Max hopping sideways in the lane on a reverberating blast of air.

"Fitz! Wake up!" A hand reached blindly for the front of his shirt, shaking him. "We're going to die."

"W-what?"

Ren clutched at his collar. "I don't want to die!"

Adrenaline sent a bolt of electricity into his veins, and he was immediately alert, looking frantically at the situation around them. They were in the middle lane on a three-lane freeway somewhere between Kansas City and St. Louis, completely boxed in on all sides by irate drivers. A woman in a cream Cadillac swerved around them, leaning out her window and yelling, "Get off the road!"

"What's going on?" Fitz yelled over the commotion.

"Everyone is freaking out! It was so calm earlier, and all of a sudden all these cars showed up!" A raised truck came right up on their bumper, the driver leaning heavily on the horn. Ren screamed, slapping her hands over her ears.

"Hands on the wheel!" Fitz leaned across the console, taking over the steering, and managed to get a glimpse of the speedometer. "Ren! You're going thirty-five miles an hour!"

"Because they're scaring me!"

A man in the truck beside them was shouting obscenities out his window. A kid in the backseat of another car flipped them off as his mother drove past. The warm spring breeze that had lulled him to sleep now whipped into the car, adding chaos to the cacophony.

"Okay, listen, we've got to work together. We're going to get over into the right lane. Come here, Ren. Put your hands back up. I can't steer the car from here." Ren lifted her shaking hands and wrapped them around the steering wheel.

"Let's give it a little more gas, Sunshine." He put his hand on her thigh, pushing her leg down to lean on the accelerator, but when Max sped up, the person to their right sped up, too, vindictive and unwilling to let Ren ease in front of them.

"Oh, come on!" Fitz yelled out the window.

A car swerved around them on the left-hand side, the driver shouting, "MORONS!"

"Why are these people in such a bad mood!" Ren cried.

A truck with a bed full of onions in front of them suddenly slammed on its brakes, making Ren swerve to the left to avoid hitting the bumper as onions tumbled out, bouncing all over the road and even into the car. "I don't want to die! I've never eaten tiramisu!"

"Tira—?"

"I've never seen the northern lights!" she sobbed. "I've never been on a plane! I've never been kissed! I want to be kissed someday, Fitz! I don't want to be the girl who was killed by onions and never ate tiramisu and never got kissed!"

In the pandemonium, his brain stuttered over that one, and for some reason, he burst out laughing, pushing down harder on her thigh to encourage her to keep going. Fitz had been unable to sleep because he'd been thinking about nothing *but* kissing her. Go figure. Those unkissed lips were precisely what got them into this predicament.

An exit was nearing, and Fitz knew this stretch well; if they didn't get off soon, they'd be stuck here without another option for miles. "Check the mirror," he said. "Can you get over?"

A watery hiccup, and then, "I think so."

"Good. Turn on your blinker. Move to the right. There you go. That's it, they're letting you in." Her hands shook on the wheel, but her chin was set in determination as she eased Max into the right lane. "We'll get off at this exit."

Fitz stared at her profile, feeling something powerful well up in him. Awe. He was in awe of her.

Out of nowhere, a semi came up behind them, air horn blasting as it rocketed past. Fitz unleashed a screaming laugh as Ren veered to the exit, slowing at the bottom of the slight hill and steering off to the side of the road.

"It's not funny!" she yelled, but then she broke and was laughing, too, tears welling in her eyes as her entire body started to shake. "It's not funny," she said again, this time with less conviction, and her laugh turned less trembling and more joyous and . . .

God, she was so pretty.

Fitz reached down and pulled an onion from his lap, and she laughed even harder. There was enough adrenaline pumping through his veins that he was tempted to just reach over, put his hands in her hair, and kiss her.

Somehow, he resisted, but he did reach across the console and cup her face, meeting her eyes. "You okay?"

Ren nodded. "I think so. Did we almost die?"

"Goonies never say die."

Dust settled around them, and when she smiled, her cheeks filled his cupped palms. "You've seen *The Goonies*?"

"Every true movie fan has seen *The Goonies*, Sunshine. Do you realize we've just survived the *Clueless* on-ramp scene and lived to tell the tale?"

"You're right." She laughed, closing her eyes, and Fitz remembered the way Mary used to lean in and kiss each of his closed eyelids when he was scared.

He searched around for the cynicism he needed, the pessimistic reminder that this was all a terrible idea, but the call went unanswered. What he was feeling had wiped it all away, and the only thing he felt was hope.

He let go of Ren's face, reeling in an epiphany that made him feel lightheaded. He'd been wrong last night. A chance to be with Ren—for three months, a week, a day, an hour—was worth the risk of getting hurt. For her, he would willingly walk toward that blind turn. But he couldn't do it without her knowing the truth about him.

He just had to figure out how to tell her.

CHAPTER TWENTY-THREE

REN

By her own admission, Ren was the most romantically inexperienced twenty-two-year-old in the world, but even so, she was pretty sure a concrete wall would be able to read the flirtation in Fitz's eyes today. He said she could keep driving if she was up for it, but after their near-death experience, Ren eagerly handed him the keys. Back behind the wheel, Fitz teased her about the freeway adventure, but he did it sweetly, with laughter and glances from those happy, crinkly eyes. And he touched her. He touched her so much that she wondered whether she'd imagined the way he'd bolted away from her touch last night, feigning a coughing fit. She'd lain awake in bed, curled away from him, torturing herself by sifting through every embarrassing thing she'd done that day, when he'd clearly been trying to tell her that they were only friends.

So . . . was this how Fitz was with his friends? To him, was this kind of contact casual? And if this was casual contact, how on earth would she someday survive a real kiss, a real embrace?

Whatever was happening, Fitz seemed to melt somehow. He would reach out and squeeze her thigh to take the edge off a joke. He'd tweak her ear, poke her dimple, tuck her hair behind her ear. When she recounted the sequence of terrifying vehicular events that occurred while he'd been sleeping, he reached over and put his hand on hers. It felt like he was finding every possible excuse to touch her as much as possible. As soon as they were settled in tonight's hotel, Ren promised herself, she would point-blank ask him what it all meant, and why he was running hot and cold constantly. She didn't know how to play this game.

So, of course, the first time she really, really hoped they'd be forced to share a room again, the hotel in St. Louis had two available. It was clean, it was ready, and it was cheap. They still had plenty of money left from the Screaming Eagle, so unless she was ready to fess up about wanting to room together, there was no way for her to turn it down.

"Great," she said with false brightness. "I'll take it."

The man with a handlebar mustache and bow tie tucked her key into one envelope, tucked Fitz's into another, and wrote down their room numbers on each. Ren peeked over to see if they were even on the same floor.

They were not.

Using a pen to point to a small map printed inside the key envelope, the gentleman showed them where their rooms were. "Breakfast buffet opens at six thirty. Elevators are here, general store is over here, and our heated pool and hot tub are on the first floor, which is one floor down from where we are now." He looked up at them and smiled. "Our pool is great. You'll need your key to access it, but definitely give it a try if you can."

Her brain screamed at her that hunger and sleep could take a backseat to time spent in the hot tub with Fitz.

The man closed their envelopes and handed them over. "Welcome to St. Louis," he said as they bent to pick up their bags.

"Finally," Fitz said in the elevator, "I can stretch out in bed, take up the entire thing."

This made her laugh. "You'll still sleep on your side anyway, completely immobile all night."

He glanced at her sidelong. "You been watching me sleep, Sunshine?"

Heat rushed up her neck. "Definitely not."

He was still looking at her when he said, "Maybe I'm really just looking forward to walking around the room naked."

The words landed just as they arrived at the fifth floor. Ren stared at her reflection in the metal of the doors as they slid open, her body immobile, brain caught in a nuclear meltdown. Fitz held his arm out, pinning the elevator open. "This is you. I'm one more up."

When the doors began to loudly beep, she startled into motion, stepping out into the hall. But then she turned, summoning a rush of courage and stopping the elevator doors from closing again. "Wanna meet at the hot tub in ten?"

Fitz's expression went blank, and then he took a step forward. She released the doors to close just as his answer burst free: "Absolutely."

Ren stood in front of the mirror, tugging on the thin fabric at her hip. What on earth was she thinking? A hot tub? With Fitz? She'd worn a bathing suit exactly one other time in her life, and now she was just going to—what? Walk around in front of him like she was some kind of supermodel? He'd probably dated the prettiest girls in school, in every school he ever attended. No—he'd probably turned down the prettiest girls in school because there were prettier girls somewhere else. Staring at herself now, Ren registered that she'd made an enormous mistake.

Once every few months, Miss Draper over at the Finders Keepers thrift shop in Troy would let Ren go through the bins of new donations and keep a few things in exchange for helping her get them washed and mended and ready for sale. Never having had a sibling to give her hand-me-downs, it was the easiest way for Ren to get new clothes when she'd outgrown her old ones. Sometimes the boxes would overflow with so many nice choices, and she'd want to try on all the silly impractical things—tube tops, tiny shorts, soft fluffy sweaters—but in the end Ren would take only what she needed. A bathing suit wasn't ever in that category; Ren always swam alone at Finley's Pond or at their secluded creek, anyway, and would just strip down to the buff and jump right in.

But when the bikini came through in the donations, she'd pulled it free from the pile and couldn't let it go.

It had been two skimpy red-and-white-striped triangles for the top and a tiny scrap of blue polka-dot fabric for the bottom, and every part of her wanted it desperately. She knew Gloria would never approve of something so flimsy, so she'd kept it hidden high in a tree she knew Gloria would never climb, waiting for the days that stretched long and sultry, when the air shimmered with the heat of summer.

Ren was fifteen when she was riding her bike home from the market and followed the sound of voices down by the town watering hole. A group of kids about her age were swinging off a rope tied to a giant oak tree. Their laughter drew her closer, and their delighted screams as they soared through the air and splashed into the still-cold lake made her desperate to join in. She couldn't get to her hiding spot quick enough. Ren shucked off her clothes, put on the bathing suit, and raced back. She swam in the sun-warmed water and splashed with the other kids. The suit was a little big—the top seemed to slip down and the bottoms crept up—but she tightened the straps and waited with bated breath until it was her turn at the rope. She'd never experienced anything as exhilarating as swinging through the air and letting go. She felt alive. She felt free. She felt very, very naked: Ren made it back to the shore long before her top did.

The one she was wearing now was newer—to her, at least—and fit better. She'd picked it up at Finders Keepers in January, just before she'd left for Spokane, after she'd seen that the school had a pool on campus. It was simple and yellow—Miss Draper called it a halter neckline—and had about three times as much fabric as that old bikini did. Unfortunately it was still a bikini, but it was the only bathing suit in Ren's size at the thrift store that day. While she was tying it more firmly around her neck, her pulse seemed to sprint away inside her chest, tiny feet hammering down a path of incessant worries. What if history repeated itself, but this time she ended up naked in front of Fitz?

"You won't be swinging from a rope," she reminded herself with a laugh. But then her thoughts turned down a new path. What if Fitz didn't like how she looked in it?

Ren drew her eyes up over the reflection in the mirror. "Knock that off," she said to the woman standing there. "You look perfectly fine. No one can make you feel bad about yourself if you feel good."

Ugh. She was taking too long, agonizing over nothing. It wasn't like Fitz was going to notice her anyway. He was probably down at the pool, effortlessly shirtless in his swim trunks, scrolling on that phone of his and not thinking about her at all. She'd walk in and he'd say *Hey* and she would feel stupid for putting even this much thought into it.

She tugged on her T-shirt and shorts and padded out of the room.

Ren could smell the pool as soon as the elevator opened on the bottom floor but was grateful for it; turned out she didn't like riding the elevator alone, felt weirdly claustrophobic without Fitz.

She swiped her key at the door and pushed in, seeing no one else in the long, dim space. The air was heavy and humid, filled with the chemical smell of chlorine and wet cement. And just like she expected, at the very back of the pool room, she found him slumped in a chair, scrolling on his phone. She was relieved to see he wasn't shirtless yet.

His eyes dragged upward when she approached wearing her too-big T-shirt and sleep shorts. "You swimming in that?"

Ren worked to not fidget with the hem of her shirt. "No."

He cocked an eyebrow, a silent *Well?* But Ren needed another second to find her courage.

In front of them was a large, lit rectangular swimming pool with a spillover feature, like a tiny waterfall, that filled the space with the sound of splashing water. On the other side of the deck was a steaming hot tub. Refracted light bounced off the pool's surface and shimmered along the walls, the ceiling, and rows of empty lounge chairs. Lapping water echoed in the quiet.

Fitz stood, walked to grab a couple of towels from a rack, and came back over, dropping them onto the chair. Without ceremony, he reached for the collar of his T-shirt, tugging it off, and for a second, Ren lost her breath.

His torso was so much better than she'd remembered. And that all made it so much worse.

With her pulse rioting in her throat, she threw her gaze to the other side of the room. "I thought there'd be more people in here."

"We can leave if you want," he said immediately, a frown in his voice. "We don't—"

Before he could finish, she shoved off her shorts, peeled off her shirt, and turned to him. "I'm good."

Ren didn't miss the way his mouth went slack and his eyes dropped to her feet before slowly climbing up her bare legs. When his attention moved to drag up over her stomach and across her chest, her skin felt like it was covered in sweet, licking flames. Turning to keep him from looking any further, Ren cannonballed into the pool.

She was still underwater, arms and legs flexing out and back as she kicked to the surface, when there was a smooth missile under the water, and Fitz's hand came around her foot, playfully tugging.

Ren emerged at the surface, screaming out a laugh, and he broke through right after her, hair slicked back and lashes heavy with glimmering water droplets. With his eyes full of mischief, Fitz dove back under, wrapping his arms around her waist and hoisting her up, hurling her screaming in delight across the water. Ren ducked under, minnowing past him, dodging his grasp, and coming up behind him. With a laugh, she dunked his head underwater as he let out a laughing shout.

She'd spent countless hours swimming, but none in an actual pool, and rarely with anyone to play with like this. For what felt like hours they chased each other, wrestling, grabbing, tugging limbs and hands and toes. He practiced launching her with one foot in his joined hands until she'd made a perfect dive into the deep end. They raced—his strokes clean and practiced, hers unpolished and instinctive, but Ren won half the time anyway. They did handstands and underwater somersaults and competed to see who could stay under the water longer until they gave up nearly at the same time and pushed together, breathless, to the side, arms bent and chests heaving.

"You're strong," Fitz managed between labored breaths.

"You bet I am."

He leaned his cheek on his arm, gazing at her with a glimmer that she didn't want to believe was interest. Okay, that wasn't exactly true. She wanted to believe, a little too much. Ren blinked away, feeling a shiver pass through her.

"Cold?" he asked and surprised her by sending a gentle hand down her bare arm.

Ren was anything but cold after he did that, but nodded anyway, and Fitz pushed his upper body out of the water, hopping a leg up like he weighed nothing. He bent, dripping, and extended a hand to help her climb out. "Here."

Ren hesitated, but not for any reason that made sense in her head. She simply didn't know what to do with herself—with her hands and face and legs and thoughts that still seemed to be tripping over the feeling of his slippery skin against hers underwater, the size of his hands and how they slid up her legs to take hold or tickle her, the hard planes of his back and chest and arms.

"Don't you trust me?" he asked, and it unlocked something in her brain, releasing her arm from its weird, infatuated paralysis and reaching so he could pull her up. Ren scrabbled the rest of the way out of the pool on her own.

When she straightened, it was the first time they really saw each other in their suits, stealing glances as they trailed wet footprints across the concrete.

Fitz tiptoed over to the control panel on the wall to turn on the Jacuzzi jets, and when his back was to her, Ren measured the width of his shoulders with her eyes, mapping the shape of his back, and mentally painted the way water sluiced down the center of his spine. His suit was wet, plastered to his backside, and the deepest ocean blue. It made his tanned torso look golden. When he turned around, her eyes landed directly on his toned stomach, smooth and defined. Her own stomach took a screaming nosedive.

If Fitz's smirk told her anything, it was that he knew exactly what she'd been doing.

With the hot tub now gurgling between them, Ren walked to the edge and stuck her toes in the water, testing. It was so hot, it took her breath away.

"Go slow," he said quietly. "This isn't a jump-in kind of pool."

Ren nodded, looking up to find his gaze trained on her outstretched leg, eyes glazed. A rush hit her, something new and untamed, and it took her a few seconds to register what it was. For the first time since they'd been together, she experienced a tiny surge of power over him. She stepped one foot in, and then another, and couldn't help the groan that escaped. At the sound, her cheeks went instantly hot in mortification, but she didn't look at his face, couldn't log his expression. Instead, she slowly lowered herself to one of the tiled steps, watching Fitz as he followed her in.

His calves were strong, his thighs thick. Those swim trunks hung so low on his hips—inches below his navel—Ren wasn't sure what was even keeping them up. His chest was geometric and tight; she was fascinated by the angles of muscle and bone, the line that ran from his abdomen up the center of his pectorals. His nipples . . .

God. She'd never really looked at a man's nipples before.

"You okay there, Sunshine?"

Ren sank further into the water, turning her attention to the plaster ceiling above. "I'm great."

Steam twisted between them, and she didn't let herself look again until he was safely underwater. Fitz dropped to the bench across from her and the water was displaced, jostling her in her seat and rocking Ren back against the hot tub wall. Her face positively flamed at the images that flooded her head. Legs bracketing hips, wet skin against wet skin. He groaned in relief, and her stomach tightened in response. Ren had an overwhelming need to clench her legs together. He wasn't touching her, but it didn't matter; it felt like his hands were everywhere, all over.

"That feels good," he murmured.

Not helping.

She'd thought about him—of course she had—but she'd never mapped out the mechanics of touching him. Or of him touching her.

Right now, it was all she could think about.

She desperately needed to think about something else.

"What's your favorite thing about Nashville?"

Fitz dragged his eyes up from the water bubbling at the surface, visibly thrown. "What?"

"Nashville. What do you love about it?"

He closed his eyes, leaning his head back so that his Adam's apple pushed forward.

Not helping.

"The food. The music. The feel of being outside on a warm spring night." He lifted one shoulder in a lazy shrug. "It feels more like home than home does."

"Is it your mom's side or dad's side?"

"What's that?"

"Your family there," she said. "In Nashville."

"Oh." Fitz lifted a hand and dragged his fingertips through the bubbles. "Um . . . mom." He smiled, but it didn't look happy. "Nashville isn't really Robert Fitzsimmons's style."

"What's he like?"

He exhaled a dry laugh through his nose. "Rich."

"Really?" She laughed incredulously. "That's the only way you'd describe your *father*?"

"Well, no," he said, dragging a hand through his wet hair. "He's also disciplined. I'm sure I'll grow up to be a very productive member of society, thanks to him."

"That doesn't sound very warm and cuddly."

"That's not really his way," he said.

Ren hadn't known him long, but she liked to think she was figuring him out and knew when it was time to stop pushing. "Okay, next question. What's—"

"No," he interrupted. "It's my turn now."

She swallowed. "Okay."

"What do you find attractive in a person?"

She didn't even have to think. "Kindness. In the eyes, especially."

"Kindness, huh?"

Ren grinned at him. "Broad shoulders and big hands don't hurt, though."

Fitz laughed. "There it is."

She gnawed her lip, dropping her gaze to his neck, because she couldn't look him in the eye when she asked, "What about you?"

He gave a little shrug and stretched an arm across the back of the hot tub. "I like people who are good." She looked away from how the movement elongated his muscle, his pectoral twitching just below the surface of the water, and squeezed her legs together again. "Opposites attract, you know."

She stared at him, knowing he expected her to call him out for this self-flagellation disguised as cockiness. "That wasn't the answer I was expecting," she said instead. Glimpses of his genuine depth still took her by surprise.

"You thought I was going to say boobs or asses or something like that."

It took all her strength to not cross her arms over her chest. "Obviously."

"Right," he said darkly, "because I get in everyone's pants."

"If you say so."

"I never said so. You did."

"I thought we weren't supposed to talk about this," she reminded him. "Rule number eleven."

"We're practically naked together in a hot tub. Road trip rules are out the window right now."

"Okay, then," she said bravely. "Do you have a girlfriend?"

His answer was clear as a bell: "No."

"Oh." It was like every bone in her body liquefied.

He leaned forward again, his smile wide and wicked. "My turn," he said.

"No," she protested. "It's my turn now. You asked about what I found attractive."

"And you just asked whether I have a girlfriend."

She frowned. *Dang it.*

"In the car," Fitz began, "you said you couldn't die before you were kissed. Is that true?"

"Is what true? That I don't want to die? Yes, it's true."

He laughed. "No, wiseass, is it true that you've never been kissed?"

She took a beat to steady her voice. "Yes."

He looked away, squinting in the distance at the wall on the far end of the room. After a deep breath, he turned his eyes back to her. "We could fix that, you know."

A thunderbolt cracked through her torso. "What?"

"I could be your first. You know, to get it out of the way."

"You?"

"Yeah," he said, and smiled. "Why not?"

"Why not?" she repeated. There was a storm of words in her thoughts. "You're confusing, that's why."

Ren noticed that he didn't ask her what she meant. He only said, "I'm sorry." He lifted a hand, dragging his fingertips through the bubbles again. "If it helps, I want to be less confusing."

She swallowed, shaking all over, wanting to dissect that but not having the faintest idea where to start. "It's a very nice offer, but I don't know how to do it, and I wouldn't want you to have to suffer through my fumbling."

"I would show you. Nobody's suffering here."

She blinked and looked away. Was this a normal thing to

offer? He said it like it was, just threw it out so casually. Inside her, hunger violently thrummed just beneath the surface of her skin. She wanted this. She wanted him. Even if that was all it was—a lesson in kissing—she wanted to feel it, just one time. "Okay," she said finally.

For a split second he looked shocked. And then his shoulders relaxed, and he reached for her. "Then come here."

She jerked her head back to stare at him. "Wh— *Now*?"

"Why not?"

Across the expanse of the hot tub, he found her hand and tugged her through the bubbling water to rest between his parted knees. Her own knees hit the bench and he shifted, gripping the backs of her thighs and floating her easily onto his lap, so that she was straddling him, with one knee on either side of his hips.

The air rushed from her lungs in a gasp, and she reached for his shoulders to keep from sinking down fully onto him.

"This okay?" he whispered.

She'd never been so close to anyone before for more than the duration of a brief hug, and her mind had gone completely blank. She nodded.

"Words, Sunshine. Lesson one: When you're with a guy, you need to tell him that what he's doing is okay. If it's not, he should stop."

"It's okay. I'm okay."

"Good." He swallowed, finding the fingers of one of her hands on his shoulder and guiding them higher. "Maybe you want to cup his face, like this." He brought her trembling hand to his jaw. Her eyes followed the movement, riveted, as he set her fingers on his skin, molding them with his own hand. Without thinking, she brushed a thumb over his cheek. His skin glowed under the dim lights, his eyes darting to hers.

"Sorry," she whispered.

"No. It's good. Do what feels natural."

With that permission, she moved an inch lower, drawing the pad of her thumb across the swell of his bottom lip. It was so much softer than she'd imagined, so smooth and full. He pressed a kiss there and she looked up, meeting his eyes.

"Good," he said, eyes dark. Her other hand slipped absently down to his chest. She could feel the pounding of his heart under her fingertips. "Still okay?" he asked.

He had one hand on her lower back, the other wrapped around the top of her thigh. His body was strong and steady beneath hers. Ren swallowed, starting to answer only with a nod, and then remembered: "Yes."

"How does it feel so far?"

"Really nice."

He smiled at this. "Good." He began to close the distance between them, so close that he was out of focus, and she had to shut her eyes. She could feel his breath on her parted lips, the way his fingers had slid higher and curled around the back strap of her bathing suit.

"You're doing so good," he whispered, just an inch away. "And remember," he said, so close, so quiet. His nose brushed against hers, and his other thumb moved in soft circles near the crease of her thigh.

"Remember?" she repeated mindlessly, breaths short and stuttering.

"When you do this," he said, and his lips just barely brushed over hers, "you can stop whenever you want."

"I don't want to stop."

She sucked in a breath at the first full press of his mouth; the sensation inside her felt like falling. She'd never ridden a roller coaster before, but she imagined it was something like this, right at the very top, a free fall into joyful abandon. Her stomach had to be somewhere near her throat; she couldn't get enough air into her lungs. Fitz pulled away like he wanted to check in, but Ren slid her hand to the back of his neck, pulling him close again. The heat pressing up from beneath her skin felt almost unbearable, and when he carefully swiped his tongue over hers, she felt a different kind of hunger, a new kind of need. She'd never experienced this sweet tension spiraling through her body, heavy and warm.

He moved a hand to cup her face and tilted her head to fit him better, the hand on her back moving to her hip to pull her closer. She was so conscious of every tiny movement and point of pressure—his thighs beneath her, the power of his arms, the gentle scratch of his stubble against her lips and cheeks. She understood now on a deeper, savage level why people did this, why people fought for it, lost themselves in search of it.

Languid minutes passed as he showed her so many different kisses—deep ones and tiny, soft ones; teeth-dragging ones and lip-sucking ones. Steam swirled around them, decadent fingertips brushing their skin, leaving them dewy with sweat. She felt his kisses in every nerve ending in her body, felt the growing points of contact between them, how she moved closer and closer until they were touching from chest to hips, moving, rocking.

She understood how they'd fit together.

Slowly, with his breaths gusting against her lips, Fitz pulled away, stilling her with a thumb set gently on her chin. This close, she could see that his cheeks were flushed, his lips wet, so pretty and pink. His chest rose and fell like he'd just done laps around the pool.

"We should stop," he said, voice tight.

"Did I do okay?"

He blinked, and met her eyes, giving a quiet laugh. "Yeah. You did great."

Seconds ticked by before he cleared his throat, and the glassiness in his eyes slowly sobered. She grew conscious of their position, the feel of that part of him, the reality of what they'd done, and shifted her hips back, half floating, half perched on his knees.

"See?" He reached up, tucking a wayward strand of hair behind her ear. "Now you can't say you've never been kissed."

"You're right." Her lips still tingled, and she bit the lower one, dragging it through her teeth. He watched. "Thank you, Fitz."

He closed his eyes and let his head fall back against the side of the hot tub, his smile slowly fading. Worry tightened his brow, but he curved a hand around her side and murmured quietly, "Trust me. It was my pleasure."

CHAPTER TWENTY-FOUR

FITZ

Even with all the crazy shit in his past, Fitz had never had an out-of-body experience before. But when he and Ren climbed out of the hot tub, put themselves back together in silence, eyes averted, and stepped into the elevator, it was like everything that happened in the previous hour existed only in a vague fog somewhere behind them. Gone was the loose-limbed heat of the hot tub; their shoulders were now squared, gazes pinned on the closed doors as they rose through the building.

He felt trapped in his own head, unable to think of the best thing to say. She had to know what that was, right? She had to know that he didn't just want to teach her how to kiss, he *wanted* to kiss her. He wanted *her*.

No matter what you're thinking right now, that was the best kiss I've ever had.

I want to see you again when we both get back to Spokane.

It wasn't until Ren got out on the fifth floor with a quietly mumbled "Good night" and the doors closed again that the truth hit him like a slap: A better man would have said these things out loud to her. Kissing Ren had been the first thing he'd done in a long time that wasn't motivated by resentment, revenge, or fear. And right now, Fitz stood squarely at the fork in the road.

In his own room, he looked around at the empty darkness,

imagining the rest of the night spent alone, with room service or snacks from a vending machine, the television on in the background, a vague, muted drone. A shapeless sadness began to take root, and when he imagined Ren doing the same thing, the amorphous feeling spiked into a pulse of anxiety.

What was he thinking, kissing her and sending her off like that?

He showered at light speed, pulled on a pair of shorts and a T-shirt, and took the stairs two at a time to the fifth floor and room 546. He knocked once, then again, and leaned in closer to the crack in the doorway. "It's me, Sunshine."

A few seconds later, Ren pulled the door open, her hair still loose and wet, a clean towel in her hand. "Hey."

She stared up at him in confusion, and yeah, he got it. He was being confusing again.

"I was just about to get in the shower," she told him, waiting for whatever it was he'd come there to say.

"My room was so big and quiet," he explained, stepping past her. "And it was sort of boring up there alone." He flopped back onto her bed. "I thought maybe you wouldn't mind some company."

She let the door swing closed but hovered in the entryway, studying him. "I'd be okay, Fitz," she said finally. "You don't need to worry about me."

"Who says I'm here because I was worried?"

She walked deeper into the room and stood at the foot of the bed, cheeks pink, lips still a little swollen from his gentle attack on them not ten minutes ago. "Come on."

"What would I be worried about?" he asked, knowing his face wasn't masking a thing he felt for her.

She laughed. "You're going to make me say it, aren't you?"

He grinned. "Yeah."

"You're worried that I'm here feeling confused after . . ." She pointed down to the floor, indicating the lower level. "After that."

"A wise woman once told me, if I can't talk about it, I shouldn't be doing it."

"A wise woman, huh?" Ren asked, pinning him with a raised brow.

He swallowed, warring with the instinct to take back the way he'd opened the subject. Finally, he said, "Her name is Mary. She's one of the reasons I'm going to Nashville."

"Is she a friend?"

Friend, mother, savior . . . His thoughts trailed off. "She's a lot of things," he admitted.

Ren's expression crashed, and Fitz realized how it had sounded. "No, no. Mary is in her sixties," he told her, and he could immediately see the way her eyes grew hungry, wanting more. But his stomach growled loudly, and they both laughed. "For another time, apparently." Ren looked like she wanted to protest, so Fitz spoke before she could. "How about we order room service and have a slumber party?" He patted the mattress at his hip. "We get to Nashville tomorrow. You're going to miss our roomie routine."

"You can't be serious," she said, but she was grinning. "This is only a double bed."

"Like you said, I barely move all night anyway."

"Yesterday you looked like you wanted to crawl out of your skin because we had to share a bed twice this size."

"Because I wanted to kiss you so bad," he blurted.

Ren's lips parted, her hand going lax and dropping the towel to the floor. "You what?"

"Yeah, I—" He pushed up onto his elbows, skin prickling with nerves. "It was one thing to share a room before then, but in the same bed . . . I worried I'd wake up wrapped around you."

Her cheeks flushed again. "Fitz."

"I mean . . . am I off base here?" Putting himself out there was terrifying, an emotional rope bridge over a yawning canyon, but he shoved the words out. "That wasn't a normal kiss, Ren."

"It wasn't?"

He laughed out an incredulous "No way." Swallowing, he took a breath and threw himself into the void. "Are you feeling this, too?"

"You mean, am I feeling like all I want to do is be near you every second?"

He nodded, choking out a relieved "Yeah."

"Yes. I'm feeling it, too."

All of a sudden, he realized how this probably looked to her: Fitz inviting himself in, lounging on her bed. "I don't want you to feel pressured. Shit—I can go back to my room. This isn't about kissing or whatever. I mean, it is, but it isn't *just* about that. I promise I won't try anything."

She shook her head, biting back a smile at his babble. "I don't want you to go back to your room."

He exhaled a long breath. "Then go shower. I'll find us a movie to watch."

Fitz had made a lot of bad choices in his life. He'd lied, he'd borrowed a few things that didn't belong to him, he'd talked his way out of trouble or into places where he should never have set foot. The first time he clearly remembered breaking a rule was in the second grade. He'd just been placed with Mary. His pants were too short, his ears were too big, he'd been to three different schools that year alone and was just plain lonely. Bullies can smell that kind of desperation, and Fitz absolutely reeked of it.

When a couple of older kids sat next to him at lunch, he was starstruck. He hadn't yet mastered the art of indifference and was immediately and clearly on board with whatever it was they had in mind.

Turns out what they had in mind was that it would be funny if they all pulled the fire alarm. It wasn't the kind of thing Fitz would do, normally—he'd bounced around the foster system for four years by then, and if anything, his vibe was more to fly under the radar whenever possible—but it seemed like a worthy price to pay to gain a few friends. Unfortunately, when the siren blared and everyone began filing into the halls, Fitz was the only one left standing near the alarm. His wingmen had left him holding the figurative bag and fled to their respective classrooms, where they would be accounted for. Fitz was suspended for a week.

But there was an unintended consequence. The fire department came, and everyone got to go home early. He was in trouble, sure, but suddenly he was also cool. People wanted to be his friend. He learned a lesson that day that has served him well: Sometimes bad decisions can turn into something very, very good.

In the clear light of morning, he wondered if coming down to Ren's room should be lumped in with this brand of bad decision. Because waking up curled around her, with his hand beneath the hem of her shirt and resting against the warm, soft skin of her stomach, all he wanted was to bail on every other plan he'd made for the week—for his life—and stay in that bed with Ren forever.

The instinctive thought pushed in, that he should call his father, that he was off track and a few minutes on the phone with the elder Fitzsimmons's disappointed silence and passive-aggressive advice would remind Fitz exactly why he was on this road trip in the first place. Robert Fitzsimmons wasn't responsible for Fitz ending up in foster care, but he was the reason Fitz had lost the only real home he'd ever known. If his father taught him anything, it was that the only person Fitz could depend on was himself. Ren made him want to forget all of that. He couldn't afford to.

But then she rolled over, sleepily humming into his chest, and every other thought evaporated into the ether.

He'd been on his best behavior last night, though at the time it felt like it might kill him. They watched a movie, then brushed their teeth in the new side-by-side routine they'd fallen into. They climbed into bed, and he kissed her only once. Just a simple peck. When she pushed up, wordlessly asking for more, he admitted he was worried it wouldn't end there.

"Is that bad?" she'd asked.

"No, of course not," he'd told her. "But you only get these firsts one time. We shouldn't blow through them."

"You mean *I* shouldn't blow through them," she'd said into the darkness.

"No, I mean we. These are firsts for me, too."

He hadn't known what she'd thought of that, because she hadn't said anything else. He didn't even know what *he* thought because he didn't give himself time to examine it too closely. It felt too soon to say it, too heavy, but Ren had only ever been fully herself with him, and so he tried that type of bald honesty on with her like a borrowed coat. It felt good. It felt so good that they'd both fallen asleep the way a match goes out, a gentle, soundless surrender into darkness.

When the sun streaked across the foot of the bed, though, Nashville called, only a handful of hours away. Fitz felt the pull of two directions again: forward to the next step of his plan, and down, rooted to the bed and the promise of things he'd never let himself hope for. He wasn't sure how to handle the way this new, hungry feeling mixed with the sour cocktail of all his old ones, so he did what he did best: He pushed forward.

“Wake up, Sunshine,” he told her, kissing her neck. “We gotta hit the road.”

CHAPTER TWENTY-FIVE

FITZ

It was only when they pulled up in front of the hotel in Nashville that Fitz remembered how he'd splurged on this one, anticipating the way doubt might creep in at the last minute before his internship interview, hissing in his ear that he wasn't law firm material, that a kid like him couldn't begin to hang in the world he hoped to conquer. It wasn't the Ritz, but it was a heap of steps up from where they'd stayed so far, and he could see the intimidation flood Ren's posture the moment she stepped foot in the lobby.

Everything was marble, crystal, brass. The atrium had towering ceilings, with a glass dome far up in the air. To one side was an imperial staircase, on the other was a cluster of plush seating areas. There were urns spilling fresh flowers everywhere, uniformed employees hovering near every wall, ready to jump to service. The lobby was full of guests, too, chatting in small groups, greeting each other across the space, embracing. The park outside was full of booths and tents and chaos that spilled into the hotel. There was definitely some sort of event happening, that much was clear.

"Holy cow, Fitz." Ren stepped closer, sliding her hand into his. "Are we staying here?"

"We are."

"You really are rich."

There was no edge in her words, only awe, but for the first time in years, it bothered him that someone thought Robert

Fitzsimmons's money was his, too. He'd let so many omissions and white lies linger between them. He should clarify right there, should tell her that the cash she got at the Screaming Eagle was the most cash he'd ever held in his life, that he was a scholarship kid, too, that everything was riding on his grades, and that's why she found him in Audran's office that night. But instead, he swallowed it all down, squeezed her hand, and led her to the reception desk.

Ren's attention was behind them during check-in, watching all the bustle in the hotel lobby with rapt attention.

As soon as the woman stepped away to program the keys to their room, Ren tugged on his arm. "Fitz. Look."

He followed her gaze to where a handful of people pushed carts loaded with boxes through the front lobby doors. Others were still checking in or chatting in the adjoining coffee shop, with brightly colored cowboy hats tucked under an arm or wearing flashing LED necklaces around their necks.

"Four hundred people checking in today alone," the clerk said wearily. "You here for the festival, too?"

"Festival?" he asked.

"Beer, Bubbles, and Barbecue."

Ren stepped forward. "Bubbles?"

"Champagne," Fitz told her, and watched as the woman looked up from her monitor, her gaze doing a slow, fascinated sweep of Ren's hair.

"It's the biggest downtown festival of the year," the clerk told them. "Two music stages. Vendors, food trucks, fireworks. Loads of these people are still setting up."

"Then yes, we are absolutely here for the festival," Ren said confidently.

Worried she was about to be disappointed, Fitz reached for her hand. "It's probably sold out."

"Actually, it is," the clerk said. "But because we're going to be in the middle of the whole thing, the hotel got an allotment for VIPs. I might have a couple left if you're interested. Let me check." She disappeared into a back room.

"She called us *VIPs*," Ren whispered.

"In fact, I think her implication was that real VIPs didn't want these tickets."

"Well, *we* do!"

Fitz looked down at her. "You really want to go?" If this was his last day with Ren, he wanted her all to himself.

"Don't you?"

"The title names three things, and two of them are booze," he said. "If you want to hang out with a bunch of drunks, we can watch *The Hangover* in our room and order champagne."

Ren chewed on her lip and stared up at him. "It's just that I've never been to a festival before."

"It might be crowded. You might hate it."

"I assume it's a lot like a fair, but with less manure. And it's free." Her eyes grew round and pleading.

"This is emotional manipulation," he whispered, fighting a laugh.

Doubling down, she pushed out her full bottom lip. "Come on, Fitz. I just want to see it. Please."

She clearly saw what that *please* did to him because her expression went from pleading to triumphant in a blink.

"Fine," he said finally.

Grinning, she pushed up on her toes to press a kiss to his cheek. A strange feeling was carving out a space in his gut, like a door had been blown open in his torso. He didn't have time to examine it because the clerk was back.

"You're in luck. The last two. Because they're VIP, they'll get you side-stage access to most of the shows, a discount on food"—she leaned in—"*and* access to air-conditioned porta potties."

"Doesn't get much fancier than that," Fitz said.

The clerk slid the tickets and a flyer across the counter. "Welcome to Nashville. Have fun, and enjoy your stay."

Fresh from a shower, Fitz buttoned up his jeans. Ren had wanted them to dress up a little for the festival and had dragged him to a thrift store a few blocks from the hotel. The jeans were a clean pair of Levi's he'd brought with him, but the shirt currently folded on the bathroom counter was new. Well, new to him, at least, and a fancier brand even than the interview suit he'd splurged on two weeks ago in Spokane. In fact, when Ren handed him the shirt over the dressing room door, he'd recognized the designer as one he'd find in his father's closet.

God, his father. Fitz hadn't thought of him all day. Or Mary—who was only a twenty-minute drive from where they were staying. His twin motivations in life: revenge and restitution. In the past seven years, had he ever gone longer than an hour without thinking of one of them?

It was all because of Ren. Thinking about her was so much better than anything else.

Fitz imagined telling Mary about how things had changed with his road trip tagalong and felt the warm glow of embers behind his breastbone. But the sensation cooled as he thought about everything he still needed to tell Ren.

He'd never kept secrets from Mary, and he'd never felt bad about keeping secrets from anyone else. But Ren was different; everything was different now. And as he met his own gaze in the still-foggy mirror, he made a silent vow to talk to her as soon as she was finished dressing in the other room. No more chickening out, no more lies. No more pretending.

There was a knock on the door, and when he opened it and saw her standing on the other side, every thought melted from his brain. Her hair was braided in a delicate crown atop her head, with a few silk flowers tucked between the plaited strands; beneath it, her skin seemed to glow. Her sundress was lavender with thin straps and a soft, sloping neckline. The fabric looked delicate and breezy and fell just to the tops of her knees. She wouldn't let him see it at the store and told him only that it was simple, and it was, but simple was a lie. The dress was made for her. For a few painful seconds, he forgot how to breathe.

"I worried you got sucked down the drain you were taking so long," she said.

He tugged her inside with him, and she let out a little squeak as he closed them into the steamy space.

"You're supposed to put on that shirt." Her eyes were fixed on the ceiling, very pointedly not on his bare torso.

He pulled her closer, drawing her hands up to rest on his chest. *Touch me,* his mind screamed.

"What are we doing in here?" she whispered with a smile, looking to her fingertips as they traced the line of his collarbone. She was getting the flush he'd seen a couple times now, whenever her thoughts seemed to drift to everything they could do when they were this close.

"Well, I did want to kiss you," he whispered back, bending just shy of resting his lips on hers. "But also, I had something very important to say."

She blinked up, meeting his gaze. "What's that?"

"That you look amazing. Nobody's even going to notice the

fireworks tonight with you there."

She bit down on her bottom lip, and he reached up, freeing it with his thumb, staring. She kissed it and then pulled away, smoothing the front of her dress. "You really like it?"

He pretended to consider her, but in reality, he was afraid of the sound that would come out if he opened his mouth. He was sure he'd never seen anyone so beautiful before. "It's not an oversize T-shirt and cutoff shorts, but it's pretty good."

She grinned and turned toward the mirror. He reluctantly let her go, watching as she examined her reflection. He liked the way they looked together. "My shorts would at least have somewhere to put my room key."

"I'll carry the key." He came up behind her, bending to kiss the nape of her neck.

She put her hands over her mouth to hide her smile. "I've never worn anything this pretty before." Turning away from the mirror, she sent her arms around his waist. "Thank you for doing this with me. And for letting me come along on your road trip."

"I didn't let you," he reminded her, kissing the crown of her head. "You forced me."

She rested her cheek against his bare chest. "This has been the best week of my entire life."

For a moment he wasn't sure what to do with his hands. Something inside him wanted to shy away from the weight of her confession, from the tender clench of his heart that felt a little like an exposed nerve. Being soft and open with people had never given him anything good. But with a deep breath he pushed all that down and leaned in to hug her back.

If Ren had had access to Google her entire life, she'd probably be president by now. By the time they made their way to Public Square Park, where the festival was being held, she'd already learned the names and significance of the surrounding buildings, what bands were performing on which stage and when, located the food booths she wanted to visit, and read enough reviews of last year's festival to know where each and every portable toilet could be found.

Thank God she used her powers for good.

Nashville reminded Fitz of Vegas, with less neon and a lot more cowboy hats. The sidewalks were packed, the streets blocked off now as the sun began to set, and the sound of tuning guitars could be heard through the cacophony of crowd noise.

They exchanged their tickets for VIP lanyards and a stack of free food and drink coupons, which they used right away at a food truck called Fire-N-Smoke. When they were done eating, Ren tugged him toward the main stage, where a band he'd actually heard of was in the middle of a song that had been on every playlist already that year. And yet he barely noticed any of it, his thoughts full only of Ren dancing and jumping and singing along to the handful of words she'd managed to pick up in the chorus.

When the set ended, they wandered around the festival. It was fully dark now, and strings of glowing Edison bulbs shone overhead, illuminating the crowded park. Fitz held her hand as they wound their way from one vendor booth to the next and she told him about the fairs back home, and how she'd wanted to stay late and join in the festivities, but they always packed up as soon as they were done. Fitz promised himself then and there that he would stay as late as she wanted.

Ren never moved from his side, silently drinking in every sight: A couple kissing enthusiastically. Two kids playing with a puppy. A group in Dolly Parton cosplay. Ren pointed to a man making rainbows and giant flowers out of colored clouds of cotton candy, but then their attention was drawn to a news crew and a crowd of protestors with megaphones and signs just outside the park, their shouting drowned out by one of the bands.

Ren frowned as she scanned the signs. "They don't approve of the festival?"

"Looks that way."

"What exactly do they think is happening in here?" she asked.

"The devil's music and fornicating."

"But people are just having fun." Her frown intensified, and he wondered if she was thinking of her parents and what they would think of all this. Would they be holding signs and protesting, too? Probably not, and only because they'd never let Ren this close to begin with. That's when he noticed the cameras capturing footage of the crowd, and an uneasy chill made its way down his spine.

"Let's go," he urged softly, pressing a kiss to the side of her head, and gently led her away.

Determined to bring back her smile, they shared fried Oreos, and Fitz bought her a tiara with PRINCESS twinkling in golden LED lights across the top. And he couldn't seem to stop touching her.

Another band was playing on a smaller stage surrounded by tables and a makeshift dance floor. Fitz left her just long enough to grab them each a glass of champagne and handed one to Ren.

"Ooh, champagne!" Ren took the plastic glass, lifting it to watch the never-ending path of bubbles from the bottom to the surface. "Was it expensive?"

"I bought it from a guy wearing a T-shirt that said SUDS AND BUDS. I'll let you answer that."

"Would you be surprised if I said I've never had champagne before?"

"Not even a little bit. Should we make a toast?"

She sucked in an excited breath. "What should we toast to?"

"How about adventure?"

"To adventure!"

They clinked glasses and then she tipped hers back, eyes going wide as she swallowed a huge gulp.

"Careful," he said, laughing. "Champagne hits people differently."

"Even cheap champagne?"

"Especially cheap champagne. You could be on the floor in an hour."

Ignoring this, she cheekily drained the glass and set it on a table before tugging him out to dance. "Then you'd better be there to hold me up."

Fitz tried to resist but, unable to deny her anything, let her lead him into the crowd. They danced and drank and laughed as the music played around them.

"You know, for someone who's never been to a festival before, you're a natural," he said, twirling her and pulling her back in.

"Are these things always this fun? Is this what I've been missing?"

The music slowed, and he placed his hand on her lower back, tugging her closer. "Sunshine, I don't think anything has ever been this fun."

"Why do you call me that? You only say Ren when you're being serious."

He stiffened. "Do you not like when I call you Sunshine?"

"I do. I like that you give me nicknames. I'd never had one before. . . ."

She trailed off, and he placed a finger under her chin, tilting her face up to his. "But?"

"But I only call you Fitz. I don't even know your first name."

His blood cooled. He'd put the Fitz mask on for the first time seven years ago and never once took it off. But with her staring up at him like that, it hit him that he wanted more than anything to feel safe being the real him.

"Edward," he told her. "My name is Edward."

She met his eyes, and, as hard as it was, he held the contact, letting her recalibrate with this new name on her tongue.

"Edward," she said, and her fingers brushed through the back of his hair. "I love it." Ren closed her eyes. "The origin is English. The name means 'guardian, protector, wealthy.'" She snorted, opening her eyes again. "I guess that fits."

It was funny how not funny it was. He was none of those things, but of course Ren wouldn't know that. "You are an encyclopedia of random information." He grinned down at her. "How about more champagne?"

Ren gave him a dorky thumbs-up. "Champagne is my favorite."

"Stay here, and I'll grab us a couple glasses."

But when he returned, she was gone. Things were really in full swing now, loud and riotous. There was a fiddle player on the stage and people clapped along, faces rosy from drink, noses sunburned. The dance floor was almost completely obscured by moving bodies, and right at the center was Ren, dancing with a crowd of men and women who had brought her into their circle, arms around each other.

He found a chair on the side and sat down to watch. She was a blur of lavender and gold, arms over her head as she spun, blond strands of hair slipping from her intricate braid. A bottle of pure sunshine uncorked, spilling across the park. The song ended and the dance floor exploded in applause for the band, for each other, for the experience they were all sharing. People hugged Ren, touched her hair in wonder, took her hand, and brought her back to the floor for another song, and then another, until finally she escaped, tripping in a giddy tangle over to Edward, where she fell across his lap.

"There she is," he said, catching her.

"I love dancing!"

"I can tell." Gently, he brushed a few sweaty strands of hair from her eyes. Her tiara was crooked, and he smiled, straightening it. "If only you were more outgoing."

"That was the nicest group of people. I'm so exhausted, though."

"How many proposals did you get out there?"

"Only a few." She fixed her focus on his lips. "Came over to hear your offer before I went back with an answer."

He looked closely at her, at the tipsy glassiness of her gaze and the blissful elation in her smile. "Then I guess I can't let you go back out there."

"Is that right?"

"That's right."

He wanted to kiss her—to really kiss her like he had last night in the hot tub, with depth and heat and hunger—and knew that if he sat here much longer, he would. He would tip forward, fall into her, and maybe never be able to find his way out again. He'd started to lean in when the first firework shot across the sky, signaling the end of the festival. They both blinked away, looking upward to where a flash of color exploded overhead, followed by another, and another. They watched for a moment, Ren having gone still in his lap, before she looked over at him, a halo of golden sparks raining down behind her.

"I didn't think this night could get any better," she said.

"Proposals and fireworks. That all it takes?"

"I never did hear yours, by the way," she said, running her finger along his jaw.

"How about this: We get out of here and go back upstairs, put on our pajamas, brush our teeth, and have a slumber party?"

"No one made an offer even a fraction that good," she said,

closing the distance to kiss him. "Take me upstairs, Edward."

CHAPTER TWENTY-SIX

REN

Never in her life had Ren so ardently wished for the gift of telekinesis. With such a power, she would simply reach over with her mind and tug the hotel curtains closed. The blinding stretch of light between the drapes stabbed like a hot spear through her skull, even with her eyes closed.

Desperate for relief, she rolled over, colliding with a wall.

No, not a wall. Fitz's bare chest. Ren groaned as rising consciousness brought with it a pounding headache. "Ow."

A laugh vibrated behind Fitz's breastbone. "She wakes."

She groaned again.

"Stay here." Fitz rolled from bed, blessedly removing the cloying heat of his body, and she stretched out, seeking the relief of cooler sheets. Water ran, bare feet padded across the floor, and Fitz was back, a demon, turning on the light.

"No. Darkness only."

Another rumbling laugh. "Take these, and drink this." She heard him set something on the bedside table.

"I think I'm sick," she mumbled.

"I think you're hungover."

"Why aren't you hungover?"

"Because I weigh fifty pounds more than you, and we only had two glasses of champagne."

Weakly, she pushed up on one elbow. When a cool breeze from the air conditioner blew over her bare arms, she realized she was in her usual pajamas. But Fitz wore only those brain-melting shorts he slept in. And nothing else. "You're shirtless," she said, staring as it sank in: She'd slept pressed against his skin all night.

"Thanks to you."

Her gaze jerked to his. "You mean I took your shirt off?"

He planted two fists at the edge of the bed and smoldered at her. "You were very insistent."

She let herself imagine pulling his shirt off, reaching for the button of his jeans. Her face flamed. "I was?"

"Yes. But I stopped us." He leaned closer, whispering, "When we do those things, I want you to remember how good it was."

She fell back down face-first into the pillow, mumbling, "Don't be sexy when I might throw up."

Fitz laughed, straightening. "You feel terrible because you're dehydrated, and your blood sugar is tanked. You'll feel better with some carbs and caffeine in you, I promise. Come on." He gently urged her to sit up and take the painkillers. "We'll take things nice and slow and see how you feel. Okay?"

"I feel like a new human," Ren said, dropping a wadded-up wrapper on the tray.

"McDonald's is the hangover cure straight from the gods."

"I think I read that somewhere: The first ever golden arches were on Mount Olympus." She drained the last of her Coke, and Fitz laughed, standing to take their tray to the trash bin. "Fitz!" she called, and handed him her empty cup. She noticed there was something in his posture, a tiny hitch in his shoulders, that made her feel like she'd just done something wrong.

It poked like a thorn in her palm as they walked back to the hotel, and even though they were talking and laughing and everything in his demeanor seemed fine, she knew him well enough to know how easily he put on a smooth cover, how the Fitz he showed to the world wasn't the Edward he showed to h—

She stopped abruptly in the middle of the sidewalk. He jerked back when their joined hands pulled tight and turned to look at her. "You okay?"

As she stood there, frozen, it all came back in a blurry rush. The consuming heat of his kiss in the elevator last night, the pressure of the wall at her back once they got to their room, the way his mouth moved down her neck, wild. The fever of her hands moving up under his shirt, feeling the warm expanse of his torso. His insistence that she drink some water, go put on her pajamas, brush out her hair. Standing side by side in the bathroom, brushing their teeth, and then finding him in the darkness, pulling him close again, wanting more. The way he let her climb over him and pull off his shirt, the way they kissed and the desperation in his touch before he carefully rolled her to her back, his chest heaving as he reminded her that they had time to take it slow.

"I think you're my favorite person," she'd said drowsily into his neck. "Edward, Edward, Edward."

"I like that you call me that," he'd admitted. "It feels really good that you know my name."

It was the last thing he'd said before she fell asleep.

"I called you Fitz in McDonald's," she said now. "I'm sorry. I forgot."

A smile slowly curved his perfect mouth, and he took a few steps toward her, cupping her cheeks and bending to kiss her. "Does this mean you're remembering last night?"

She sensed the way her face heated under his palms. "Yes."

"So you know why I stopped us. I meant what I said. I want us *both* to remember when those firsts happen."

Her stomach dropped as the buildings of downtown Nashville seemed to loom overhead, crowding into her visual field. "When?"

His flirty smile slowly straightened as he searched her eyes. "When what?"

"You said when, not if."

"Sunshine, I'm okay with if, too. We can do as much, or as little as you want. But we won't do any of it drunk."

She nodded and pushed up on her toes to kiss him again. They started to walk, but the sights disappeared around her, the tourists banished by the whirlwind of her thoughts. She wanted more with Edward. If she was being honest with herself, she wanted to explore it all. But when? Nashville was the final dot on the map for him, but she still had one more stop. Would things be the same when they got back to Spokane? Or would he go back to being Just Fitz, even with her?

And she'd been so wrapped up in the excitement of the trip and the heat simmering between her and Edward that she hadn't thought—really thought—about what the next phase of her journey looked like. Suddenly, the idea of leaving him today and heading into the foggy unknown of family secrets felt so overwhelming, Ren got dizzy.

With a flush of panic, she came to a stop, tugging his hand. "I don't want to go to Atlanta today."

With a look of confusion, he turned to face her. "You want to stay another night? In Nashville?"

"Yes, but . . ." she began, suddenly aware that she might be imposing, that she had no idea what he had scheduled here. "Of course I don't want to mess with whatever your plans are."

"I, uh . . ." He trailed off, swallowing. "I have a thing on Thursday. I had some other stuff I was going to do in town, but

Thursday is the only thing I can't miss."

A thing? Some other stuff? Frustration simmered in her belly. They could kiss and sleep wound around each other, but he was always so vague. Maybe this was how it worked, though. Maybe sexual intimacy came first. It felt so backward.

"Then yes," she said. "I need to be on a bus back to Spokane by Wednesday, probably. But I want to stay another night."

One more day with Edward sounded like not nearly enough, but she'd take whatever she could get. She had bigger things to think about, but she'd never felt like this before. She wanted to stay in it a little longer, to savor it. Especially today.

"You're sure?"

"Yes," she said, confident again, and stepped forward, tilting her chin to look up at him. "Nothing sounds worse than getting on a bus, hungover, on my birthday."

CHAPTER TWENTY-SEVEN

REN

Ren kicked off her shoes and looked over at him. "Turn around."

Brow sweaty, breaths ragged, Edward slowly lowered his water bottle and gazed at her with concern. "Turn around why?"

Gesturing out to the lake ahead of them, Ren communicated the answer in her expression: *Isn't it obvious?* After making all the unnecessary noises of someone who unknowingly missed a birthday, Edward had asked what she wanted to do. She'd admitted she'd never really celebrated her birthday before, not in a way that mattered, so she had no idea. Sitting at a sidewalk café, they'd searched his phone for local options: Centennial Park, the Country Music Hall of Fame, a distillery visit, the Grand Ole Opry, or even a tractor tour. But when a series of stunning photos for Harpeth River State Park popped up in the browser, Ren was sold.

It took some work to get there, but after a winding hike over a deserted trail, the trees had finally parted, revealing a wide blue lake. Apparently, it was once a quarry but in the 1930s the bottom was sealed, the water filtered, and the area became a resort. But at the beginning of World War II, it closed, the buildings left to decay without human interference. Now, the swimming hole was completely secluded, closed in by steep rock walls and leggy trees that blocked the view from anyone standing on the ledge above.

To Ren, it was the perfect spot for a swim.

"But we don't have suits," he said slowly.

"Do we need them?"

"Generally, people who aren't routinely naked together wear suits when swimming, yes."

She smiled at him. "We have underwear, you know. We can swim in that."

"To be clear," he said, turning his back to her with a lingering grin, "I wasn't complaining."

Relief washed over her; it was unseasonably warm, in the low eighties, and after the steep hike where she'd had a near-constant view of the flexing and bunching of Edward's muscular thighs, she felt overheated and jittery. Thankfully they'd brought enough drinking water, and they'd just devoured the lunch of sandwiches and chips they'd picked up at a deli on the drive over, but the idea of diving into the calm, deep blue water made her feel like she'd had another two glasses of champagne.

Quickly, she unbuttoned her shorts and kicked them off. Her top was next. She folded them both and set them on a rock at the edge, then looked down at herself, dressed in only her simple bra and panties. They covered as much as her swimsuit, so that was fine, but she didn't have anything to change into, and she didn't relish the idea of driving back in wet underwear or walking through the busy hotel lobby braless.

She glanced at Edward's back. "I'm taking my undies off, too," she told him.

His spine stiffened. "Oh, so we're doing the full monty."

"I don't know what that means, but if it means fully naked, then yes." Unfastening her bra, she slipped it and her underwear off before tucking them both inside her shorts.

At the edge, she dipped a toe in. It was surprisingly warm and clear, and any lingering hesitancy slipped away. With a tiny yelp, she waded in a few steps before steeling herself and taking the plunge.

"Oh my God," she groaned as cool water slipped over every inch of her skin. She ducked under and kicked until she was farther out. When she surfaced again, Edward was still facing away. "I'm covered now."

He turned slowly, as if unsure of what he might see. She was submerged from her neck down, but she grinned at him and waved. "You coming in?"

The water lapped at the edge of the meager beach, a breeze rustled the trees overhead, wood creaked under the weight of lush branches. All of them awaiting his decision.

He drew circles in the air with his index finger, playfully indicating that it was her turn to look away now. Her laugh echoed in the stillness, bouncing back to them, but she did, moving to face the opposite shore. Ren continued to tread water, and as the breeze settled and quiet fell, she was vaguely aware of his shoes landing with a thunk against a fallen log, a zipper drawn down, the rustle of fabric, and the soft scratch of feet moving along the sandy shore. She thought she heard him stop at the edge, testing the temperature. She was about to tell him to stop being such a baby when there was a large splash and the call of birds as they scattered from the trees overhead.

She briefly imagined him swimming to her below the surface, wrapping his arms around her hips and then her torso before pressing his naked body to hers.

"Okay," he said from somewhere behind her. "I'm in."

She turned to see him about ten feet away. His hair was slicked back and darker when it was wet, brown eyes greener and framed by spiky lashes. Water ran down his face and neck and pooled in the hollows of his collarbones. He was blushing to the tips of his ears.

"Doesn't it feel amazing?"

"*Amazing* is one word. *Freezing* is another."

"You call this freezing?"

"There are definitely parts of my body that find this lake water offensively cold." She stared at him, confused, and he laughed, swimming in circles around her. "You know, there are easier ways to get me naked, Sunshine."

"It's a little foggy, but I think I was trying to last night."

Edward laughed at this. "So you were."

She splashed him, and he splashed her back until they were in a full-on water fight where he was at an advantage, being able to rise and show his whole torso out of the water. Her hair covered most of her bare chest, but as he advanced, wave after wave of water towering over her pathetic attempts, she decided she didn't care anymore and went all out, shoving water forward as powerfully as she could until she didn't care what else he might see. Laughing, he covered his eyes. "You're not playing fair."

"Do you give up?"

"Yes," he cried, laughing, "because if you keep going like that I won't want to blink, and all that water hurts my eyes."

They seemed to realize in unison that his hand was wrapped loosely around her wrist, keeping her from splashing him, and they were so close that her forearm rested against his chest. With the gentlest swell, the current could bump her into him, sending all of her bare skin right up against his.

"We can stand here," he said, and planted his feet, his chest rising several inches out of the water, which, when she stood, lapped gently at her chin. Trying to quell the vibrating hum beneath her skin, she spent a few seconds appreciating his broad shoulders as he breathed rapidly, catching his breath.

When she dragged her focus up his neck and higher, she found him watching her with an intensity he immediately wiped away. In a blink, his expression returned to his trademark breezy playfulness. "How does this compare to your swimmin' hole back home?"

"About ten times larger, but far fewer trout."

He shuddered.

"We stock the pond," she explained. "There are so many, I can catch them barehanded."

"That is . . ." He shook his head. "I don't know what that is."

"I believe the words you're looking for are *impressive*, *athletic*, *superhuman*."

"Yes, yes," he said, laughing. "All of those."

"From about June to late August, I swim every day."

"By yourself?"

"Usually."

"Doesn't that get lonely? Or at least boring?"

Ren shrugged under the water's surface. "If you're raised with lots of things—people, money, games, distractions—it's hard to live without them. But if you're raised simply, the way I was, that's all you know. That's all there is."

The reality of her life back home suddenly pressed down like a rain cloud.

"You haven't talked about them much the last couple days," he said quietly. "But I know you're thinking about your parents a lot."

Ren looked up at him. She was, and she wasn't. Edward seemed to take up every corner of her mind these days, but the silent, pulsing heartbeat in the background was her parents, Christopher Koning, the mystery of it all, the truth she hoped to find.

"I know my parents will always be there for me. Or I hope they will, even if I don't always do things the way they would want me to. But being away from home has made me realize how much more there is for me out here. That I can love being out in the world and love being on our land, too." She felt his attention on her as she tilted her face to the sky, closing her eyes. "But, wow, do I love our land. During the summer, I swim at night, and I'll float on my back, just staring up at the stars. You wouldn't believe how many you can see out there, where there's no city lights. I spend all day working my tail off, just so excited for the reward of getting into the pond and staring up at the stars."

"Is that why you draw fireworks around everything?"

She looked at him in surprise, having forgotten he'd seen her drawings. "No. I've always drawn those. My earliest memory is standing in a field, and there's a big crowd of people. I'm holding a sparkler in one hand, and it feels overwhelming until a big hand comes around mine and all of my worries go away. I hold my sparkler up and stare at the sky behind it, exploding in fireworks."

"Whose hand was it?"

"I don't know. I always assumed it was Steve's, but we've never set off fireworks. To him, it would be like lighting your money on fire. Also, I can't remember him ever holding my hand." She inhaled slowly as hope seemed to balloon in her throat. Another life unfolding. "When I got those results back . . ."

"You thought it might be a memory. With Christopher Koning."

"Yeah. That night . . . It was magical. The flowerworks seemed to go on forever. It's like I can still see them when I close my eyes. I dream the sky is full of them."

"They're beautiful, Ren."

Her stomach warmed with the compliment. "Thank you." She stepped forward, setting a hand on his chest. "I think *you're* beautiful."

Edward frowned, glancing down at the water lapping gently against her fingers, his chest. He seemed to sense the transition in her, the suggestion that they could stop talking for a little while.

"You know, what we were talking about back there," he said,

tilting his head closer to shore. "About how I stopped us from going too far last night . . ."

She waited, but her heart did an uncomfortable stutter, watching him piece together the words.

"I don't want you to regret anything after this trip," he said, finally, and the intensity seeped back into his eyes. "From blackmail to a sort of truce to hot-tub kissing to voluntarily sharing a bed . . . It's been a wild ride for me—I can't imagine what it's been like for you."

"*Wild* is one word for it," she agreed, laughing.

"I don't want you to jump into anything you'd look back on and wish you hadn't done."

"Like what?"

"Having sex with me," he said bluntly, and heat flashed across her skin.

"What about falling for you?"

"Oh." He swallowed, wincing. "That too, I guess."

She made herself maintain eye contact, even though her hand was trembling on his skin. "I won't deny that I have feelings for you. And I don't know how they compare to what's normal because I've never done this before. But I know my heart well enough to know that I won't fall in love with someone I don't know very well. And I barely know anything about you yet." She blinked down, distracted by the bob of his throat when he swallowed. "I do know that we're from very different worlds. You were raised in a rich family, and I—"

"About that," he said, cutting in gently. "I think you have the wrong idea about me. I think," he amended in a rush, "I've *let* you have the wrong idea."

"What do you mean?"

He pushed away, swimming backward and then returning, but still staying several feet from where he'd been. Keeping some distance. He tilted his face to the sky. "I'm at Corona on a scholarship, just like you."

"A scholarship? Why do you need a scholarship?"

"I'm not the biological child of Robert Fitzsimmons." Finally, he looked at her again. "I didn't even meet him until I was fourteen. I was fifteen when he adopted me."

Shock sent a numbing wave down her body. She didn't know how to react. "What?"

"There's so much more I want to tell you," he said quietly, coming closer until he was standing in front of her again. "I've wanted to for so long . . . you don't even know." He set his hands on her shoulders and slid them underwater down her arms until he took her hands in his. "It's okay if you're not sure you want to fall for me, but I think I want to fall for you." His words pulsed between them, sending ripples through her veins. "Unfortunately, I've never been good at talking about my past—I've never tried. Out loud."

"What do you mean?"

"Everyone who knows me at school knows me as Robert Fitzsimmons's son. They all assume that I was born rich, and I've let them. Every teacher, every roommate, every friend." He paused. "Every girlfriend."

Her stomach turned sour, and he studied her expression.

"I never wanted to tell anyone the truth, because people look at you differently when you're a kid raised in the foster system, who's adopted by a rich guy so he can get some good press."

Ren frowned. "'Some good press?'"

"It's not important right now." He squeezed her hands. "I'm telling you this because I've never liked someone the way I like you." He delivered this with a flirtatious smile that he tried to hold on to, but it loosened into a grimace. "Which means that I want you to know the truth, but as you already know, I'm really bad at talking about stuff. Even thinking about telling you everything makes me feel sort of panicked." He took a deep breath, releasing it slowly. "If I tell you and you don't like me, then you don't like *me*. Not just the story I made up."

"I don't mean to pressure you," she said. "I'm not in a hurry. I just want to know you. It doesn't have to happen right away if I know that you're trying. That you want to be . . ." She couldn't seem to get the rest out.

That he wanted to be with her.

"I do," he said, picking it up anyway.

"Even when we get back to school?"

His brow furrowed, like he didn't understand. "Of course. You think I only want you in secret?"

She shrugged. "I don't want to assume."

"With me," he said steadily, "assume. Assume I want you. Assume if I'm actually saying it that it's real." He bent a little, so their eyes were level. "But I've done some bad things, Ren. Some really shitty things. It's hard to feel like I deserve good things. And you . . . you're the best thing."

"Have you been in trouble with the police?"

A sad smile flickered over his lips. "Define trouble."

She knew him. He was good all the way down to the marrow of his bones. "Have you killed anyone? Assaulted someone? Held someone at knifepoint?"

Edward pulled back, quickly shaking his head. "Ren—"

"Traded organs on the black market? Posted racist tirades on social media?"

A tiny smile. "Uh, no."

"Abandoned puppies at the side of the road?"

"I might be an asshole sometimes, but I'm not a monster."

"Then whatever it is," she said, cupping his face and pulling him in for a kiss, "I can handle it. I just want to be with you."

CHAPTER TWENTY-EIGHT

EDWARD

Well.

It was a start. At least he could say that much.

But he could also say that it was only a few tiny truths, and he was left feeling completely depleted afterward. So drained, in fact, that he was tempted to let Ren drive them back into town just so he could close his eyes and not think for half an hour.

Edward wished brains had power-down mode. He wished life had an edit feature. He wished time had a pause button. He would hit it and close the door of their room in Nashville behind them and give them each another week in which they didn't have to think about everything still coming their way.

He looked up when Ren clapped her sneakers together beside Max's passenger door, trying to shake out all the mud they'd accumulated over the last bit of their hike. She leaned against the side of the car, her hair damp and loose, and looked up at him in playful despair. "We might need to go back to the secondhand shop and get me some new shoes."

He nodded in agreement. "Based on your thrifting skills, you'll go in for Keds and walk out with Prada."

Ren pointed over his shoulder. "Look."

It had started to rain on their way back—just a drizzle—and now he turned to find a rainbow arcing brightly overhead, not even trying to be coy. In fact, he'd never seen a rainbow like that, so thick and vivid it looked drawn onto the sky. He could clearly make out each individual color; it felt so sharp, so real, he'd swear that if he walked up the hill behind them, he could reach out and touch it. He briefly wondered if seeing it would make him lucky. Wasn't that what people said? He'd never thought about luck or wishes before—what was the use, really—but the appearance of Ren in his life had changed a lot of things, he guessed. "That's insane."

"Isn't it?" She dropped her shoes and looked down at them before seeming to give up, peeling off her socks and walking over to him barefoot. "Sometimes I can't believe that two different people can see the exact same thing." Her fingers found his and threaded between them. "Of course, maybe your red looks different from my red, and your green different from my green, but I don't think so."

"I don't think so, either."

"Sensation has to be universal." She looked at him so squarely, like there wasn't a thing in the world she needed to hide. God, he wanted to know what that felt like more than anything. "Like when you gave me my first kiss?" He nodded. "It wasn't your first, but I swear you knew what I was feeling."

He couldn't help but watch her mouth while she spoke. "I did."

She stretched, sliding that mouth over his. He pressed her to the side of the car, kissing her deeply, and fell into the sensation of melting from the inside.

"How's the birthday so far?" he asked when they finally came up for air.

"Easily in the top three of all time."

"Top three?" He walked around to the driver's side. "Okay, that's it, I'm taking you to my favorite local place for dinner. I'm getting that number one spot before the day is over."

Ren clapped happily, climbing into the passenger seat. But when

Edward turned the key, nothing happened.

He groaned. "Come on, Max. Don't be jealous." He tried again. Nothing. "Shit."

While he pulled his phone out and began searching for Triple A, Ren got back out of the car and walked to the front. He rolled down the window. "What're you doing, Sunshine?"

"Pop the hood."

He pulled the latch, and Ren propped it open. He started to climb out. "No, wait," she said. "Stay there. Put it in neutral and turn the key."

"Ren, I have Triple A. They'll come handle it." And his dad would find out that he was in Nashville, but there wasn't much he could do about that. He could call Mary for a ride back into town, but she would want to help with whatever repairs Max needed, and Edward would not ask her for a penny, not ever.

"Let me look first." Ren reached up, tying her hair into a bun atop her head. "It might be something super easy."

Reluctantly, he sat back and did what she said. The engine remained silent, but he could hear her voice, soft and gentle. "Okay, Max, what's going on with you, buddy?"

Edward leaned out the window. "He's pouting, that's what. I told you not to call him old. Though right now, I might have to agree with you."

"He didn't mean that," she murmured to the engine, and then looked over at Edward. "Do you have a toolbox in the trunk? Maybe a screwdriver?"

Meeting her at the back of the car, he pushed some things aside and pulled out a black emergency tool kit. Inside were a pair of jumper cables, some pliers, an adjustable wrench, a jack, a tire pressure gauge, emergency reflectors, and—he pulled them free—a set of screwdrivers.

"Perfect."

Passing her the flathead, he followed her back to the open hood. "What're you doing?"

"This is the solenoid relay"—she used the screwdriver to point to something in the engine—"which is basically an electromagnet and a couple of contact points inside a metal canister. They use a small amount of power to connect to a big amount of power." She bent, fidgeting with something. "Inside there are two contact points, and they're spring-loaded so they stay apart. When you apply power to the electromagnet, they close." She held a hand out to the side, squeezing her thumb and index finger together to illustrate. "When they close, they connect this wire here." Ren leaned to the side so he could see and pointed to what she meant. "Which is connected to the positive terminal on the battery, this terminal here, which runs down to the starter."

He laughed, already lost. "You could be making all of this up, but it sounds amazing."

"Long story short, I'm going to use this screwdriver to bypass the solenoid relay switch."

"You're sexy when you're being a gearhead." He leaned in closer, whispering, "Please don't electrocute yourself."

Ren laughed. "I'm only willing to try this because your screwdriver has a rubber handle."

"If this works, I'm taking you out for a fancy dinner after."

"I thought you were doing that anyway." She grinned over her shoulder, teasing and flirty, and she probably had no idea the power she had over him. When she finally learned how to harness it, he was done for.

"Extra fancy, then," he answered.

She nodded for him to go back inside the car. "Keep it in neutral and turn the key to the on position, just so everything lights up. Let me know when you do."

He kissed the top of her head and then ducked into the driver's seat. "Okay," he called to her.

"Go ahead and turn it all the way."

He closed his eyes, hoping he didn't manage to inadvertently zap his new girlfriend, but he heard her happy whoop when Max's engine roared to life. Ren closed the hood and bent to kiss it, saying, "Good boy."

Three hours later, Ren fell back in her chair, clutching her stomach and groaning happily. "That was the best meal I've ever had in my entire life."

Dressed in a new set of secondhand clothes that they picked out on the drive back from the lake—a cream silk skirt and green top that complemented Ren's eyes, a nice pair of jeans, and a linen button-down that she'd said made Edward's tanned skin look golden—they'd parked along a quiet street lined with older homes and small businesses and walked to a brick building fronted by a mixed garden of flowers and vegetables. Inside, the decor was as welcoming as being in someone's home. Heavy dark tables encircled an open kitchen with a wood oven in the center, its copper chimney stretching to the ceiling. Ren had been delighted, fascinated by the staff waiting and busing tables, by the food she could see being prepared and how much organization it took to make something like this look like no work at all. Observing the world through Ren's eyes made Edward realize how often he didn't really pay attention to what was going on around him. He moved through life constantly on the offense and went into every interaction with an objective. It meant he missed the details, missed the moments that made life worth living.

Edward gazed at the destruction all around them: crumbs from the world's best salted butter rolls, only a tiny fatty scrap of an impeccably cooked steak, some stray radicchio from a delicious salad, a few tendrils of linguini, and two empty red wineglasses. There wasn't birthday cake, but the waitstaff lit a candle in the center of her decadent Bananas Foster bread pudding. He'd pulled out his phone to capture her expression as they'd set the plate in front of her, the candlelight reflected in her wide, tear-rimmed eyes. That was one moment he wasn't going to miss.

Now she looked at him from across their small table. "You've absolutely ruined me."

That was too tempting a sentence to dwell on. Planting his elbows on the table, he leaned in. "Did I hit number one yet?"

She winced, clucking her tongue. "It's going to be really hard to beat the year I turned thirteen and Steve let me drive the truck to and from town, and then I saw a meteor shower that night when I was out at the pond."

"Skinny-dipping, engine victories, and those buttery salted rolls don't beat that?"

She pressed her lips together, fighting a laugh. "Mm-mm."

He drummed his fingers on his chin, pretending to think. "Okay, I have one more idea." He tossed the napkin to the table and reached for her hand. "Let's go."

The field was dark and deserted—just like he'd expected. With a tiny, nervous smile, Ren climbed out of Max, but stayed close to the door. "Where are we?"

"It's called Percy Warner Park," he explained. "It's huge, and I knew it would be pretty empty tonight—perfect for what I want to do."

"Hmm." She squinted out into the darkness while he grabbed a blanket, a sweatshirt, and her gift from the trunk. "I haven't seen any, but I've read that this is how horror movies begin."

"I'll protect you." He gently tugged her forward, using the flashlight on his phone to lead them to a paved trail and out onto the lawn, where they hiked up a small hill.

Edward spread the blanket on the soft, dewy grass. "Did you bring me out here to see stars?" she asked.

"Not exactly." It was true that the stars were more visible here than downtown, but excitement rose in him as he pulled her gift from his back pocket and turned to shield it from her view. Opening the box, he pulled one long stick free and slid the purple Bic lighter out of his other pocket to ignite it.

Light popped and sizzled, and he held it up to Ren, witnessing the moment her eyes went round and then immediately filled with tears. She clapped a hand over her mouth, turning to look at him, the sparkler reflected in a million golden flashes in her eyes.

"Happy birthday, Sunshine," he said quietly.

She reached out, grasping it, and then held it in front of her, staring in awe. Tentatively, she waved it around, drawing a figure eight in the air. It burned down to the end and her expression fell. "That was so beautiful. Thank you so much, Ed—"

He lit a second sparkler and handed it to her.

She gasped. "Another?"

"I got a box of a hundred," he said, laughing. "It'll take us an hour to get through all of them."

And it very nearly did. They lit two at a time and wrote their initials in the sky. He handed her two, one for each hand, and she stood, waving her arms wide, forming perfect circles while he captured the image on his phone: her beatific smile and the two cones of fire on either side of her. They ran streaks of light down the hill and back up again. And every time they were ready to light a new sparkler from an old one, she said, "Let them kiss."

When they lit the final one, she watched it burn all the way to the end before releasing a tiny, happy cry. "That is absolutely the best present anyone has ever given me."

"Number one yet?" he asked, and she turned, sliding her arms around his neck, burying her face there.

"Number one, forever," she said, voice muffled. "Thank you."

They stretched out on the blanket, staring up at the stars, and Ren pointed out the constellations they could see: Hydra, Leo, Leo Minor, Sextans, and Ursa Major. She told him about the kinds of things she would normally do on a birthday—go for a longer walk than usual around the property, be allowed to nap out in the field without being scolded for missing chores. It occurred to Edward that every time she shared something about herself was an opportunity for him to reciprocate, but he hadn't taken any of them.

They fell quiet, his brain lighting up with everything he wanted to say. He wanted to tell her about Mary, how close he'd been to having a family and how it had fallen apart, how angry he'd been for so long and how he'd spent the last few years plotting something he wasn't even sure he wanted to carry through anymore. He'd carried anger and hurt for so long, wrapped himself in them and used them to keep others away. Something about Ren made him want to put it all down.

"Ren—" he began, just as she said, "Do you—?"

She squeezed his hand. "Go ahead."

"No, you first."

"I was just going to ask—if it's even okay to ask this—whether you know who your birth parents are."

A shadow passed through his chest. "No . . . all I know is that they relinquished custody of me when I was three, and that's when I went into the foster system. They handed me over to the Spokane Fire Department."

"But you have family here?"

He nodded. "In a sense."

She'd given him an explicit opening, and still, he couldn't step through the door. How did Ren make opening up to him look so easy?

"Mary," she guessed.

"She was my foster mother," he said, relieved at her gentle prompt. "She moved to Nashville a couple years after her oldest son graduated high school—which was right around the time my adoption went through. I have a job interview here on Thursday. I'd set it up forever ago, knowing I eventually wanted to be closer to her."

"Oh my gosh, Edward, this is so much. We could have spent today with her."

"No, there's time for me to see her while I'm here. Seriously, she's fine. I wouldn't have wanted to do that when we could be doing this."

"Do you know where your birth family is now?"

He paused, staring up at the sky. "No. But I was hoping there would be at least some genealogy stuff for me when we did that test in Audran's class."

"I'm guessing there wasn't."

"No. Nothing."

She reached over, squeezed his hand. "I'm sorry."

"Yeah."

"That's what I was expecting, too," she said, laughing wryly.

"Nothing. And here we are."

"I envied you," he admitted, rolling to his side and propping his head on a hand. "But you know what's funny?"

"What?"

"Now that I know you better, I'm surprised you did the test at all. I can't imagine Gloria and Steve would've given the green light."

"I've thought about that a lot—why I did it so readily." She rolled to face him, too. "I never disobeyed my parents before, but with every day I've spent away from them at school, I started questioning more and more why so many of those rules were there in the first place. I started pushing, a little at a time. I did the interview with the school paper, I made friends in study groups, I did the test. I've wanted to experience everything, because deep down, part of me knows they won't let me come back next fall. Once I'm home again over the summer, I think they'll see how much I've changed. They definitely won't let me finish out the semester if they find out about this trip."

His stomach bottomed out. When he first met Ren, he didn't think she'd last the week. Then, when she started to show him up, he wished he'd been right. The thought that her parents wouldn't let her come back felt too real, if he let his thoughts linger on it. Given how controlling they were, Fitz wasn't sure how she'd manage to keep any of this from them. Whether or not Ren found Christopher Koning, whether or not he was even her father, he knew it didn't matter. She had already changed from this experience, and there was no universe in which her parents wouldn't see that.

And another thought landed, and this time, his stomach twisted tightly and he let out a guilty groan. "I made so many rules," he said quietly.

Ren frowned at him. "What?"

"For the trip. I made those rules. No bowing, no talking, no eating, no singing. All your life you've been living under Steve and Gloria's rules. Then you were sent to college with more rules. And then you leave with me and—again, rules." He closed his eyes, wincing. "I'm such a dick."

"It's okay," she said immediately, instinctively.

"It *isn't*." He opened his eyes, met her gaze. "It's shitty. I'm so sorry."

Ren looked at him, really seemed to be trying to see him. "You do a lot of things to keep people out. The rules were about your boundaries, not about me. I got that."

Edward stared at her, reeling.

"I would only be mad about them if you were still speaking to me in riddles," she continued, smiling. "But you're telling me about yourself. I know how hard that is."

He let out a soundless laugh of disbelief. "I am so crazy for you." Edward ran his hand down her arm, feeling the goose bumps there. "Cold?" he asked, reaching for the sweatshirt and draping it over her.

"Cold," she said, and grinned in the darkness. "And crazy for you, too."

"Are you nervous?" he asked. "About tomorrow?"

Ren laughed tightly. "Nervous doesn't even cover it. It's like I start to imagine it, and then my brain powers down and everything just turns to fog, and I can't breathe."

The words rolled out of him, finally. "Can I come with you?"

She went quiet, eyes wide, watching him. "To Atlanta?"

"Yeah."

"What about your interview?"

"It's only a four-hour drive. I'd just need to drive back up here Wednesday night."

"You'd do that for me?"

He laughed because the surprise in her voice was so genuine. "I got naked in a freezing lake for you. You think I won't drive a few hours to make sure you get to Atlanta sa—"

His words were cut off when she pushed forward, pressing her mouth to his and rolling him to his back so she hovered over him. Her hair had come loose and formed a soft curtain around them as they lay, alone on the hill, kissing and kissing and kissing.

It occurred to him later, when they were in the hotel brushing teeth side by side, that he'd been lucky three times in his life: The day he met Mary. The day he met Judge Iman. And the day he met Ren. Being there with her, he didn't know how to go back to being Just Fitz. He hadn't thought about his five-year plan in days. He'd had a whole spiel memorized for his interview on Thursday, but now he didn't even know what he'd say. All he wanted was to run away with her.

So, in a way, they did.

CHAPTER TWENTY-NINE

REN

"Wonder if Max'll start this morning."

Ren looked up at the sound of Edward's voice, finding his eyes already searching her face with concern. Only now did she realize how tense she'd been, how she'd barely spoken or looked up all morning. Her voice came out scratchy: "He's the best boy and will start right up."

And, oh. Now that she was looking, she noticed how good Edward looked. She'd been so in her head she hadn't realized he was wearing a hunter-green T-shirt that made his brown eyes seem hazel, that he'd combed his hair off his forehead and looked so polished and grown-up. She hadn't taken a moment today to relish the thought that this man was her boyfriend. Her anxiety had become a physical brick in her stomach, not leaving room for anything else.

"How're we doing?" he asked, bending to meet her eyes. She wondered if anyone else at Corona knew how gentle he could be.

"I'm okay."

He seemed understandably skeptical. "You sure? You're a little pale. Want something to eat before we hit the road?"

The thought of food made her stomach lurch. "I think I just want to get there."

He smoothed her hair back, tucking a strand behind her ear. "Okay, you're the boss today."

"I still don't know what to say," she admitted, leaning back against the passenger door. "Do I just walk up to his door and say, 'Hi, are you by chance missing a daughter'?"

"It's not the worst idea." Edward smiled and then bent in, giving her a long, lingering kiss. "Ready?"

"Ready."

He rounded the front of the car, giving Max an encouraging little pat on the hood as he passed. The second Edward turned the key in the ignition, Max roared to life.

Last Tuesday felt like a lifetime ago, but it had been only seven days. Ren remembered waiting at the curb for Fitz to show up, feeling nervous and guilty and queasy from the enormous lie she was about to tell her parents. She imagined having the entire trip to think about what she would do on Christopher Koning's doorstep, what she would say. She thought she'd have time to mentally and emotionally prepare to hear that there was no way she was his daughter, or—even more world rocking—to hear that she was.

But instead of focusing on finding her father, the trip had become less about what she had ahead and more about what was right in front of her: Edward Fitzsimmons. What started so rocky and contentious had melted into comfort and passion and honesty. It was overwhelming, the way her heart was discovering love at the same time her mind was contemplating the possibility that her entire life had been built on a lie.

"I'm so glad you drove me down," she told him. "I'd be so nervous alone."

He glanced away from the road, smiling. "Me too. I'd be useless today if I was up there and you were down here without a phone."

A phone. It hadn't even occurred to her that if they were separated for any reason, she'd have no way of getting in touch with him. They'd ditched the burner from the Screaming Eagle bounty; Fitz explained it could have been used for all kinds of illegal things, so it now lived in a dumpster in Rapid City. The realization that Ren would probably need to buy one made a second bolt of awareness land, and she took a minute to piece the words together, staring out at the road ahead of them. "Would it hurt your feelings if I wanted to go up to his house by myself?"

"Of course it wouldn't. You mean you want me to wait nearby, right?"

She considered this. As comfortable as she was with Edward, and as much as she knew she'd want to tell him everything about what happened, she wasn't sure she wanted him there to witness it if she was turned away. Everything—even this—was too new. She knew she'd want to deal with it on her own first, even if she needed him nearby.

"I think it'd be better if you went and checked us into the hotel, and I called you when I was ready for you to come get me."

He was quiet for a few seconds. "You don't have a phone, Sunshine."

"I know, but you can give me your number. Even if he's not my dad, he'd let me use his phone, don't you think?"

"Let's just go grab you a burner and come back."

She shook her head. "I'm too nervous. I want to do this now. I'm sure I can use his phone."

"I'd be more comfortable if you took mine." He reached for the console and handed it to her before wrapping his hand around hers, squeezing. "I'll call this line from the hotel and leave the number so you can call me when you're ready."

Ren was pretty sure she'd never be ready, but it didn't matter, because they pulled up at the curb of the tree-lined street in Atlanta and it was right there, 1079 Birchwood Terrace. The house was blue, with white trim and a sunny yellow front door. The neighborhood was beautiful, with vibrant greenery and seductive, heavy buds bursting on every branch. It looked nothing like she'd been imagining from her years of reading Toni Morrison and Flannery O'Connor. But this was modern-day suburban Atlanta: Yards rolled down from beautiful homes to the sidewalks; flower beds were immaculate, bordering tidy verdant lawns. Trees lined the sidewalks, throwing soft shade over rooftops, their branch arms reaching for those of their cousins across the asphalt.

She could tell this was a neighborhood full of homes—not simply houses—where families met at a table at six sharp for dinner, where daughters learned to play catch with their dads and sons learned to ride bikes with a mom chasing after them, struggling to keep a steadying hand on the seat. It was so different from her own upbringing that she felt momentarily split down the middle, facing this alternative reality. She imagined playing in a yard like this, going to a real school, and being driven around in a shiny sedan instead of a rusty old pickup. She didn't want to change how or where she was raised, but she hadn't realized until she'd left how lonely she'd always been. Her only friends had been pigs and chickens, cats and cows.

Edward pulled a half a block farther down the street and parked at the curb. "You sure you don't want me to come with you?"

Ren gazed out the window, staring behind them. "I'm sure."

"Look at me, Ren."

She turned, and he leaned over, kissing her once. "I'll call as soon as I'm at the hotel with the phone number and our room number so they can connect you. I'll have them text it, too, just in case." He reached over, silencing the ringer. "It won't ring—I don't want it to distract you—but it'll vibrate when the voicemail is there. Okay? You know the passcode and how to get to my voicemail? My texts?" She nodded numbly, and he made her repeat the plan back to him.

"You'll leave a message with the phone number for me to call," she said, showing him that she knew where to access the voicemail on his phone. "You'll tell me our room number so I can have them connect me."

"Call me either way," he said. "If you stay for dinner, call me. If you need a ride immediately, call me. Actually, as soon as you have a sense of how it's going, call me. Just keep me updated. Please?"

"I will. Thank you." She reached over the console, cupping his cheek, then took a deep breath before climbing out.

Edward called out to her. "Ren!"

She bent down, peeking back into the car to find him leaning across the console, staring up at her. "I . . ." His smile straightened, eyes searching hers. "I wanted to tell you . . ."

"Tell me what?" she asked.

Finally, he grinned, making a fist of solidarity. "You got this."

"I'm going to take your word for it. I'll see you soon." With a weak smile, she waved, closed the passenger door, and waited with a strange sadness as he finally drove away.

Even the air smelled different here, thick with a sweetness she couldn't immediately name until she saw the iconic white star flowers crawling up trellises and weaving through arches over doorways.

Jasmine.

She slipped Edward's phone into her pocket, feeling comforted by the weight of it against her hip. She wanted to feel like herself today, so she'd dressed simply in cutoff denim shorts and a cropped T-shirt, her hair back in a smooth braid. It felt like they'd only driven ten seconds past the blue house with the yellow door, but the walk back seemed miles long. As she passed others—a yellow house with white trim; a white house with green trim; a green house with blue trim—she tried to imagine five-year-old Ren running across these lawns, eight-year-old Ren getting on a school bus, thirteen-year-old Ren sunbathing in one of the huge backyards. She was so lost in her own head, imagining her fictional life here and her actual life thousands of miles away, she swore she could almost hear Gloria's voice.

"Ren."

She froze on the sidewalk, awareness dawning that it wasn't her imagination at all.

"Ren Gylden, you look at me right now."

Ren spun slowly, heart plummeting into her stomach.

Gloria's hair was jet-black and glossy when Ren was little, but it was gray now, salt-and-pepper curls she wore half up, half down, the long waves cascading to the middle of her back. She wasn't wearing her good clothes that she'd normally wear for a trip into the city; she was in jeans and a button-down shirt, the same thing she'd wear to work their booth at the fair or make deliveries in town. Instead of gardening gloves and a big sun hat, she had a canvas purse over her shoulder and a pair of sunglasses on her face. Ren could see her own reflection in the lenses; she looked small and terrified.

Her worst nightmare had come true. Gloria had found out. Gloria was standing right in front of her in this sleepy Atlanta neighborhood. "What are you doing here?" Ren asked.

Gloria took her sunglasses off and dropped them inside her purse. She smiled with saccharine brightness. "Aw, sweetheart, I just came to ask you how midterms are going?"

"I promise, I can explain."

Gloria's expression snapped closed. "I don't need an explanation. I know exactly what you're doing here."

"You do?"

"Of course I do, you silly girl."

Sweat prickled at her scalp and at the back of her neck. Everything, everything was going wrong. Why did she let Edward leave? He would help her. He would know how to navigate this.

Ren tried to channel his easy confidence. "I'm actually fine handling this on my own."

"On your own? Is that right?" Gloria batted Ren's bravado away like a lion swatting at a buzzard. "Yesterday, I took an unplanned trip into town for supplies and Tammy had the TV on behind the register. You'll never guess what I saw."

"I don't—I don't know. What did you see?"

"Just you and some boy holding hands at a party in Nashville, Tennessee."

Ren's stomach dropped. She remembered the music, the dancing, the champagne. They'd been watching the protestors when Edward had abruptly suggested they move, distracting her with a kiss to the side of her head and a skewer of fried Oreos. World-weary Edward had seen the cameras and known the danger they presented. It had never occurred to Ren. If there was ever a sign she was destined to be caught, this was it. "Oh."

"Yeah, 'Oh,'" Gloria mocked, and laughed harshly. "Tammy was so excited she took a photo of you on TV. She even printed me out a copy, and you better believe I used it to get that boy's name. We got on the next plane." Gloria saw them on TV in Nashville yet knew exactly where Ren was headed. Right down to the very street? Understanding was like a door kicked open. Ren snapped to attention at her mother's voice: "Ask me how much I liked having to do that."

"Gloria, you didn't have to come for me. I would have come back. I promise."

"You think after all the time and effort I put into raising you free of all this"—she gestured to the beautiful street around them—"I'm going to be fine with you hitting the road with some stranger and driving to Atlanta? I trusted you to go to that school, to hold true to the values we brought you up with, Ren. And the first time you're away from home, you do this? Lesson learned."

"Everything would be the way it was before! I just . . ." Ren took a deep breath and looked her mother in the eye. "I need to know the truth, and I worried that if I asked you, you wouldn't let me go back to school."

"The truth," Gloria said, taking a step closer, her expression softening. "Ren, do you think that I would have kept something good from you? Do you think if there was something good for you to find here that I wouldn't let you go? You think so little of me?"

"No, Gloria, I—"

"Did it not occur to you that I was trying to protect you?"

Ren paused, frowning. "Protect me from what?"

Gloria glanced at the house two more doors down and took a deep, shaky breath. "From a very bad man. Steve may not be your blood, but he's the best father in the world to you and loves you like his own. He saved me from the hell of my first marriage."

Confirmation of this felt like a knife in her side. "Why didn't you tell me?"

"Because it didn't matter," she said. "You were so young, it didn't matter that Steve wasn't your biological father. We found a better place and made a better life, free of that man." She tossed the last two words toward the house where the very bad man must have been.

"It's a pretty place," Gloria allowed when Ren's gaze tracked down to the blue house with the white trim. "He was always very skilled at playing the part in public. Just know that dark things lurk behind these doors, Ren. You're my only child, my baby girl, and it took a long time for me to get free of his clutches."

Ren shivered, instinctively taking a step closer to Gloria and meeting her eyes. They were shiny, filled with unshed tears, and maybe a little afraid.

Ren had only seen her mother cry once, and it was when her favorite mare colicked and passed overnight.

"I didn't know you were in a bad relationship before Steve," Ren told her. "We never talk about that stuff."

"For good reason." Gloria reached down, taking Ren's hand. "Please, baby girl, don't bring him back into our lives again. I need you to trust me."

Ren lowered herself to the curb and put her head in her hands. She knew now that her mother had been wrong about some things, but she loved Ren, wanted what was best for her.

"We have three tickets to fly back tonight," Gloria said, rubbing Ren's back.

"What about Edward?"

Gloria gaped at her. "Ren, you can't be serious. I—I thought—" Gloria swallowed hard, frowning. "Please tell me that boy was just your ride out here."

"It started that way," Ren told her. "But it turned into more. He's a good person, Gloria."

"A good—" Gloria laughed, a single, harsh sound. "He's a criminal, Ren. A con man." She shook her head. "I don't know why I'm surprised. I guess we were both bound to make the same mistakes, get mixed up with the wrong kinds of men." Gloria sat on the curb next to her. "Thank God I got here in time."

"You don't understand. He made some mistakes back when he was younger, but . . . He's a scholarship student just like me."

"So you know he's not really that rich man's kid?"

"I know. He told me everything."

Gloria swallowed, gazing at her with part concern, part pity. "Everything? Did he tell you about the trouble he's been in?"

Suddenly, Ren wasn't sure. Edward had given her pieces of his life, like bread crumbs. Maybe he hadn't told her everything yet. But no, Ren *knew* him. Lifting her chin, defensive heat flashed through Ren's chest. "Yes, I know there's a lot in his past, but he's a good person." He was, even if he didn't always believe it. She met her mother's eyes, willing her voice not to shake when she said, "He's my boyfriend, and I trust him."

"Well, then." Gloria stared at her for a long beat and then blinked away, reaching into her purse and pulling out an envelope. "I'm glad to hear none of this will surprise you."

Ren opened it, pulling the single sheet free. At the top was a photo of a younger Edward—scruffy, filthy, long haired, eyes wild. The fury in his gaze was disorienting.

It listed what she assumed was his legal name—Edward Pryce Fallon—his date of birth, and a few other numbers Ren assumed were record numbers in the Washington State Child Welfare system. Below all that was a list about fifteen lines long. She scanned it quickly:

9A.56.065.................... Theft of a motor vehicle
9A.56.068.................... Possession of a stolen vehicle
9A.56.330.................... Possession of another's identification
9A.56.340.................... Theft with the intent to resell
9A.56.310.................... Possessing a stolen firearm
9A.56.346.................... Robbery in the first degree

There was more, but Ren stopped, a quiet moan escaping. "This isn't right. This can't be— How did you . . ."

Her heart thundering, Ren thought back to their conversation in the lake, both naked, both vulnerable. He'd been trying to tell her something, had started by saying he'd done bad things, and she'd asked him if he'd ever been in trouble with the police, fully expecting him to say no. But what had he said? He'd looked in her eyes and said—

Define trouble.

Ren's heart sank. He hadn't admitted to anything, but only because she hadn't asked the right questions. He knew Ren wanted to see the best in him, and he let her.

"It's him, Ren." Gloria put her arm around Ren's shoulders. "Baby, it's him. Men like him are good at fooling women like us. Of taking advantage."

Ren felt like she might throw up. The father she came here to find had been an abusive husband, and the boy she'd fallen for was a criminal.

She turned Ren to face her, expression soft as she read Ren's silent spiral. "Now, you listen to me. You can't blame yourself for this. This is just what I did—met a boy, fell in love in a matter of days. You're human. But this boy is bad news. He's a criminal and knows how to tell you what you want to hear, how to get you to trust him. Look at that rap sheet. Robbery? Possession of a stolen firearm? This boy didn't just steal a pack of gum. Who knows what he would have done to you. Or *us*."

Ren didn't know what to think. She'd assumed Edward had been a foolish kid and his troubles were over something trivial, not something dangerous. Certainly not something involving a firearm. How did she not see this coming? Ren hadn't learned an ounce of judgment in her time away from the homestead. She was just as naive and ignorant as ever.

Reeling, she remembered the Polaroid. He'd been cheating.

She'd caught him cheating, and somehow, over the past few days, she allowed herself to forget all about it. Miriam had warned Ren that very first day, hadn't she? She was right; everyone was right. Edward was Fitz, and Fitz was a liar.

"You didn't tell him anything about us, now, did you?" Gloria asked gently. "Nothing about where we live? We don't want him to find us."

Ren thought back. "Maybe I mentioned the five-and-dime," she admitted. "I think I told him about Corey Cove."

Gloria took a long, deep breath. "All right. Thank you for your honesty."

Ren leaned into her mother's arms. "I feel so stupid."

"None of that." Gloria helped her up and turned them toward a small blue rental car parked down the street. "Let's go pick up your dad and get you home."

CHAPTER THIRTY

EDWARD

Edward wasn't generally a guy who panicked. He'd learned early in life that there were two human emotions that served no purpose whatsoever: worry and regret. But when six o'clock rolled around and he hadn't heard anything from Ren, he felt the cold tendrils of unease take root at the base of his spine. They'd hit the road early; he'd dropped her off just after ten in the morning. That was nearly eight hours of silence, and even if she'd forgotten that he wanted her to keep him updated, and even for someone who wasn't used to calling and checking in, it didn't feel right. Unfortunately, he couldn't track his phone without his iPad or laptop, and he didn't have either of those things right now. So he kept calling. He would call and the phone would ring and eventually go to voicemail, and he'd leave yet another message.

But the first time it went *directly* to voicemail—indicating that it'd been turned off or the battery had finally died—was the moment unease morphed into true panic. He had no way to reach her, no way to know whether she was safe.

At seven, blood heavy with anxiety and dread, he headed to the lobby, deciding to wait for her there. With every car that pulled into valet, he'd think, *Maybe that's her in a cab. Maybe that's her father dropping her off.*

An hour went by, and still no sign of her.

He approached the check-in desk. "Have you seen a woman, early twenties, about this tall?" He held his hand about chest high. "Very, very long blond hair?"

It was at that description that the woman's face relaxed. "Can I get your name, sir?"

"It's Edward. Edward Fitzsimmons."

"Thank you. Yes, she left several hours ago with an older couple." The woman bent, opening a drawer, and then set his phone on the counter. "And she left this for you."

Edward took the phone, numb, and walked in a daze to the elevator. Back in their room—nope, *his* room, he thought bleakly—he lost track of time, staring at the floor, trying to sort through every possible scenario.

Older couple could have meant Gloria and Steve, but he didn't know how they'd find Ren here. It could mean Christopher Koning and his wife, in which case Ren might have opted to stay at their house for the night. But then why not call?

No matter which way he broke it down, something wasn't right.

And the only place he knew to start was at 1079 Birchwood Terrace.

The street was so different at night. Or maybe that was just his mood, reading everything with suspicion. To an anxious mind, what looked like utopia during the day looked like a neighborhood that could easily mask darkness, could effortlessly let an innocent twenty-something vanish.

There were lights on inside; they were warm and soft, and from the porch he could hear music. Closing his eyes, he took a slow, deep breath.

Calm down, Edward. There's an explanation. You'll find her.

He lifted his fist and knocked. The sound of small footsteps pounded on hardwood, and the door swung open, revealing—holy crap—a tiny Ren in pajamas and slippers.

Golden hair spilled down over her shoulders. Wide green eyes gazed up at him. What felt like a spear passed through his chest. "Hi," he said, offering a friendly smile.

"Mommy, there's a man at the door!" she yelled in response and ran back down the hall.

A woman leaned through a doorway in the distance and gasped, "Oh! Emily! Wait for Mommy or Daddy before answering the door!" Wiping her hands on her apron, she approached, calling back over her shoulder, "Honey, someone is here!"

In the other room, a male voice murmured something, and Edward caught only "Sweetheart . . . door . . . always . . . me or Mommy . . . safe."

Edward's heart was a roaring beast in his chest. This didn't feel like a house of shady abductors. But it also didn't feel like Ren was there, either. She would have come out at the mention of a man at the door, he knew she would.

The woman met him at the doorway and smiled. "Hi, can I help you?"

Edward tried to smile warmly, to take the edge of hysteria out of his eyes. "Hi, yes, I was wondering if a Mr. Christopher Koning lives here?"

The woman's expression stuttered. "Yes, that's my husband. Let me—" She stopped, looking back and seeing him already coming down the hall, and said, "He's asked for you."

The man in front of Edward looked just like the printed photo that Ren brought with her—blond hair, green eyes, hopeful smile. But the resemblance to his daughter was even stronger in person.

Ren had his nose: narrow and gently turned up at the end. They shared the same coloring, the same arch of their brows. But there was something else, some undefinable aura about him that *felt* like Ren, too. Whether it was the kind eyes or the patient smile that said he was in no hurry for Edward to put his words together, he wasn't sure. Edward's head was spinning.

"I'm Chris," the man said. "How are you?"

Edward shook his extended hand. "I'm good, thanks. My name is Edward." Edward swallowed, unable to predict how this was going to go. "I'm sorry to show up on your porch like this. I have a strange question."

Chris smiled and stepped outside, closing the front door behind him. "Let's hear it."

"Did a young woman come to your house today?" Edward asked.

Chris frowned. "No . . ." But then something seemed to land, and his shoulders squared as he took a step closer. "Who did you say you were? Who came here today?"

"Her name is Ren." Chris didn't show any sign of recognition, but his eyes were wild now, searching Edward's. "We drove across the country to find you."

"How old is she?" Chris asked sharply.

"She just turned twenty-three." Edward winced. "I dropped her off earlier to talk to you, but she never returned to the hotel, and I got worried."

Chris was white as a sheet, and Edward pulled out his phone, opening his photos to show him a picture of Ren at dinner the other night. He swiped through photos of her at Mount Rushmore. "This is her. This is Ren. Ren Gylden?" Pausing, he added quietly, "She—she thinks you might be her father."

With a shaking hand, Chris took the phone and stared down at the smiling girl. "Gracie?"

Edward went still. "What did you call her?"

When Chris looked up again, tears streamed down his face, and he pointed to the screen. "That's my Grace. Oh my God." A sob escaped his throat. "That's my girl. My daughter. Becky! Come here!" he yelled into the house, before turning back to Edward, a world of devastation in his eyes. "She was taken twenty years ago."

On their dining room table, Chris and Becky Koning spread out every document, photo, and newspaper clipping they had and told Edward the story of the disappearance of Chris's three-year-old daughter Grace Koning at a Fourth of July celebration in a local park. Chris, at the time recently divorced from Ren's mother—Aria, a petite blond woman—had taken his daughter to see the fireworks and, distracted by the question of a man nearby while looking for his daughter's sweater, turned back to find she was no longer at his side.

What followed was an all-out manhunt lasting nine months and spanning eight states. But Grace was never seen again.

"Over the years," he said, carefully moving his hands over his collection of documents, "there have been nearly ten thousand calls in to the hotline we set up, but only a handful of credible leads. For years I'd think I'd see her in every crowd. I think that feeling of needing to look for her every second I was out started to wane maybe eight or nine years ago." He looked to Becky, who nodded, rubbing his back. "All this time," he said, "she's been all the way in Idaho." He laughed, a sad, sharp exhale. "So many nights I'd wake up wondering if I imagined her. I'd get up and look at these pictures and try to figure out how I could possibly keep moving forward if I never got to see my little girl again."

Edward glanced around the house. It was cozy and warm, and from his chair he could see into a large great room with a TV and two big, pillowy couches. There were toys on the floor and a collage of construction-paper artwork covering one wall, a cluster of family photos covering another. Besides Christopher and Becky, there were some of the little girl who had answered the door, and older photographs of another girl Edward assumed was Ren. His phone buzzed in his pocket, and he pulled it out immediately, hoping it might be her. Seeing it was his father, he silenced the call.

"I don't understand, though," Becky said. "If you dropped her off here, where did she end up?"

"I dropped her off a few doors down, yeah," Edward said, wishing he'd put up more of a fight and insisted he go with her. "I only know what Ren told me, but Gloria seemed really controlling. If I had to guess, I think she was waiting and probably told Ren a good story that made her question whether she wanted to talk to you after all."

His phone buzzed again, but he ignored it once more. This was the part he didn't totally understand. Why would Ren come back to the hotel and leave his phone at the front desk? He could only assume that Ren had insisted, knowing it was expensive and he didn't have the money to replace it before his interview. But why would Gloria agree? She must've been so convincing when getting Ren to leave with her that she wasn't even worried a chance run-in with him would change Ren's mind.

"Do you know where this homestead is?" Chris asked, pulling Edward from his thoughts. "It's taking everything in me to not pack up tonight and go there."

"I know generally. At least," Edward said, "I know it's in Idaho. I know they go to a farmers market in Latah. There's a five-and-dime near them. . . . I think I could probably narrow it down based on some of the descriptions she gave me."

Again, his phone vibrated in his pocket, three rapid pulses. Begrudgingly, he pulled it out to see texts from his father.

Answer your phone, Edward
Explain what the hell is going on
If you don't answer this phone right now I'm
canceling your cards and

He stopped reading and stood. "I'm sorry. I need to make an urgent call."

Chris stood, too. "Is it her?"

"No, sorry, it's my father. I'll be right back." Stepping out onto the porch, Edward pressed the contact for his dad. He picked up on the first ring.

"Edward, tell me where you are right now."

He frowned, glancing down the block. "I'm in Georgia. It's a long story."

His father was incredulous. "Geor—? You know what? I don't even care. But I would like you to explain to me why the financial office at Corona called to tell me there's evidence that you've violated the terms of your scholarships and have one week to appeal your expulsion."

His heart came to a violent, shuddering stop. "Violated? What evidence?"

"I don't think they have it yet. Apparently, some girl caught you cheating. Her mother called the school."

He pinched the bridge of his nose, his stomach dropping. "Dad, this is absolutely not what you're thinking."

"Save the fiction, Edward. I don't care what scheme you've got going or how you fix this, but that's what you're going to do. Straighten this mess out, because if you get expelled, I'm not pulling strings to get you back in. Do you understand?"

"Yes, sir." His heart lurched forward before tumbling over a beat, faster and faster, as his father's words rolled around in his head.

Ren didn't do this—Gloria did. He knew it. If Gloria kidnapped her own daughter twenty years ago, she wouldn't leave anything to chance. This was a warning shot: Stay away from Ren and stay away from Christopher Koning, or you lose everything.

She didn't know that Edward was already there, that he already knew who she was, and that he'd throw everything away in a heartbeat if it meant he'd get Ren out of her hands.

CHAPTER THIRTY-ONE

REN

Once their old truck turned off the asphalt, Ren knew it was only another five minutes until she was officially home. She'd been on this dusty stretch of road more times than she could count. She'd climbed the trees that wrapped it in shade, she'd ridden her bike over its rocky surface and shoveled enough snow to build her own mountain. She knew every bump and curve, but it all felt different. Ren felt different.

They'd landed in Lewiston just over an hour ago. The old Ren would be babbling nonstop about her first plane ride, about being on board an actual 737-900 aircraft, about the sheer scale of the Atlanta airport. She would have begged for the window seat and pointed out every visible landmark; she would have made friends with the flight attendants and marveled at the free snacks and been bursting with excitement.

Instead, she felt numb with shock. Sadness ate at her belly until she was burning from the inside and had to excuse herself to the tiny airplane bathroom to lose the water and meager bites of food she'd managed that day.

Now she barely remembered the flight or the short layover in Salt Lake City. She barely remembered the drive to the homestead or the occasional murmured conversations happening around her. She was trapped in her head, tangled in thoughts about what had happened that day. The revelation about Gloria's first husband; the revelation about Fitz's criminal past . . .

But as Ren sat with it all day, something in the timeline didn't feel right. The idea of Gloria being married before Steve itched at her brain. Gloria had told Ren that she and Steve met in college, and Ren knew Gloria had her when she was thirty-six. So had Gloria left Steve at some point, married Christopher Koning, had Ren, and Steve and Gloria rekindled their romance after Ren was born? Or did she and Steve not meet until they were older and they only told Ren they'd met when they were younger, wanting to erase this Christopher Koning from their history? Ren wanted to ask but knew it was too late. Her window for those questions slammed shut the moment she agreed to come home.

And worst of all was the way Edward's eyes from his mug shot haunted her. Dark and bleak, they'd initially looked so foreign and unfamiliar that the menace in his expression had scared her. Sitting on the curb in Atlanta, she'd felt like she was looking at a stranger. But the image lingered in her mind, just as vivid every time she closed her eyes. The more she saw it, the younger Edward looked, the more desperate. He'd been only fourteen, still a child, and Ren hadn't even let him explain what it all meant.

It was late, too dark to see much as they came around the last corner and the bulk of their homestead came into view. Steve pulled the truck to a stop, and they wordlessly climbed out; nobody had said much since they left Atlanta. In fact, she didn't think Steve had looked at her once.

Her feet touched the ground, and the scent of damp grass and alfalfa filled her nose. Maybe it was the smell of home or really seeing the full sequined map of stars overhead for the first time in days, but some of the static was blown clear from her head. Her shoes crunched on gravel as she walked to the bed of the truck for her bag, only to see that Gloria already had it.

"I'll put this inside," she told her, and Ren nodded. "Some of the new chicks have figured a way out of the chicken coop, so I want you to check on them before you come inside. Make sure they're accounted for."

The only thing Ren wanted was to disappear under her comforter, but the soft down of newborn chicks wasn't the worst welcome home. "Yes, ma'am."

Ren turned to leave but stopped when she heard Steve murmur, "There's no sense putting this off. She'll find out in the morning anyhow."

Ren looked between them. "Find out what?"

"We're moving," Gloria said, meeting Ren's gaze. "We have an appointment with a real estate agent in town tomorrow to list the homestead."

"Moving?" The ground beneath her shifted. "Moving where?"

"Not sure yet," Gloria said with a simple shrug.

Ren's mouth opened, but no words came out. Moving. No family discussion, no asking how she might feel about it, just stated as fact. Already decided. Ren looked out over their land, at the trees they'd planted, the fields they'd worked, and the cabin they'd built by hand. She'd always assumed that even if she were to leave this place, she'd at least be able to come home. The way they'd always talked about it, Gloria and Steve planned to live there forever, wanted Ren and her future family to live there with them.

"Is this because of what I did?" Ren asked. "Is it a punishment?"

"Oh, Ren, come on, now. We wouldn't sell our land as punishment for your impulsive decision." Gloria turned toward the house but stopped. "We're moving because it's the right thing to do. Maybe we need a fresh start, to get back to what matters. That's this family, right here."

No matter what she said, or how for just a moment in Atlanta it felt like she and Gloria had connected, the edge of accusation cut through any argument Ren might muster. A few days ago, Ren wasn't sure she wanted to come back to the homestead; now the idea of leaving for good felt like losing an organ. These were the only stars she'd ever known, and they wanted to take it away, all because—what? She'd disobeyed them?

"I don't want to move."

"This family is moving. If you want to continue being part of it, then so are you."

"Gloria—"

"This discussion is over," Gloria said. "We have an appointment in town tomorrow, and you'll be coming along. Go blanket the horses and check on the chickens, then get inside to bed."

That night, surrounded by the familiar sounds of crickets and the purr of Pascal curled at her feet, Ren let herself cry, quietly so nobody could hear.

She missed Edward. She couldn't stop thinking about his face in the mug shot and the wide, defensive eyes of a kid left to fend for himself for far too long. She knew he had more to tell her, knew there were things in his past he was ashamed to say. When she thought back to the conversation in the lake, she realized she hadn't *let* him explain. She'd been so insistent that she didn't care—that she wanted him no matter what—she hadn't let him get a word in edgewise.

By his own admission he'd told her he wasn't good at opening up, and she'd promised to be patient. So why, when Gloria came to find her, had Ren been so quick to assume he'd keep this from her indefinitely? Yes, she'd been panicked at the sight of her mother. Yes, her blood had already been flooded with adrenaline over the prospect of approaching Christopher. But to doubt Edward so immediately felt devasting to her now. He'd have told her everything in time, and she'd just taken off. Ren abandoned him, just like everyone else had.

Gloria thought Ren was naive, and in many ways, she probably was. But no matter what anyone said, Ren didn't think she was naive about Edward. Yes, he had a criminal past. Yes, she'd caught him cheating. But even so, she didn't think she read him wrong. He wouldn't let her sleep in the car. He protected her with his own body whenever they were out in public together. He paid for her meals, he went out of his way to show her parts of the country she'd never seen before. He didn't take advantage of her when she'd been drinking; in fact, he was always the one to slow things down when she wanted more. No, Edward wasn't a threat to her. She might not know much about the world, but she knew that. She'd never, not once, felt anything but safe with him.

Rolling over, she released a mournful groan into her pillow. She didn't know if she'd ever see him again. She could hear his voice now: *You're an adult, Sunshine. You don't need their permission to go to school. You don't need their permission for anything.* And while that might legally be true, she wasn't ready to sever her family ties just because she wanted to see Edward again.

Even so . . . there was something deeply wrong with those family ties. Why couldn't Ren stay in both worlds? Why did it have to be all or nothing? She felt so intensely uneasy that she couldn't stop shivering, even beneath the warm blankets.

When she finally did sleep, her dreams were restless. She walked for miles up an endless grassy hill, and with every step, the top seemed just a few yards in the distance, always just out of reach. She fell back, tunneling down into darkness, and—for the first time in her life—the flowerworks exploding all around her weren't a balm; they were unsettling. Unease scratched at her throat, trapped there in a silent scream. This time there was no big, warm hand to take. It was only her.

CHAPTER THIRTY-TWO

EDWARD

Edward was losing his mind, stuck without any way to reach Ren, impotently pacing a path in the Konings' living room rug. The revelation that Ren had been kidnapped when she was three years old, and that Gloria wasn't even her mother—had in fact been lying to Ren her entire life—ignited a bomb in his bloodstream. The moment it became clear that Steve and Gloria could be taking Ren anywhere right now, that they were unlikely to be easy to find again—might move to a new place, take on new names, forever remain off the grid—the situation turned urgent.

Chris had no idea who Gloria and Steve might be, Edward had never seen them, and they were unlikely to be traveling under those names, so unless they were walking through airports with Ren's golden hair flowing down her back, finding them would be like looking for a needle in a haystack. Chris called his contact at the FBI, and Edward had recounted every detail he could remember about Ren's descriptions of home: a couple hours outside of Moscow; a place called Corey Cove; the small town nearby with the Hill Valley Five and Dime; a big plot of land with a pond and the cabin with the rock chimney, a red barn, and picket fence.

Anxiety pulsed like a twin heartbeat—*Go now. Go now. Go now*—but unfortunately, they'd missed all of their fastest options; there were no flights to Idaho until morning. The contact assured them that agents in the vicinity would keep watch for someone matching Ren's description until the bureau was able to get a full team in place. Edward had no idea what exactly that meant or when that might be. Would they be going, too? Whether or not that was the FBI or Chris's plan, it was definitely his. Every second that passed was the second when Ren could vanish forever.

Becky put their daughter to bed and came down to kiss Chris good night. "Keep me updated," she told him, and the reminder of Edward's own plea to Ren earlier that day sent a spear of frustration straight through him. She didn't leave anything on his phone—no text, nothing in his notes, nothing emailed. What on earth did Gloria say to make Ren walk away without even a glance backward?

Chris collapsed into the sofa, pressing the heels of his hands to his eyes. "I'm going crazy."

"Me too."

"I just wish I knew who these people were. Did they know us? Was it random? Why Grace? Who does that? Who takes a little girl watching fireworks with her father on the Fourth of July?"

"Monsters, that's who."

"Her mom and I had divorced," Chris said. "Gracie's mom, Aria . . . She—I mean, I'll admit it, she was a bit of a mess. She drank too much. The woman was terrible with money. All that's what ended us, and I'd filed for full custody, and it hadn't been a battle. But then Aria came back into the picture. She'd show up at all hours, banging on the door, wanting to see Grace. A few times she was so drunk and disruptive, I even had to call the police. So, of course, when Gracie went missing around that same time, we spent two months just looking for Aria, thinking of course she'd taken her, thinking that was our path to Gracie. But then one night Aria just showed up on the porch, wanting to see our girl, and after some pretty intense interrogation by the cops and checking all of her alibis and locations, it was clear that she'd had nothing to do with it.

She'd just gone on a bender. We'd lost so much time looking in the wrong place."

"That's just—" Edward didn't have words for how awful it was. "What a shitty time to go off on a bender."

Chris laughed darkly. "You're telling me." He leaned forward, propping his elbows on his thighs and staring bleakly at the floor. "I knew it would be hard, you know? Taking care of her all alone? But I was doing it. I wasn't bad at it. I certainly didn't lose my daughter," he said, voice breaking, and Edward could see that for all the hope he felt, the prospect of finding her was unearthing the pain and guilt all over again. "But she was taken from right next to me, and do you know how hard it is to reckon with that? How easy it is to lay that blame at my own feet?"

"None of this is your doing."

"I'd have given everything up for her. I had a plan in place for how I could manage as a single dad." He sniffed, wiping his eyes. "Had neighbors who pitched in," he said, "but I was managing. And when Gracie disappeared, everyone came together. Everyone put up posters and walked the streets and did everything they could. I felt—" Chris cut off, and then straightened. "Oh my God."

Edward stopped pacing and turned to face him, skin prickling. "What?"

Chris walked to the window and looked out at the house across the street and a couple doors down. "I've spent twenty years thinking about this. I've spent twenty years considering every possible angle. I've thought about who knew us, who loved us, who showed up when Gracie disappeared. But I never thought about who didn't." He looked over his shoulder at Edward. "I think I just realized who took her."

CHAPTER THIRTY-THREE

REN

Ren was up with the sun, and elbow deep in chores long before breakfast. Hard work was preferable to the nonstop reel of doubt playing in her head, and so for a few brief hours she let herself get lost in feeding and watering the animals, collecting eggs, and taking care of nesting boxes. She came inside to shovel a bowl of granola in her mouth between tasks, but Ren might as well have been invisible. The lectures and new rules she'd been convinced were coming never materialized.

Instead, Steve and Gloria talked as if she wasn't even there, discussing water rights in Oregon and the Portland Farmers Market as they pored over survey and plat maps spread out on the table between them. When Gloria sent Ren to the cellar for peaches, there were already boxes waiting to be packed up to move.

Ren couldn't wrap her head around it. Her parents were not impulsive. Look up the word *cautious* and their faces would be right there next to every possible definition. It took them a year to decide where they wanted to dig the pond, and twice as long to finally break ground. They had the same breakfast every morning, went to town the same days every week, and wouldn't replace something if any amount of duct tape would hold it together. She'd never heard them so much as mention leaving, but now they were already partially packed up and ready to go?

Back in the kitchen, she wished again that she could talk to Edward. The weight of his absence sat heavy in every one of her thoughts as she stood over the sink, the dishwater growing cold in front of her. Whether he was Edward or Fitz, he was still the same man who watched movies he'd seen a dozen times because she never had, suffered through tourist traps so she could have an adventure, and couldn't stand the idea of sharing a bed because he wanted to kiss her so badly. He was the person who showed her how to kiss, how to cuddle, and how to open her heart to someone new.

He was also the one who drove her to Atlanta to meet her father and insisted she call him and keep him updated, and she never did.

God, what must he be thinking? She needed to let him know that she was okay. She needed to tell him that she was sorry. She needed to figure out how to do that. No one had mentioned a thing about her returning to school, but her trunk was still in her dorm room, full of her things. She was pretty sure nobody would be willing to take her there again.

Ren would have to move with her parents or leave on her own, possibly losing them forever.

The sound of Steve pushing away from the breakfast table snapped her back to what she was supposed to be doing. She set her dishes in the drying rack and wiped her hands, happy to retreat to the barn, where she could lose herself in chores again and figure out a plan. Gloria's voice stopped her on the way out.

"You can finish your chores later," she told her, rolling up the maps and fastening each with a rubber band. "Help me load stuff into the truck. We're headed into town."

It might not have been intended as punishment, but when Ren's parents pointed to a bench outside the realty office and told her to stay put until they were done, it certainly felt like one.

The Realtor's office was in the same tiny storefront as that of the seamstress and the notary, because they were all the same person. Just next door was the bakery owned by Miss Jules, who also doubled as childcare for a handful of younger kids in the area.

Until recently, Ren's tiny town was the only one she'd ever known; seeing it with new eyes was disorienting. The turnoff from the highway to Main Street had always been exciting. She liked the people, liked seeing how the storefronts slowly changed, liked the novelty of being somewhere different, even if she'd been there a hundred times. Now she imagined Edward sitting next to her and trying to understand how on earth people lived someplace so isolated. For the first time she saw the dents and scuffed paint, the cracked asphalt and crooked shop signs. There was no Starbucks or twenty-four-hour anything. It felt claustrophobic with its cracked one-lane road and single, swinging traffic light. Edward didn't belong in a place like this. He wouldn't fit; he'd be too big and worldly for her sleepy town. And the more she thought about it, the more she wondered if she'd grown too big for it, too. With a population in the low triple digits, everyone there knew everyone else and could spot a stranger the second they stepped foot on Main Street. Even a private letter in the mail didn't go unnoticed.

Mail . . .

The word poked at the back of her head as her gaze swept to the five-and-dime, just across the street. Ren paused, awareness landing. At the very least she needed to let Edward know that she was okay. She didn't have a phone and wouldn't know his number even if she had one. As long as she was here, her parents controlled every aspect of her life, but there was one thing they couldn't shut down. If she hurried, there might be time.

Knowing the trouble she'd be in if she left without alerting someone, Ren ducked into the bakery. "Miss Jules?" she called out.

"If you see my parents, can you let them know I ran into Jesse and Tammy's shop for a minute and will be right back?"

Jules looked up from her game show reruns and gave Ren an arthritic thumbs-up. "'Course, Ren."

She jogged across the street and ducked into the dark interior of the little store. Soft country music played from a set of speakers attached to ceiling tiles overhead, and Ren scanned the aisles, spotting Tammy where she was on a stepladder stocking an endcap with canned beans and a sign that advertised a buy two, get one free sale.

"Tammy!" she said brightly. "Hi!"

"Ren! Oh my goodness! Look at you!" Tammy climbed down and pulled Ren in for a hug. "You look like a real college girl!"

"Just the same old Ren from a couple weeks ago," she said, laughing.

"No way." Tammy held her by the shoulders at arm's length, "There's something in your eyes that wasn't there before."

Ren was sure Tammy was right.

Hooking her thumb over her shoulder, Ren asked, "My folks are over at Belinda's. Would it be okay if I used the restroom?"

"Of course you can, sugar. Come on, let's grab the key."

As she followed Tammy through the store and down a narrow hall to the back office, Tammy talked about all the town happenings since Ren last saw her—the new hair salon that opened down the street, Jules's new scone recipe, and Old Donny's run-in with a moose. The office was a small room with an ancient copy machine and a long table in the center littered with signs and labels and small boxes of supplies. Easter bunting adorned a robin's-egg-blue refrigerator, its surface littered with schedules and random flyers. Two desks were pushed against opposite walls. Softly humming on one of them was a computer.

Tammy pulled a bright orange coiled key ring from a hook just inside the door and handed it to Ren. "Here you go."

Ren took the key with a smile.

"I think there's some Girl Scout Cookies in the freezer if you're hungry," Tammy said. The bell over the front door rang, and the older woman squeezed Ren's shoulder. "Help yourself, Ren. Good to see you, sweetie."

Ren smiled at her retreating form but, instead of heading to the bathroom, moved straight to the old computer.

She'd been in this room hundreds of times over the years doing odd jobs for Tammy and Jesse, so she entered the password from memory, waited for the browser to open, and quickly logged into the Corona student portal. Ren's email address at the Corona College domain was rgylden and she assumed all students had the same format, so she was going to try him at efitzsimmons and hope it worked. But the second she opened her email, her eyes immediately settled on a message at the top from Dr. Audran, with the word URGENT in the subject line.

> Ren,
>
> I realize class hasn't reconvened yet, and I hope you're having a pleasant and well-deserved break. I wouldn't normally email about something like this, but I don't have a phone number on record for you or your parents, and I consider it quite urgent. I received a call from your mother, who conveyed to me that you'd witnessed Edward Fitzsimmons cheating on his exam. First, I want to assure you that anything you say to me will be held in the strictest confidence. The university takes these things very seriously. We will ensure that you in no way suffer any sort of retaliation should you corroborate her story.

But because of the gravity of this situation, there are certain procedures we have to follow, and I do need to verify the information with you. Can you contact me via telephone as soon as possible? My information is below, and again, I'm sorry for disturbing your break.

Best,

Michel Audran

Ren took a breath, trying to slow her racing heart.

Gloria called Dr. Audran? Ren's stomach plummeted as she remembered that, in a moment of devastation in Atlanta, she'd told Gloria about the cheating, about the Polaroid. But why on earth would Gloria bother to call the school to report it? Ren had about a hundred questions and zero time to answer any of them. All she knew was that she couldn't involve Edward in any of this mess with her mother. This was between her and her parents.

With her fingers on autopilot, she hit reply, and typed out the fastest email of her life.

Dr. Audran,

Thank you so much for emailing me. Let me assure you, this story is completely false. I never witnessed Fitz cheating. I never told anyone that I did. I don't know the intent of the person who called you, but it certainly wasn't my mother, because that conversation never happened. I'm sorry you were taken away from your own well-deserved break. I hope it is okay that I have answered you here via email, as I do not have access to a telephone.

Happy Spring Break!

Ren Gylden

Her hands shook as she pressed send, and with a leaden weight landing in her belly, she remembered Gloria taking Ren's bag yesterday. Did Gloria take the Polaroid? And if she had, when would she have called the school? They didn't have a landline; even if Gloria had a secret cell phone, they were so far out of range she wouldn't have been able to do it from the homestead. At least Ren didn't think she could. . . . Ren never had a cell phone to try. Maybe Gloria called from a phone at the airport when she went to the restroom. But why? Ren pressed her hands to her eyes, bewildered. Why on earth would Gloria go to all that trouble when Ren was already home safe? Why would she go after Edward at all?

Queasy with dread, Ren moved the mouse to start a new email to him but froze when the bell over the shop door rang again.

"Hey, you!" Tammy called out.

"Hey, Tam," Gloria answered. "Jules said Ren stopped in. She here?"

Ren's heart dropped through the floor. Standing on shaky legs, she quickly turned off the computer monitor.

"She sure is." Tammy's voice carried down the aisles as Ren tiptoed across the floor. "She's just in the back using the ladies' room."

Ducking out of the office, Ren raced to the bathroom and opened the door, backing into the doorway as if she were just coming out, right as Gloria turned a corner and came into view.

"Hi," Ren said, closing the door behind her. "You guys all done?"

Her mother eyed Ren for a long beat before glancing to the open office only ten feet away. "We are."

CHAPTER THIRTY-FOUR

REN

Ren cleared dinner as quickly as she could manage without looking like she was trying to hurry through it. The last thing she wanted was for her internal frenetic energy to bleed to the outside, raising her parents' antennae. Though it might be too late for that, Ren reasoned. It wasn't that Gloria was paying her more attention than usual, it was that Ren sensed something when her mother *did* look at her, some question in her eyes that hadn't been there before. It would explain why Ren had barely had a moment to herself since they got back from town. She'd already helped unload the truck, then been sent to the cellar to start packing up preserves and to the barn for inventory. But with the sky dark and the final dinner dish put away, she saw her chance. Steve and Gloria were busy with whatever information the Realtor gave them, so Ren excused herself to get ready for bed and padded quietly to her bedroom. A quick rifle through her backpack revealed that the Polaroid photo was gone. With her breath held tight in her throat, Ren slipped down the narrow hall, and into her parents' room.

On the top shelf of their closet was a flat box that held all their important documents. Ren had seen Gloria open it on occasion, but it always had that *Off Limits to Ren* feel about it.

That never seemed weird to her until now.

Silently, she slid the box from the shelf, setting it down on the bed. Ears perked, she strained for the sound of footsteps coming toward her but could still hear their voices on the other side of the wall, talking.

Lifting the lid, she peeked inside. The thick stack of papers was so much bigger than she expected, given their small lives. She sifted through the pages, past animal records, her birth certificate, the titles and registrations for various pieces of farm equipment, and then there, deep down in the stack, she stopped on a marriage certificate, with the Fulton County Clerk's seal.

In search of a date, she pulled the paper free and tilted it to read by the meager light coming from the front porch outside the window. She couldn't believe what she was seeing. Just like she'd feared, it was dated eight years before she was born. Could Gloria have married Steve, left him, married Chris Koning, given birth to Ren, left Chris Koning, and remarried Steve? It was possible. But plausible? No. It felt too slippery, too convoluted.

Another detail caught her eye and she had to blink, make sure she was reading the correct line on the document. Because it wasn't Gloria's and Steve's names in front of her. It was a marriage certificate for two people named Adam Zielinski and Deborah DeStefano.

Frantic now, and with the icy tendrils of awareness pushing at her thoughts, she shuffled through the other pages. There was a birth certificate for Gloria under the name Gloria Smith, and one for Steve Gylden, too. Her hands shook as she pushed them aside, digging past registrations, loose pages of equipment warranties, and invoices to where she found two more birth certificates, folded in thirds and faded with age. Carefully opening them, Ren stared at the names there: Adam Zielinski and Deborah DeStefano. And at the very bottom of the box were passports.

Her fingers barely cooperated as she flipped one open, clapping a hand over her mouth when Gloria's much younger face looked back at her. Just beside the photo was the name Deborah Louise DeStefano. Ren dropped it into the box like she'd been burned and looked around the room in a panic.

All this time she'd been focused on the possibility that Steve wasn't her father; now she wondered what else they weren't telling her. Was Deborah her mother's real name? And if so, why had she changed it to Gloria? Why had Steve changed his from Adam? In one numbing, pulsing heartbeat, Ren suddenly wondered . . . were *either* of them her real parents?

She felt boneless, her blood staticky as she fumbled to find the Polaroid and then gave up, straightening the pile to put everything back, just the way she'd found it. With her heart hammering in her throat, she slipped out of their room and the few steps back down to hers, looking there one more time. Her bag was on the floor near the foot of her bed, and she dug into it again, this time dumping everything out and tossing it to the floor—her T-shirt and sleep shorts, the book of monuments Edward got her, the gift card and the watch from the Screaming Eagle. But the Polaroid was gone.

"Looking for this?"

She jerked around to find Gloria in the doorway, the photo of Edward in her hand.

"Gloria," she said quietly. "What are you doing with that?"

Gloria stared at her for a beat, then stepped into Ren's room and sat on the bed. "It's our little insurance policy."

Dread sent a shiver through her, and she wrapped her arms around herself. She needed to leave. She might not know all the details, but every cell in her body screamed that she needed to get away. Anywhere. "Insurance policy?"

"We're going to move and start over. You're not going to try to find Christopher Koning. You're never going to mention that name again."

"Are you even—"

"And if you do," Gloria cut in, waving the photo, "I'm going to send this everywhere and tell the administration at that school how this boy abducted you and took you across this country. How he abused you."

"That—that's insane," Ren stammered, hysteria bubbling up in her throat. "That didn't happen. I'll just tell them you're lying."

Gloria's face softened. "Oh, honey, then I'll tell them it's just the trauma talking," she said with saccharine sweetness, the concerned-mother mask slipping into place. "'Oh, we are so worried about Ren. All those specialists we took her to told us that she might want to protect him. We told her not to worry. She's safe now. We won't ever let him touch her again.'"

Ren felt the tears when they broke, streaking down her face. "I don't understand why you're doing this."

Steve appeared in the doorway. "What's all the fuss in here?"

Gloria looked up at him. "Ren's upset that we're not letting her see that boy anymore."

"You think that's what I'm upset about?" Ren said through a watery laugh. "I don't actually know who either of you are!"

They both turned their eyes on her. "What did you say?" Gloria asked, eyes hawkish.

"I looked in the box in your closet. I was looking for the photo, but there was a lot of stuff about you and Steve in there that I didn't understand." She turned her eyes to him. "Is that even your real name?"

His eyes narrowed and he sucked his teeth, looking at Gloria, who held out a steadying hand. "What are you saying, Ren?" she asked.

Ren took a slow, deep breath. "I'm asking whether you're really my mother."

Gloria laughed. "Do you hear yourself? Of course I'm your mother."

"So who are Adam Zielinski and Deborah DeStefano? And

when again, exactly, did you marry Chris Koning?"

"How about you get some sleep," Gloria told her. "We'll talk in the morning."

"I don't think that's a good idea." Steve took a step into the bedroom and looked out her small window. "I'm telling you, Gloria, we gotta leave tonight."

Tonight? While they talked, Ren looked around the room, trying to formulate a plan, a voice inside her head whispering the same word over and over: *Run*.

"We aren't even close to ready," Gloria argued. "Even if that boy manages to narrow it down, we're not easy to find."

That boy. Edward.

Ren's pulse rocketed. She filed back through every story she'd told him, every detail she'd given him about the homestead and the little town. Could he figure it out? Could he find her?

Steve shook his head. "I have a bad feeling about this. We gotta go." He nodded to Ren. "She knows now, and others might, too. What do we do with her?"

Ren's head snapped up. "*Do* with me?"

"We take her," Gloria answered. "No one else knows it's us but her."

Gloria's words sent a wave of nausea rolling through her, and for a few staggering breaths Ren thought she might not be strong enough to process what she meant. *No one else knows it's us but her.*

A whistle cut through the sky, followed by a deafening crack that shook the entire cabin. They fell to the ground, each of them covering their head as light spun across all four walls of the small bedroom. When Ren chanced a glance up, the darkness outside had been blown apart, light flashing in intermittent starts and stops.

Gloria rushed to the window as a streak of gold whistled through the sky and exploded in color immediately overhead. More of them came, one after another, explosion after explosion filling the sky with color.

Fireworks.

Steve turned, yelling at Gloria. "You see that? Gloria, they know!"

Before Ren could make sense of anything, she was shoved to the bed, and Gloria loomed over her. "Stay put. Do not test me, Ren." And then she turned to Steve. "Get the guns. I'll get the keys."

They ran out of the room, and Ren looked around frantically, trying to form some sort of plan. Steve had said, *They know*. Did that mean these fireworks were for her? Her heart screamed his name—*Edward*—but her mind slapped the fantasy away; he was on the other side of the country. Even if he did figure out where she was, she'd left him—why would he come here?

When a burst of orange and gold erupted in a shot of sound outside, Ren looked out the window and down the front drive, trying to figure out what direction the fireworks were coming from.

But it wasn't just fireworks. In the distance and around the bend of the long drive were the pulsing, rhythmic whirls of red and blue.

The police were here. It had to be him. It had to be. Who else would know where to find her?

Adrenaline dumped into her veins, a starter-pistol blast jolting her to action. With Gloria and Steve occupied, screaming through the cabin to each other to pack up their guns and clothes and money, Ren gripped the sill and tried to pry the window open.

"Please, please, please," she whispered, panic rising like an ocean swell in her chest. It didn't budge. Ren scrambled to her small desk, finding a metal ruler to wedge in the frame and use for leverage. Quickly, she worked it around the edges of the frame before wedging it beneath the bottom, seesawing the ruler up and down. Finally, the sill gave the tiniest bit, groaning with a winter's worth of stiffness, and Ren winced, listening for the halt of movement in the rest of the cabin. As quietly as possible, Ren worked to get the window open wider, finally giving up when she hoped it would be enough and wedging her body into the narrow opening, pushing her head and shoulders through.

Behind her, she heard Gloria's surprised "Steve! She's going out the window!" Panic swelled, and Ren pushed harder, feeling the wet slide of blood down her neck as she scraped her chest against the sill, shimmying to get out her waist, her hips, her thighs—

A strong hand clamped around her ankle. "No you don't," Gloria growled, and leaned back, tugging hard.

Ren kicked her legs and reached for anything she could find, trying to get leverage to pull herself free. Gloria's grip tightened, and she shouted for Steve to go out the front and catch Ren on the other side.

With panic sending fire into her pulse, Ren screamed in the quiet between fireworks, the two hopeful syllables cutting a shrill knife through the air—"EDWARD!"—and finally managed to wrench one leg free of Gloria's grip. She kicked once more—hard—and felt her foot connect with something soft. A groan sounded from inside, and then Gloria's hands fell away and Ren tumbled to the ground just as the front door opened.

Steve's eyes met hers. "Stay right there, Ren," he warned, racing down the front steps, but she scrabbled to her feet, pushing off into a sprint down the driveway. In the distance, she could see a line of cars, flashing lights, and the silhouette of figures.

"Edward!" she screamed, praying he was there. She had no one else. Nothing else. He was the only person who hadn't betrayed her. "EDWARD!"

In the moonlight, she saw a commotion and then two figures breaking away from the line, sprinting toward her. Instinctive fear pulsed for a flash before an explosion went off overhead, the gentle raining of blue and silver illuminating the homestead. She could see them. They'd broken free from the barricade and were sprinting right for her.

"Ren!" Edward yelled. "Run!"

Gunfire sounded behind her; a whistle seared past her head, close enough to send goose bumps down her arm.

Another voice. A man's voice, one she knew somewhere, deep in the marrow of her bones. "Gracie!"

Thirty feet from the two figures . . . twenty feet . . . ten . . .

Another bullet kicked up dirt beside her feet just as she collided with Edward's chest, his arms coming around her, pulling her tight into him, before someone else captured them both from the side, tackling them into the brush just as gunfire rained down on the cabin.

CHAPTER THIRTY-FIVE

EDWARD

Edward didn't care about the thorns or the branches or the cold. He was never letting go of her.

Voices rose, footsteps pounded toward them, muted shouts and directions. Ren was curled into a tight ball in his arms, hands over her ears, shaking violently. "Ren, shhh, I got you," he told her. "I got you. I got you."

"What's happening?" she asked into his chest. "Where are they? Are they coming?"

"You're safe," Chris said, sending a careful hand over her back.

"They were shooting," she sobbed into Edward's chest. "Were they shooting at *me*? *Were my parents shooting at me?*"

Edward's helpless gaze met Chris's over the top of Ren's head. Panicked, he shook his head, not knowing what to say.

"The police are here," Chris said softly. "Lots and lots of them. It's going to be okay."

Edward knew Chris was probably right, but Edward wasn't entirely convinced yet. There was a lot of yelling, and something somewhere was on fire. He was aware of a handful of SWAT officers moving past them down the driveway, the dark, ominous sound of gunfire, and then the piercing, high-pitched misery of Gloria's scream.

Ren violently flinched in his arms. "What happened? Oh my God, what's happening?"

He craned his neck, trying to see anything, but it was suddenly impossible, with another cluster of bodies in dark combat gear jogging past. All he could sense was that the energy had shifted, and everything quieted. And then two medics sprinted past with heavy bags.

"I think they've got the cabin surrounded," he told her.

"Is Gloria okay?" she asked. "Is Steve okay?"

Edward looked over the top of her head to meet Chris's eyes again—because honestly, he wasn't sure that everyone in that cabin was going to make it out—but Chris was staring at his daughter in Edward's arms, tears brimming.

"Hey," Edward said gently, urging Chris to look at him. "Should we move back there?" He lifted his chin to where the police cars, ambulances, and SWAT vans were parked in the darkness.

Just as he said it, a low voice came from beside them in the bushes: "Guys, we gotta move you out."

Movies always made the climax of a story seem so tidy, so compact. Police surrounded the suspects, apprehended them, carted them away in cop cars, sirens wailing victoriously. The victims were tucked safely in the back of an ambulance with a cup of tea and a blanket over their shoulders. Viewers caught up four months later with the characters, now smiling and healthy, walking in the park with a new puppy.

In reality, it wasn't anything like that. In reality, the supposed climax was confusing, cold, dark, and time passed without any obvious plan or momentum. After the agents brought Ren, Edward, and Chris back to the protected line of cars, vans, and ambulances, she was quickly whisked off to the care of a pair of emergency medics; Chris was led to another ambulance a bit farther down the road, and

Edward was asked to wait, out of the way, for further instruction.

Out of the way could mean a lot of things, he thought, and he moved so he was near the driver's-side door of Ren's ambulance. He eavesdropped while they spoke to her in low, calming voices. He could hear others nearby, too. Cops and medics and federal agents and all the various special-ops people they brought in to face any potential insanity on the homestead, all speaking too quietly for him to make out, but the movement around him gave him some clues about what had happened. Police tape was unrolled liberally, cordoning off large swaths of land. Dogs were brought in to search the premises for drugs, guns, maybe even people. He had no idea. With Ren shielded from view by a van, Gloria was escorted into an unmarked car and driven away—he caught only a glimpse of wild eyes and tousled hair before she was somewhat roughly guided into the backseat—but Steve's whereabouts remained a bit of a mystery. That was, until a CSI van backed down the driveway and the coroner arrived.

The idea of this, that the only mother Ren had ever known had just been arrested, that the only father she'd known was leaving his property in a body bag, was too much. He couldn't stay out of the way anymore.

Edward walked to where Ren sat in the back of the ambulance, partially hidden by the medic who was carefully dabbing at two large scrapes across her arm. She looked tiny and terrified, dwarfed by the big flannel blanket around her. She glanced up as his shoes crunched through the gravel, her eyes watery and bloodshot: a portrait of grief and confusion.

"Hi," he said, and the single syllable felt heavy in his mouth.

"Hi." She swallowed a sob. "How did you get here?"

"Airplane," he said. "Then cop car." In an effort to diffuse some of the tension, he whispered, "For once, I was not in handcuffs."

Ren gave a watery laugh, and when the medic stepped away,

Edward offered her his hand. She grabbed it between both of hers, wordlessly tugging him forward, needing a hug. Without hesitation, he wrapped his arms around her while she shook. "I'm here. I got you."

"I don't understand," she said, but he knew that she did. She did, but it was too terrible to comprehend, and there was nothing he could say to make it any less horrific. Slowly, she pulled away and tilted her face up to his. "Who was that in the bushes? Was—"

"Yeah."

"My dad?"

He ran this thumb over her cheek, wanting to protect her, wishing she got to hear this in a way she'd want to hold on to and remember. He nodded. "Yeah, Chris. He's been looking for you for a very long time."

"He's not a terrible man?" she asked, chin wobbling.

Edward frowned, fury at Steve and Gloria rising in him anew. "No. He isn't. He's a good man who had something deeply precious stolen twenty years ago."

Her tears spilled over, streaking down her cheeks. "Can I see him?"

Edward turned, searching in the darkness, and found Chris about ten feet away, standing unobtrusively next to a patrol car. It was all over his posture, the way he wanted to burst forward and hold this grown-up version of the little girl snatched from his side nearly two decades ago, but he approached slowly when Edward waved to him, correctly reading the shock all throughout Ren's posture.

"Hi, Ren," he said, calm and simple, just like the agents had suggested on the drive here from Lewiston. *Use the name she knows,* they'd told him. *Don't expect much right away. She may not want to talk, or she may need you to lay it all out immediately.* There wasn't one way this would go down, but this was what he needed to remember:

This will be much more of a mixed bag for her than for you. You've just got your daughter back, but she's losing the life she's always known. Go slow. You do whatever she needs.

"I'm Chris."

"Hi, Chris." She tried to smile, and this glimpse of the Ren Edward adored, this earnest effort, sent a painful ache through his gut. "Thanks for coming."

His laugh was carried on a sob. "Are you kidding? I've been looking for you for twenty years. I would have flown to Siberia a hundred times over."

Ren stared at her father, and Edward knew what she was seeing, how it was undeniable who he was. In the flashing lights, he could see the tears streaming down both their faces, and as Chris stepped forward to give her a careful hug, Edward blended back into the mass of bodies all around them.

KIDNAPPING VICTIM GRACE KONING FOUND ALIVE TWENTY YEARS LATER, RESCUED IN DEADLY SHOOTOUT IN IDAHO

by Tustin Wilkes and Dawn Meyer, Associated Press

Updated 3:14 a.m. PDT

Grace Koning, the young girl who vanished nearly twenty years ago from a park near her home in Atlanta, was rescued last night in a shocking confrontation at her alleged kidnappers' homestead in rural Idaho that left one man dead and a woman in police custody.

Deborah DeStefano (59) and Adam Zielinski (61), living under the assumed names Gloria and Steve Gylden, abducted Koning on the Fourth of July as she watched fireworks with her father, Christopher Koning. According to news articles from the time, Mr. Koning let go of his daughter's hand to dig into his backpack for her sweater, and when he turned back to her, she was gone. An official search for the missing girl lasted nine months and spanned several states.

DeStefano and Zielinski reportedly brought Koning to Zielinski's rural land in Latah County, Idaho, where they raised her as their own child, hidden from society.

As of just over a week ago, Koning, now twenty-three, was attending Corona College as a freshman under the assumed name Ren

Gylden. "Ren said it took her a long time to convince her parents to let her go to college," classmate Jeb Petrolli told the Associated Press. "Knowing what we know now, it's wild they ever agreed. I guess they must've figured everyone forgot about Grace Koning and they'd get away with it."

According to a campus student profile, Grace Koning had never been to school prior to her arrival in Spokane but was self-taught in subjects such as calculus, physics, Mandarin, and chemistry. And she made quite a positive impression on her peers. "She was absolutely a fish out of water," a classmate told the Associated Press, asking to remain anonymous. "But once you get to know her, all the hype is real. She's great. In hindsight this all makes sense, but at the time we just figured she'd had an alternative upbringing and was just sheltered."

But after barely two months at school, Koning suddenly left campus a few days before spring break with another student, twenty-two-year-old Edward Fitzsimmons. The purpose of their trip remains unknown. Officials at Corona College have not replied to AP's request for comment.

At some point in the trip, DeStefano and Zielinski intercepted Koning and brought her back to their homestead in Idaho, where authorities surrounded the area and rescued Koning in a shootout that left Zielinski dead.

DeStefano remains in custody. A spokesperson for the FBI told AP she would be arraigned within forty-eight hours.

Although it was unclear why Koning left Spokane with Fitzsimmons, the Associated Press has learned that he is the one who alerted the authorities to Grace Koning's probable location. Fitzsimmons and Koning's biological father, Christopher (52), were apparently on-site for the rescue.

Neighbors of Christopher Koning report that DeStefano had once lived in the Atlanta neighborhood across the street from the Koning family. "She wasn't really involved in neighborhood activities," longtime local resident Annabelle Cleff told the Associated Press. "She mostly kept to herself."

According to multiple sources, Christopher Koning and his ex-wife, Aria Miller, divorced just before Grace was two. Mr. Koning was awarded custody, but Miss Miller would make frequent attempts to see her child. "She was troubled," Cleff said. "Addiction issues. Sometimes she would cause a scene. I remember standing at the curb one night when the police were called, and Deborah came out of her house, and all she said was 'That poor little girl.' She hadn't spoken much to any of us up to that point. Didn't even think about that again until all this happened."

Multiple residents recall DeStefano's relationship with Zielinski, who lived with

DeStefano in the Atlanta neighborhood for some time. Jimmy Murphy, Mr. Koning's next-door neighbor, remembers Zielinski as "a quiet man who had no love for city life or city folks." When the couple moved away, residents figured they'd gone somewhere that suited them better than the suburbs.

"They moved before Gracie went missing," Murphy said. "They must've come back for her. No one even thought about them, not once. And to think, all this time they had that little girl. I'm sure glad she's alive, but Chris'll never get those years back."

Grace Koning is reported to be healthy, with no major injuries. She, Mr. Koning, and Mr. Fitzsimmons have been moved to an undisclosed location for protection.

This is a developing story.

CHAPTER THIRTY-SIX

EDWARD

The authorities put them up in a hotel in Boise, a swanky one, with giant suites and soldiers outside of their rooms. Before she would agree to go, Ren insisted she check the animals and speak to whoever would be caring for them. She gave them a list with each animal's name, their allergies, and anything important to know about them. Edward imagined it gave her a tiny sense of control; her world had been turned inside out, but this one thing she could manage.

The leaks about the story were already creating a frenzy online. Edward scrolled through some of the trending tags—Grace Koning, Ren Gylden, Georgia abduction—but eventually put his phone away, feeling restless and panicky, wanting to find Ren but not sure where they'd put her in the hotel. They'd been driven in an unmarked van, two agents with shotguns up front and one sitting in the back with them. Beside Edward, Ren almost immediately fell asleep, slumping over onto his shoulder. But the second they pulled up in front of the hotel they whisked her inside, and he hadn't seen her since.

At the very moment he thought he might burst out of his skin, tempted to break their rules and begin wandering, a heavy knock landed on his door. In the hallway stood a man approximately the size of a refrigerator. Edward tilted his head up to meet the man's eyes. "They grow them big in Idaho."

The Fridge didn't crack a smile. "Miss Gylden wants to see you."

It was nearly four in the morning; he didn't bother getting dressed. In bare feet, shorts, and a T-shirt, he followed the Fridge to

Ren's room, where the guard knocked twice, swiped a card, and let Edward in, firmly closing the door behind him.

Ren's room was a mirror image of his. There was a sitting room, a kitchen, a bathroom off the entryway, and then, through a set of double doors, a bedroom with a king-size bed, plus a master bath. He wanted to make a joke about how handy a room this size would have been out on the road, but any humor dried up when he saw her, sitting in the middle of the bed. She looked gaunt and tiny, and visibly shaken.

"Hey."

"Hey." Of the million or so questions he wanted to ask, there was only one that really mattered. "How are you holding up?"

She sniffed, wiping her nose, and then looked at him with a bleakness that made him hurt. He knew that look. It was awful. He'd worn it a time or two himself. "They asked if there was anyone I wanted them to call or bring to the hotel," she said. "I realized I didn't have anyone. Not a single person."

Edward walked to the foot of the bed and knelt on the floor, resting his arms on the mattress and his chin on his folded arms. "You have me."

Her face tightened in anguish, and he watched as she fought through the confusion Gloria must have seeded. "Do I? I felt like I did. But then I didn't know . . . if I really knew you."

And right then was when he knew how Gloria got her away from Atlanta. She'd found something out about him and used it to scare Ren off.

"I get why you're questioning everything," he said, gently. "I think that's the most normal reaction you could possibly have right now. But for me, everything that happened between us was real. It changed me, and I'm not leaving until you tell me to."

She swallowed, blinking down to her lap.

"Do you want me to leave?"

A tear fell on her calf, and she rubbed it away. "No."

"Tell me what you need from me," he said. "I'll do anything."

She nodded, and kept nodding, like she was trying to find her voice. "I don't want to be alone," she whispered. "I can't sleep. I'm scared. I'm so sad." A sob tore from her throat. "I feel lost."

"I know. Life threw it all at you in one day."

"Will you stay with me?"

"I'll do whatever you want."

"But I need to know everything."

"I know." They gazed steadily at each other for a long beat. "I'll tell you anything you want to know."

CHAPTER THIRTY-SEVEN

EDWARD

The first night, they started with his life up to his arrest. By the time they fell asleep, facing each other on her bed, Ren knew all about his foster mother, Mary. He even showed her a dorky photo of him in his first ugly Christmas sweater, though he'd be willing to bet it wasn't meant to be ironic. She knew that he was placed with Mary when he was seven, that his life with her and her two sons wasn't perfect, but it was good. She knew that he was loved, and that Mary had begun the long, arduous process to adopt him.

Ren also now knew that when he was thirteen, the lease on their apartment was up and wouldn't be renewed; the building was being torn down to build luxury condominiums. Mary had to pack up the three boys and move. But because she no longer had the rent-controlled two-bedroom apartment, she and her two biological sons had to move to a smaller space, and Edward's foster placement with her wasn't reapproved; the adoption process was halted.

By the time they fell asleep, Ren also knew how he'd spiraled, running away from his temporary group home and living on the streets. She knew that he'd stolen a car, not realizing there was a gun inside. And how when he was fourteen, he'd been sentenced to eleven months in a juvenile correction facility.

"I think that's enough for tonight," she said after that, and in under a minute, she was fast asleep.

They slept until well past ten. By then the news about Ren

had broken everywhere—the front page of every major newspaper, the top story on every news channel. An abducted girl found after twenty years made a pretty splashy headline. They were told by their security team to stay in the hotel.

Ren had lunch with Chris and a team of therapists in a private room, and then returned, hollow eyed and exhausted, saying only "He's very nice" before promptly falling asleep again.

Of any of the victims of this, Edward was the least of anyone's problems, but he was grateful when his assigned therapist, Lisa, asked that he stay on to support Ren through the sequestered crisis-management phase. "Quite frankly," he told her, "if you hadn't invited me to stay, I would have booked a room here anyway."

His phone rang while Ren was still sleeping, her head in the crook of his neck. He had no intention of actually answering it, but when he saw his father's name on the screen, he knew he couldn't avoid it forever. Carefully disentangling himself from her, he climbed from the bed and let himself out onto the balcony.

"Hey, Dad."

"Edward," he said. "Where are you?"

"Boise." Edward tried to work up the indignation he usually felt when he spoke to his father, the familiar anger that buoyed him and kept his eye on the endgame—Robert Fitzsimmons's downfall—but he couldn't seem to muster any. Whatever happened to him after this, whether he lost his recommendation or had to face academic or legal consequences, he knew he'd eventually be okay. Ren had changed, but Edward had changed just as profoundly. He was still terrified and had to fight the instinct to keep people at arm's length, but his doors had been blown open and he didn't want to close them again. He wanted to let go of the anger and let someone see him. He wanted to heal.

"The papers just said Idaho, I wasn't sure where," Robert said.

"Yeah, the police put us up while they sort everything out."

"And how are you? Sounds like it was pretty rough."

Edward looked at his phone, unfamiliar with the strain he could hear in his father's voice. Anger, yes. Condescension, always. But gentleness? The edge of concern? That was brand-new. "It was," Edward said. "But I'm fine. I'm more concerned about Ren. Her whole life has been turned upside down."

"I heard you figured out where she was and got the police there before it could get any worse. That was good thinking, son," Robert said, and a beat of silence passed over the line. "Whatever you did to get yourself into this, I'm glad it happened. She's lucky to have you. I'm proud of you."

Edward looked back toward the room. He could see Ren still asleep in the bed, and for the first time in his life he wished he could tell someone—one particular someone—what he was feeling. Was this what it was to feel safe? He'd share one piece of himself, and then another, and eventually the floodgates would open? He hoped so. It was terrifying, but he wanted Ren to know all the parts of him, even the ugly ones.

Edward turned away, staring, unseeing, at the parking lot and strip malls facing the back side of the hotel. Wood-scented smoke poured from the chimney of a barbecue restaurant.

"Thank you," he said finally.

"The dean should be calling you tomorrow. You're an adult, so you'll have to work out the details directly with him, but he should be offering you a leave of absence. I suggest you take it."

The authority in his father's voice was more familiar ground, but Edward would gladly take it. "Yes, sir."

"And what about your interview?"

Edward stared into space. His father knew about the interview. Of course he did; he had connections everywhere. But Edward realized it didn't matter anyway. He was done hiding from his father. "I emailed to let them know I'd need a rain check." He laughed dryly.

"They understood."

Another pause, and then, "Call me after you've spoken to the dean, and we'll figure out the next steps."

"Okay," Edward said, "I'll do that."

"Have a good night, son."

His father ended the call, and Edward stared at his phone until the screen went dark. It was the least contemptuous conversation he'd ever had with Robert Fitzsimmons, and he was unsure how to feel about it. Without the rage he'd tended for so long, he felt slightly off-kilter, unsure if he was seeing his father differently now, or whether Robert really had changed. Was that even possible? And when Edward really thought about it, did it matter? He felt like he was just stepping out of a long fog, and had many, many things to figure out. As long as he knew where Ren was and that she was safe, the rest was just details.

Inside the room again, he turned on *Clueless* but stared blankly at the screen, finally ordering room service for dinner and keeping the trays covered until she woke up, rumpled and red-eyed, shuffling to the table he'd set up.

"Those," Ren said, pointing to the pancakes when he'd shown her the options he'd ordered. "Thank you."

It was a weird feeling to be sitting across from the current most famous woman in the country, to know her better, he thought, than anyone. He mumbled a quiet, "Yeah. Of course."

She spread the butter and poured syrup and then poked at the pancakes with her fork. There was a lot on his mind, but nothing he felt he could say out loud. He didn't want to tell her how huge the story had become, how there were gigantic mobs of strangers standing in front of the hotel holding signs proclaiming how strong and amazing she was, or how people from all over the world had already donated an ungodly amount to a trust set up for her by the State of Georgia. How she would never have to worry about money again. It was already too much.

All he cared was that Ren never had to worry about her safety again.

"How are the pancakes?" he asked, stupidly, because she hadn't even taken a bite.

She looked up at him. "What happened in the juvenile correction facility?"

He smiled down at his Caesar salad, relieved to be given this prompt, relieved she wasn't scared off by what he'd told her last night. "All right. I like it. Keeping me on track."

So he picked up where he'd left off, telling her about how he learned in juvie that he actually loved school, that therapy was pretty effective, and—most importantly—that he could play by anyone's rules. He learned to leverage his greatest skill—charm—to make his life easier. He told her how he became a model inmate, how Judge Amira Iman took him under her wing, brought him to city fundraisers for disadvantaged youth to meet and talk to people in the community, and how it was there that he met the socialite Rose Fitzsimmons, and the spark of an idea struck her that she wanted to do more to help than throw money at the various foundations: Rose wanted to adopt a fifteen-year-old reformed hooligan named Edward Fallon. And then he told Ren how Rose's husband, real estate developer Robert Fitzsimmons, loved the idea of adopting him, but for a completely different reason: After a slew of lawsuits that claimed his firm had broken various civil and criminal codes, he needed an image overhaul.

And once he learned the truth about Robert, young Edward was a very willing accessory: His new father's latest project, a high-end series of condominiums, was to be built on the same city block where Mary's apartment—and Edward's happily ever after—had once stood. With the ember of loss still burning in his chest, Edward hoped he could one day gather enough information on local developers to be able to take them down one by one.

Edward told Ren about moving into the Fitzsimmons estate, about how he felt out of place from the minute he first stepped foot on the property. He told Ren how he took the opportunity whenever he could to learn how to integrate himself into every situation: fancy dinners with politicians and in the kitchen with the staff; pickup basketball games at the park and fundraisers with celebrities. He hated everything about the rich, privileged life he was living, and a plan was forming even then, one where he would use everything he learned living in that house to take down the first pillar of the big developer community: Robert Fitzsimmons.

By that point, Ren's eyes had lost some of their attentive focus, and he stood, taking her napkin and piling everything neatly on the table. "Let's get you to bed."

They rolled the room service table into the hall, where the Fridge grunted out a sound of greeting and wheeled their dinner away.

Ren put her hand on Edward's arm. "Don't go."

With a grin, he reminded her, "I'm not going anywhere until you kick me out."

This earned him a tiny flicker of a smile, and they carefully locked up, brushed teeth side by side, and then climbed back into the giant bed.

She reached over, turning out the bedside lamp, leaving only the light from the bathroom softly drifting across the foot of the bed. Ren rolled to face him, curling up on her side, hands tucked up under her chin. She was so beautiful, it made his chest constrict.

"How's my Sunshine feeling tonight?"

Instead of answering, she asked, "Why didn't you just walk away when I left you in Atlanta? Weren't you mad?"

It took immense effort to not propel his body forward and pull her into his arms. "No, Ren. I wasn't mad, not for one second. I don't trust easily, and I'm working on that, but I do trust you. If you left,

I knew there had to be a good reason. I was only ever worried." He tilted his head, smiling. "*Panicked* may be a better word, especially once we put together what happened."

She looked up at him, eyes sincere. "Thank you for being so smart."

He felt his face heat. "I just put the puzzle together. You tell a good story. Thank you for talking so much."

She smiled. "Thank you for coming for me."

"It was never a question."

"I'm sorry Gloria tried to blackmail you into staying quiet."

He waved this off. "It's fine. I was already at Chris's house by the time my father called to yell at me." He closed his eyes, searching for the sinking feeling in his stomach, the anxiety that he'd ruined his future, but it didn't come. "I didn't want Gloria to have any power over us, though. . . ." He swallowed. "I called Audran from the airport and told him that I'd doctored my scores. I explained a bit why—Judge Iman told me just before I got out that if I finished at the top of my class, she would give me a recommendation to any law school in the country. It doesn't make what I did okay, but he was actually pretty cool. He agreed to give me a zero but shut down the academic dishonesty inquiry. I'm not sure I deserve that, but I'm not going to argue. I still need to iron the details out with the dean, but it looks like I'll be taking an extended leave."

"You're not going back to school next week?"

"I think I need time to figure it all out. School feels like another planet right now."

"Everything feels like another planet." Her smile was limp. "I can barely focus on anything."

"Pretty sure there's not a soul in the world who would blame you."

She adjusted her pillow under her head. "Are you still planning on going to law school?"

He thought about how relentless he'd been, how his need for misguided revenge had driven him toward money and success, and away from depending on or trusting anyone. He felt lighter without it, unaware how heavy a burden he'd been carrying until it was gone.

"I don't know. The whole point of law school was to become powerful enough that I could take everything from men like my father." He laughed, because it sounded sad and empty, even to his own ears. "I was still holding on to what had happened to Mary, had happened to me. I wanted to destroy him and everything men like him had."

"You don't want to do that anymore?"

"I still want to take care of Mary, that hasn't changed, but with everything that's happened, the rest of it sounds kind of dumb."

Ren laughed and found his hand, squeezing it. "It's not dumb. It's very noble that you want to help her."

"Noble to live my life like the most pathetic Bond villain?"

She laughed again. "Even I get that reference."

"Maybe I don't even want to be a lawyer. I pursued that as a means to an end, but not because I'm all that passionate about it." In the darkness, his smile faded. "It seems kind of pathetic to be mad forever. Exhausting. I have meeting you to thank for that."

"Meeting me?"

"Yeah. You changed me. The way you approach the world with such optimism. Such an open heart. I want to be more like you."

Quietly, she scoffed. "An open heart feels like a curse right now."

He reached across the darkness to carefully pass a hand down her arm. "Look, I know everything is . . . I mean, there aren't words. What you're dealing with is beyond comprehension. But your fundamental goodness is why I'm so lost for you, Ren. You made me a better person, and that's why I'll be here as long as you want me."

There was shifting of the blankets, and then she scooted closer until she was carefully pressed up against him.

Tentatively, he wrapped an arm around her, urging her closer. "Are we still doing this?"

"Doing what?" she asked, but there was a teasing lean to her voice.

"Things people do when they share a king-sized bed."

She snorted quietly into his neck. "What else are we going to do? We can't leave the hotel."

"Look at you, making jokes already," he murmured, kissing her forehead.

She pulled back enough to look up at him, and in the dim light filtering in from the bathroom, he saw a tender gleam in her eyes. "I hope we're still doing this," she said. "I like you a lot."

"Trust me, I'm absolutely crazy for you. But I'll be crazy for you tomorrow, and the day after that, and the day after that. Even if we don't do anything tonight."

Ren sent a hand up his neck to his jaw, tracing his lower lip with her thumb. "I want this one normal thing."

"What's that?"

"Having a crush on a guy and using it to ignore all my other problems."

With a laugh, he bent, pressing his lips to hers.

They kissed a lot that night—deep and claiming and fevered—and it meant they were exhausted the next morning when the alarm on Edward's phone went off. But he laughed as Ren jumped out of bed anyway, and an hour later, they were walking hand in hand downstairs to meet Mary, who had arrived on an early flight.

Edward watched as the only real mother he'd ever known pulled Ren into her arms and held her in that big, warm hug that had been like oxygen to him once upon a time. He watched Ren's small, tense shoulders slowly loosen, watched her arms finally come around Mary's waist. When Ren started to cry, Mary pulled back, pushing Ren's hair out of her face. Frowning in concern, Mary murmured gently, "Well, it looks like I got another bird in my nest. It's going to be okay, sweet thing. We got you now."

That night, at a new hotel in Atlanta with the same giant guards and the same looming questions about what life looked like from there on out, Ren pressed up against him again. "Kiss me" was all she needed to say.

Daytime was for therapy and self-reflection. Nighttime was for escape, and Edward was happy to follow her lead, giving her everything she needed. Because if the news feeds were to be believed, Chris's house was surrounded by journalists hoping for a glimpse of a family member. They'd been mobbed by reporters on the short walk from the hotel door in Boise to a van waiting at the curb. It was becoming clear to Edward, if not to Ren, that there wouldn't be a return to normalcy for a while. People who went missing and famously reappeared didn't just blend back into society, especially when they were as recognizable as she was.

Their second night in Atlanta, she seemed to realize it, too.

There was a knock at their door, and the Fridge handed him a bag from CVS. "For Ren," he said simply.

Edward found her in the bathroom, brushing out her hair, and set the bag down on the counter. "Fridge brought you some stuff."

"Did you tell him thank you?"

"Uh . . . yes?" he lied.

With something between a sideways smirk and a glare in his direction, Ren put the brush down, gathered her hair in her hands, and slid the length of it over one shoulder. Then she pulled a pair of scissors out of the bag. With a deep breath, she looked at herself in the mirror before turning to him. "Will you do me a favor?"

CHAPTER THIRTY-EIGHT

REN

"Me?"

"You," Ren said, and felt Edward's eyes on her as she carefully pulled her hair back, securing it at the base of her neck with a rubber band.

"You're pretty important right now," he said nervously. "I'm sure they'd be happy to send a professional up to do this."

"I don't want a professional to do this. I want you." She walked to the bed, climbed on, and scooted to the middle, patting the space behind her. "Come here."

The mattress shifted under his weight. Ren could feel him hesitate, but then came the soft brush of his lips on the back of her neck. "Before I do this, I want you to know that I'm in love with you."

A tiny firework went off in her chest, electricity sparking through her veins like a summer sky before a storm. She wanted to say it back, could see the words drawn in thick, black calligraphy in her mind, but no sound came out.

"You don't have to say it," he said, lips brushing the shell of her ear. "I just wanted you to hear it."

She nodded. What she felt for him was more profound than anything she'd ever experienced, but right now everything was heightened. Everything was new. And, perhaps most obviously, the whole idea of love was such a scrambled, messy one for Ren. What did that word even mean?

"I want to say it," she admitted.

"It's okay. That isn't why I told you."

"I know . . . it's just . . . there are so many things I've never felt before," she said. "But I thought I'd known at least one kind of love."

Edward sat quietly, letting her organize her thoughts.

"I've been working through this in therapy," she continued. "What does love mean? Was love how Gloria and Steve justified kidnapping a little girl who lived across the street?"

From what they'd been able to parse out, Gloria—Deborah, she reminded herself—had seen a single father trying and failing to raise a young daughter alone. She'd seen Ren's birth mother, Aria, messy and drunk in the neighborhood. In whatever reality she and her husband had created, they thought they were saving Ren.

"How am I supposed to hate them if they truly were doing what they thought was right?" she asked, voice tight. "They never hit me, they never abused me. In their own way, I believe they did love me. But how could they claim to love me while lying to me my entire life?"

"I know," he said quietly.

"And then there's the love Chris has for me," she said. "I can tell when we sit together at lunch every day that he loves me deeply. That he loves me in that consuming, unconditional, instinctive way of parents I've only ever read about in books." Ren closed her eyes, thinking about how Chris listened to her like she was the most fascinating thing in the world. Steve and Gloria had tended to her basic needs, but they were always so focused on their idea of what was right and best for Ren, that they'd never once asked—or possibly considered—what she actually wanted. Now, every day, Ren registered Chris's amazement at her silliness and her curiosity, his admiration of her strength and grit, his pride in everything she'd managed to accomplish entirely on her own. He listened to her and valued her opinion. His love was as clear as a ringing bell in the crisp morning air.

"But he barely *knows* me," she said quietly. "How is that love any more believable? His memory of me is as a towheaded three-year-old whose favorite food was watermelon and favorite song was 'The Muffin Man.' His memory of me has been frozen in time, locked on the girl who liked to be read to before bed and who loved getting raspberries blown on her belly."

It could be a genuine love, she supposed. At least, eventually. The foundation was there; the desire was there to reconnect. He was desperate to build the relationship he'd always imagined. And even in this deepest part of her bewilderment and heartbreak, Ren knew she was also open and hungry for family. As far as fathers went, Chris seemed to be an ideal one. He was calm and measured; he took their therapy sessions very seriously. Outside of that, he was surprisingly funny and self-deprecating; that humor hid what Ren could tell was a uniquely sharp mind, and as she spent time with him every day, she grew to think maybe she got his curiosity, his drive. He was patient with her, warm and loving, and other than Edward, there was no one in Ren's world who made her feel as cherished and important as Chris did.

"I can understand why you wonder what it all means," Edward said carefully. "I can't even imagine what you're feeling. But I know that I'd do anything for you. I'd sacrifice anything."

"I've been talking about you in therapy with Anne, too," she said, nodding. "How it's confusing to be this happy when I feel shredded up inside. About whether at first my feelings for you were real or somehow tangled up in my excitement about being out in the world. About whether I should be starting a new relationship, especially something intimate and complicated, when I've never been with anyone romantically before."

"Yeah?" he said, gently, without judgment. "Those seem like good questions to be asking."

"Anne reminded me there were no rules," she said. "I don't have to be happy just to make sure people aren't worrying about me, and I don't have to be sad all the time, either, even though everything is objectively hard." She looked at him over her shoulder and smiled. "There are beautiful things that came out of this tragedy. The way I feel about you is beautiful to me. It feels like a gift. I want to let my heart stay open, even if it's scary to trust again."

And she did. She trusted Edward in ways she wasn't sure she could totally understand. He'd started calling their nightly conversations "radical transparency," and he always said it with a laugh, which told her it was a term his own assigned therapist was giving him. But it was working. He'd answered every one of her questions. She knew about his past, and she also knew that he was doing everything he could to figure out a new plan for his future. He'd been given an open calendar to reschedule his internship interview, but his thoughts on what he would do with a law degree were starting to change. He'd realized he wanted to help kids like himself. He knew it wouldn't pay as well, but for the first time in his life, that didn't seem to matter.

She shook her hair down her back, taking a deep breath. "Okay. I'm ready."

Edward gathered her ponytail in his hand and bent to kiss her neck again. "You're really sure?"

"I am. I've done some research and can donate my hair to an organization called Locks of Love."

He audibly winced at the first cut, but the immediate weight lifted—actually and figuratively—made tears of relief spring to her eyes. In tiny snips, Edward carefully and quietly worked until she was free, and he was left holding the long castoffs in his hand.

He passed the cut ponytail to her, and she stared down at it. It was thick, and at least a foot and a half of soft, blond hair. She ran her fingers through it.

"How do you feel?" he asked.

"Amazing." She laughed, and then reached up to cup the back of her neck. "Cold."

He ruffled her haircut from behind; it fell a few inches above her shoulders. "I don't want to declare this too early," he said, picking a stray hair off her shoulder, "but of the single haircut I've ever given, this might be the best."

She laughed, turning to face him, and reached beside him for the other objects in the bag. "And now," she said, looking down at the box, "looks like I'm going 'Downtown Brown.'"

He frowned at the box. "No."

"Yes."

He flopped back onto the mattress, but he was smiling. They were desperate to get outside, and there was only one way that was going to happen.

Their plan was to duck out in the late morning, during her father's scheduled press conference in front of the hotel, when every one of the scores of reporters was expected to be congregated at the fountains outside.

Fridge would escort, walking behind them, with another agent in plain clothes walking in front. Even though their destination was an ice cream shop only two blocks away, it was the only way the hulking guard would let Ren out of the building.

Edward stepped up beside her in front of the mirror in their room, waiting for the knock to let them know their security was ready.

"Holy sh— You look hot," Edward said, smoldering at her.

"Hot?" She covertly sniffed under her arm.

"I mean you look good," he said, laughing. "Gorgeous. Sexy as hell."

"Oh." Never in her life had she been called sexy before meeting Edward, and she felt heat climb up her neck and consume her face. She ran a hand over her hair—which came out much darker than she'd expected, but Edward insisted he loved it, saying it made her eyes seem even greener.

She didn't know if hair could be sexy, though. Just like she'd never believed that her hair could be meaningful, or hold magical, untold powers. It had always just been hair. And the minute Edward had cut it off, it was no longer even hers.

They stared at their reflections, and she wondered if maybe when he called her *sexy* he was talking about the fancy sunglasses and pretty white sundress someone brought for her to wear. She'd heard that Dr. Audran refused to hand over the Polaroid of her from his immunology class to the news, and for that she was eternally grateful. It meant that the only pictures circulating of her were the one from her student ID and an old one that Tammy took years ago when Ren was helping out at the five-and-dime, which showed a girl with very long, very blond braided hair, jean shorts, a too-big T-shirt, and sneakers, laughing as she reached for a box on a high shelf. Ren hoped the fancy outfit and radical change in her hair would keep her anonymous, at least until the initial attention let up. She didn't see herself when she looked in the mirror now, and she didn't think that was a bad thing.

She'd very much like to be someone else right now.

She looked up to see Edward's reflection smiling at her.

He'd been given a Yankees baseball hat, dark sunglasses, and a sweatshirt with an NYU graphic. She knew the torso beneath it by heart because she'd spent hours at night memorizing it with her hands and lips. His jeans hung low and slim on his strong hips. The photo circulating of him was one from last fall, midsprint on the soccer pitch. Taken together with all the media accolades that Ren would not have been found if it hadn't been for him, the bunching muscles visible in the photo made him look like a superhero. She had never wanted something as instinctively as she wanted him.

She wasn't sure she could say it yet, but she was pretty sure she loved him, too.

"You good, Sunshine?" he asked.

She turned to him, pressing up against his body. "I'm great. I'm about to get ice cream."

Ren stared out through the spotless front window, letting her feet kick against the legs of the high countertop stool. "I probably can't go back to Corona, huh?"

Edward took a long lick of his double-decker mint chocolate chip on a sugar cone, then gazed sidelong at her while he swallowed. "I think you can do whatever you want. You want to be a student? Be a student. You want to write a book and sell it for a bazillion dollars? Do that. You want to buy your own farm in New Hampshire?" He waved his hand forward, like *You get the idea*. "And you want to be Ren, or Grace, or someone entirely new? It's all up to you."

She sucked on her spoon, letting the ice cream melt on her tongue. Just outside the shop window, Fridge's towering form cast a long shadow across the entrance as he casually pretended to read a newspaper. She wasn't sure whether it was because it wasn't really ice cream weather today or no one dared cross his hulking path, but she and Edward had the whole place to themselves. "I want to be Ren."

He nodded. "Good."

"But . . . I think Ren Koning."

"You know Chris will cry when he hears that," Edward said,

eyes twinkling with a grin.

"He's tenderhearted," she said, with a sweet defensiveness.

"Now we know where you get it."

Ren smiled at this, realizing how much she was growing to like being compared to her father.

"What's your dream future?" she asked.

He pointed to himself in question, quickly swallowing another bite. "I don't think it's up to me right now," he said, adding, "nor should it be."

"But I mean, if you decide to go off and do your own thing?" she asked, and he swiveled on his stool, turning hers so that his thighs bracketed hers.

With narrowed eyes and a sneaky smile, he studied her. "Why would I go off and do my own thing? Are you trying to get rid of me, Sunshine?"

"Never."

"So then why are you suggesting I go off on my own?"

"You don't have to stick around," she said, lifting a shoulder. "I'll probably be a mess for a while." She stuck another bite in her mouth, sucking on the spoon just to have something to do. Her emotions all sat just beneath the surface, and right now, for some stupid reason, she felt like crying.

His eyes softened. "Maybe I like mess."

"Hmm."

"Besides," he said, straightening, "who else is going to help me fix my car? Max needs a lot of work."

She laughed, pulling the spoon from her mouth. "I'm sure you could find someone."

"And who else will drive around the country with me, seeing all of the cheesiest tourist destinations?"

She clicked her tongue, digging out another spoonful. "It might only be me, you're right."

Edward tossed the rest of his cone into the trash behind him and then turned back to her, reaching up to cup her face in his hands. "What do *you* want to do?"

"Have another scoop."

"And then what?"

"Not be special anymore."

"Unlikely, sorry." He kissed her softly. "And then what?"

"Go to college," she said, inhaling wistfully.

"Oh, we're definitely getting you that college degree. What else?"

"Swim in the ocean," she said, on a roll now. "Hike the Appalachian Trail. Go to London. See the Parthenon."

"I assume you don't mean the one in Nashville."

She grinned. "Maybe that one first, then the other."

"Amazing. What else?"

"Spend holidays with my father and his family. Buy food from a vending machine in Tokyo. Sleep in on Saturdays. Drink champagne on the top of the Eiffel Tower." She closed her eyes, taking a deep breath. "I just want to be free."

"I'm inviting myself along on all of these trips, by the way."

"That's a given." She smiled, but it faded. "I think I have to move somewhere totally new. Somewhere I can start over."

He nodded, leaning in to kiss her again. "That makes sense," he said against her lips. "What else?"

"I don't know," she admitted into another peck, and then he gave her a dozen tiny, soft kisses. "I think"—kiss—"for now"—kiss—"I really just want to eat ice cream"—kiss—"and wear giant sunglasses"—kiss—"and kiss your cold lips."

Edward smiled and tilted his head, gently but decisively setting those cold, smiling lips against hers.

And—after college, law school, whirlwind travel, many holidays with family, very little revenge scheming, the purchase of some land, and what Edward found to be a truly excessive number of farm animals—they lived happily ever after.

The End

ACKNOWLEDGMENTS

Let us set the stage: It's early 2014, and we recently released *Beautiful Player*, with a hero—Will Sumner—whose playfulness, ease, and charisma was inspired in part by our favorite Disney hero, Flynn Rider.

Our agent, Holly Root, knew of our *Tangled* love and that we wanted to write an actually *Tangled*-inspired book. She promised she'd let us know if any such thing came across her desk. Fast-forward a few years and we hear about the Meant to Be series and that Disney wanted us for *Tangled* as much as WE wanted us for *Tangled*. It took us a few years to land on a story that contained everything we love about this perfect movie, but then . . . we did. Now, dear reader, almost exactly ten years after we first begged to take on *Tangled, Tangled Up in You* is in your hands!

This would never have happened without our amazing agent, Holly Root. Thank you, Holly, for believing we can do (almost) anything. You are the human we measure all other humans against. PR goddess Kristin Dwyer, we wrote this book remembering how much you loved the very first book we wrote together, and hoped you'd love this one just as much. We would be lost—literally and figuratively—without you. None of our books are complete without the touch of Jen Prokop, and this one was no different. Thank you for your wisdom and brilliant editorial eye.

Thank you to our editor, Jocelyn Davies, for being patient while we found the story worthy of Rapunzel and Eugene, but also our Ren and Edward. Thank you for guiding us through this process and for every spot-on edit and enthusiastic email.

Thank you to the extraordinary team at Disney and Hyperion Avenue: Sara Liebling, Guy Cunningham, Karen Krumpak, Dan Kaufman, Sylvia Davis, Elanna Heda, Jessica Hernandez, Kaitie

Leary, Julie Leung, Alexandra Serrano, Jennifer Brunn, and Jennifer Levesque. Thank you, Andrea Rosen, Vicki Korlishin, Michael Freeman, Monique Diman-Riley, and LeBria Casher for all your work getting this series into stores.

We couldn't love our cover more, so an enormous *thank-you* to designer Marci Senders and artist Stephanie Singleton.

Julie Murphy, Jasmine Guillory, and Zoraida Córdova, thank you for celebrating the princesses we all love and setting the bar so high. It is an honor to follow in your footsteps.

To our best friends who keep us sane and deserve a smooch from Flynn Rider himself for putting up with us, we love you: Erin Service, Susan Lee, Kate Clayborn, Katie Lee, Ali Hazelwood, Sarah MacLean, Jen Prokop, Rosie Danan, Julie Soto, Jess McLin, Jennifer Carlson, Brie Statham, Amy Schuver, Mae Lopez, Alisha Rai, and Christopher Rice.

We are Disney nerds, and if we could manage it, we would put every reader, reviewer, booktokker, blogger, librarian, and bookseller in the seats next to us on Expedition Everest. We would watch fireworks together and eat Dole Whips and corn dogs. We'd shower you in Mickey ears and take all your photos in front of the castle, because what you do is magic. We couldn't do any of this without you.

To my Lo, I feel like this book is everything we love about *Tangled* and romance. We talked about it for so long and it looks almost exactly like the story we dreamed of. How often does that happen?? Thank you for always being my left quote and my best friend. I love you so much. Meet you at the Tower of Terror.

To Christina, there are so many ways that you delight me every day, but in this case, one stands out above all else: thank you for putting them in the hot tub. It might be my favorite scene we've ever cowritten. Love you to the stars and back.